MW00948354

# Beneath Us.

A novel by
John Crawley

ISBN Number
9781304564740


Book Design: Monticello House Books
Type Face: American Typewriter
Cover design by Ted Karch for Monticello House Books design studio

Monticello House Books

**Other novels and books by John Crawley**

Among the Aspen

Baby Change Everything

The House Next Door

Under the Radar

The Uncivil War

Between Sunday's Columns

The Man on the Grassy Knoll

Beyond a Shadow of a Doubt (a novella)

Stuff

Dream Chaser (a serial e-novel)

The Myth Makers

Fishing Lessons

Letters from Paris

The Perfect Food

The End

Lincoln, Texas USA (Short Stories including a print version of Dream Chaser)

Wrong Number (including the novella The Gift.)

Of Poets and Old Men (a collection of poetry)

One Elephant Too Many

The Ripple Effect

Dedicated to Caleb Pirtle.

And to all those who sit and face a blank screen or an empty sheet of paper every day in order to create.

## A few thoughts about Beneath Us.

"This is a brilliant piece of literary fiction.

The characters are strong even with their flaws and weaknesses.

Lost love that never really disappears is a theme that others have written but, I believe, not nearly as well nor as vividly as you have done.

You have created a fascinating concept, beginning with the good, bad, and ugly of a writer on the brink of success, moving to the Texas oilfield story which becomes a best-selling and internationally award winning book, then returning to the addictions, dreams, battles, and struggles of the writer. As you know, I am a child of the oilfield, especially during the slant hole days. Your movements from storytelling to developing passages within an acclaimed book is the stroke of genius.

Success never breeds the kind of happiness we expect it to. Often, it creates the turmoil that casts its characters into nightmares that threaten to ruin or destroy them.

...It is without doubt the finest book you have ever written."

**-- Caleb Pirtle's comments about *Beneath Us*, written ten days prior to his untimely passing. We will miss you Caleb.**

"Captivating. And I never expected that ending. Oh My!"

**-- Dee Leone, writer and editor**

## Acknowledgements

Henry Crawley III          editing and proofreading

Michele Stephens          editing

Caleb Pirtle          for direction and coaching (He
lived through the slant-hole days
in Kilgore.)

Dee Leone          for a critical eye and a word of
encouragement when I needed it.
(Her grandfather worked the
East Texas Oil fields back in the
day, so she knows.)

Special thanks to all the folks at Lulu Press and Monticello House Books for working to get this puppy published.

*If she's amazing, she won't be easy. If she's easy, she won't be amazing. If she's worth it, you won't give up. If you give up, you're not worthy. ... Truth is, everybody is going to hurt you; you just gotta find the ones worth suffering for.*

– Bob Marley

# Book One

**Chapter One**

Clark was alone. And that was a good thing.

He sat at the keyboard facing out into the woods that stretched beyond the isolated cabin. The soft light of morning cascaded down and among the boughs of the overhanging firs and pines, dusted by a late spring snow that had been born in a Pacific storm, now thundering its way in the distance towards Idaho and Wyoming. Tracks in the white drifts led into the dark forest from his porch. Raccoons, he reasoned. They were about his only companions. That, and whoever ventured a phone call up the mountain to his hideaway – but when he was writing, the phone was off. He wanted no distractions.

He warmed the coffee in his cup and took a slow sip, letting the steam fog his glasses, which he wore only when he was typing on the laptop or posing for the publicity shots, which accompanied his book tours. As he sipped from the cup, he eyed the table across the room and its colorful bottles full of whiskey, gin and vodka – all the time wishing for one sip. Yet, he knew he could not. Not even one. They were there as a reminder of where he had come from – who he had been once before – and the power he had over them. But it was tempting and yet, he had promised himself he would never go back there, to that dark past.

He sipped the coffee again.

The phone rang. He had not yet turned it off. On the other end was Moss, his agent. "I know you're writing, so I'll make this brief. Simpson House is requesting you come to Portland. Speak with two other authors at the university and then do a book signing. Second week in June. Can they count on you?"

"Yeah sure," he said, unenthusiastically. He hated book signings.

"Good to hear, Jack. How's it going?"

"If you'd quit calling me it would go smoother and faster."

"I'm gone, bro. Don't want to disturb Michelangelo. Peace." The line went dead. He found his calendar, marked down the date and made a few notes about which speech he would give. He had five of them; all about the same, but with slightly different focuses. He shut the phone off, making sure this time, it really was off. He then turned his attention to the work at hand.

It was quiet in Oregon that morning. He would have no more interruptions. Just as he liked it. The cabin, warmed by a gentle crackling fire in the old rock fireplace, offered the solitude for an artist and a blank canvas to merge – ready for the wrestling match called creating. He was trying to start his new book, trying to put into words everything that had transpired in the last year or so.

He took another sip of the hot coffee, set the cup down and began to write again. His mind racing ahead of his typing. Visions working themselves into words beneath his fast-flying fingers. He was on autopilot. He had tried to explain it to a writing class at one time. He told them it was as if he was only there to connect the creative muse of the universe and the computer. He was but a transmitter. An antenna – he had called it. Ideas flowed out of the ether and into his consciousness, through his fingers and then onto the electronic screen of the laptop.

He grinned. The notion would be far more romantic, for some reason, if the computer wasn't involved; but rather, a single sheet of blank paper trapped in the roller of a manual typewriter or spread out on an old desk top waiting to receive the daily hand-written dictation: visions of Hemingway typing away on an old Underwood in sultry, humid Cuba, or Steinbeck with pencil in hand in the dry and dusty American West amidst the Great Depression. That was real writing. True warriors of the printed word. He wanted desperately to be among them. So he wrote on, even if he was aided by spell check and automatic page formatting.

Every time he began to write, she would come into his vision. Clark closed his eyes. He could still see her as if it were yesterday. It was as if he shared all his stories with her. 'Come sit by me and let me tell you something.' It was his open invitation to her spirit. And in his head, she always came: sat there, still and silent and waited for his story to slowly emerge. She never grew impatient; but rather, was engrossed with what it was he was doing. Like a little child discovering something new each time they went outside to play in the dirt, she sat there discovering what it was he had to divulge to her.

He typed on, as his imaginary audience watched.

He just wished she were alive and real and next to him. Yet, powers that extended far beyond his control – beyond his reach – had seen to it that she wasn't there. The incident on the lake had seen to it – that she was long gone. Their past and the secret they shared were the only things he had connecting him to her. Wherever she might be. But after that hellish night, she was estranged from him forever.

But when he wrote, her vision appeared to him. He wondered at times if she even remembered him. If she ever thought of him. If she even knew he was a published author. Did she pass a window of a bookstore somewhere in some city or township far away and look in and see his works there, lined up in a row? Did she see his photograph and recognize him, even with his pen name?

Jack Lawrence. She didn't know a Jack Lawrence. But would she recognize his black and white picture on the jacket of the books? And would she care? Did she even read books? Did she visit bookstores?

But he had seen her in bookstores – well, not her, but rather her photograph on the cover of all kinds of magazines – mostly European fashion magazines: Vogue (The French, and Italian versions), *L'Officiel*, Madame Figaro, Elle, and Numéro. Currently she was on the cover of W, which he had on his coffee table. She had adorned the covers with evening gowns and mini skirts and even jewelry – posed with next to nothing to go with it but her soft, delicate skin. The same skin he had explored as a young man in his last year of high school. She was, by now, a very famous model having taken France and Italy by storm. She was a celebrity of sorts in New York, Milan and

Paris. She was constantly pictured on the arms of actors and ball players, rock stars and even politicians ten years her senior. Movie directors were her chosen companions of late. He had seen her on the periodical shelves in bookstores from Los Angeles to Miami; Canada to Mexico. Every time he turned around her face was staring back at him. Taunting him; 'Now you see me, now you don't.' He couldn't go through an airport without Missy Rusk spying on him from some newsstand.

He typed some more, the words flowing onto the screen. Images from his brain translated into the hieroglyphics of a printed language, every syllable of which, he dedicated in his heart to her – every stroke of the keyboard, an outreach to her soul.

He paused. One drink. Just one. A small one. He looked at the collection of unopened bottles. Then he looked away. He had to be stronger. His will had to match their draw. It was a battle he fought every day – all day. Most days he won.

He wrote:

People die. All people die. Doctors, lawyers, priests, ditch diggers, farmers, teachers, cooks, crooks, policemen, road workers, evangelists, housewives...even kings and queens...every one eventually dies. It is the rule of the game all humans play.

No one beats the rule.

Money can't beat the rule. Bend it for a time, for sure, but it can't win in the end.

Science can't beat the rule.

People die.

That's just how it is and how it is going to be.

Until we are all gone.

He decided Willie was right. He would load up the old company Ford pickup with some poles and lures and take Les fishing. They hadn't been fishing in years. Not since the incident on that dark and violent night with the lake cloaked in the secrecy of darkness.

Clark remembered when that's what his old man loved to do. Go fishing. But in recent years he had mostly hung around the clubhouse and played forty-two with his old friends, trade stories and drink beer. Lester Harvey seldom picked up a golf club anymore; especially since the stroke. And he hadn't been out on the lake for two years or more. Not since Lee died. His father's gait and his look since the stroke had changed, not that Clark was aware of it, having been away for close to two decades. His hair had turned white. His scrappy beard too, which spread-out haphazardly over his thinly stretched, pallid skin. He was much paler than Clark had ever seen him. And Willie, his wife – Clark's mother – had tried in vane to coax him out of the house at every opportunity she could, to get him up and about and active.

So Clark thought a fishing outing would be good. Even if Clark, himself, wasn't keen about spending any more time with the old man than he had to.

Fishing would be a good pastime until he died.

Everyone dies. "We all die, someday." Clark told himself, as if justifying spending time with his father out on a boat on a huge lake in East Texas. "He'll die and we can stop pretending. And stop fishing." He said it aloud to nobody. Then again he repeated it, quietly to himself, as he looked in the mirror at his parent's home, the home he had grown up in a lifetime ago. The face that stared back at him looked tired, but relieved. Relieved in that the great charade was now over.

Now it was time to wait on death to come.

It always came.

So when Clark got the word from Mrs. O'Brien that his mother was ill, he wasn't surprised, although it had been close to twenty years since he had seen his mother or even talked with her – not since he left home at the age of eighteen. He knew his parents would someday pass away. He had lost a brother, although he had not heard about it until well after the event. Clark's twin brother, Lee, after a stint in junior college, had learned electronics in the Navy then turned that into a career as a radio station engineer in San Antonio, Texas. It was there, one day, two years ago, that he was on a tower adjusting a short-wave relay system when lightning hit the pole and he was killed. He had been warned to get down because of the impending storm, but Lee was one to always finish what he had started and he wanted to finish the relay connection.

They call it clear lightning – it really means lightning out of clear air. In the dry southwest, approaching storms build up huge static electrical charges that are released ahead of the storms themselves, when cool dry air and warm moist air rush together. The power these storms produce ahead of their frontal boundaries is immense and dangerous.

Lee had been struck halfway up the tall commercial antenna and was laid to rest in the rock-hard soil of

Central Texas, his twin brother, a thousand miles away unaware of his passing.

Clark only learned about Lee's death through Mrs. O'Brien. "We missed you at the funeral, Clark," she said. "Everyone was there. The whole class I think turned out for it. Everyone loved Lee so much." Mrs. O'Brien had been the boys' English teacher in high school and was one of the people responsible for him becoming a novelist, although at the time during his school days in Lincoln, Texas she didn't think he was a very good essayist. "You're trying too hard to be creative, Clark. Just follow the rules." Clark hated the rules.

Mrs. O'Brien had spotted him at a book-signing event in Portland. Even though he published under a pseudonym of Jack Lawrence, she knew it was Clark the moment she walked in the over-crowded store and saw him, with three other authors, sitting at a signing table, his latest novel stacked beside him. *The Promised Land* was its title and it was already being talked about as a Hollywood hit movie, even though the screenplay had yet to be penned. For that matter, the movie rights had not even been sold.

The shop was crowded and stuffy. The unseen heater was working overtime against the unseasonably late spring cold outside. The shelves, lined with every book imaginable, seemed to wilt under the oppressive heat. The temperature didn't deter the line of people waiting for autographs and a word with the authors. He never understood autographs. Didn't know why people wanted them or what they did with them. Selfies, sure – hey look at me with this famous person; or in his case, not-so-famous person. He could understand selfies, but an autograph was beyond his comprehension. Why someone would wait for hours in a sultry, serpentine line to get a scribbling on a piece of paper. 'To Alice: Yours, Jack Lawrence.' But they filed past him as if by duty from some unknown order.

"Willie is ill, Clark," she said it as matter of fact, as if they had been having a conversation just minutes before, instead of several decades. She simply stepped up next in line to have a book inscribed and said, "Willie is ill." And Clark looked up and saw the face he remembered at the chalkboard during his junior year of high school. "She's got cancer. Again."

He didn't know Willie had fought two previous bouts with the disease, nor was he aware that she was losing this round desperately fast, until Mrs. O'Brien told him. And he sure didn't know that his father had had a stroke and a heart attack and two bypass surgeries. And neither did he know that his brother had been struck by lightning.

This was all news to him.

To Clark, these names – these people – were strangers. He lived far away from them and the misery they had brought him. It was the price of his freedom. But Mrs. O'Brien had changed all that. She had broken through the present and poured a heaping dose of the past back into his life.

They had coffee together after the book signing. The coffee shop was almost as crowded as the bookstore had been, but not as hot. Fresh air seeped in through the front door. Steam rose from their ceramic mugs as they danced around the stories and the time that had passed since Clark was last in Texas and saw his parents.

"Willie is quite ill. I'm afraid she won't win this round."

Clark nodded and sipped his coffee nonchalantly. He had feared the day when someone would come up to him and recognize him and say, "Hey, man, your parents are dead." But here he was hearing the words that they were still alive. But apparently just.

"Your father is weak. He had a stroke, you know, and two bypasses and still hasn't recovered. Not fully. Not like his old self. He's a shadow of the man he used to be, Clark. Not at all well. And Willie...she tries as best she can to care for him, but she's got her own battles to fight." Mrs. O'Brien let her voice trail off, or was it that Clark just stopped listening for a moment. There was a silence between them. A reader noticed him and stopped by to greet him and tell him how much she loved his work. He thanked her, signed her book, then turning to Mrs. O'Brien he finally answered.

"I'll go home and check on them."

"Yes, they'll like that. I'm sure they will."

"Will you tell them you found me and that I'll be coming as soon as I can wrap up some things here in Oregon?"

"I'd be delighted to, Clark. Jess and I will be back in Lincoln this weekend. They will be so excited with this news."

Clark merely nodded. There was a lot of rewinding to do.

The line on the blue pole's reel was fouled and needed rewinding. Its pale green filament was knotted into an eternal ball of twisting mess and was nearly impossible to straighten out. Clark was about to cut the string with his knife when the old man said he'd do it. He said it briskly. Like an order. He always was giving orders. He had learned the art in the army during the war. He had been a staff Sargent in Germany. Made it through the Battle of the Bulge as a young man, barely out of his teens himself. But a seasoned fighter none-the-less. He lived when others hadn't. That was because he was cunning. He was brave. And, as he always was sure to admit – he was damn lucky.

So Clark handed it over to him and watched as the thin fingers, shaking with the reel nestled in them, began to twist and pull at the chord and knots until, before long, the fishing line was straightened out and the old man cranked it back onto the reel. He handed it to Clark. "Here, let's go if we're going."

Clark started the old truck and eased the clutch out and headed down the hill towards the club's marina. Jimmy Earl Jackson ran it these days. His father, Bruce, had built it the year after the Corps of Engineers had finished the dam and the impoundment began to fill with water. He and two partners had foreseen the need for a country club community; complete with clubhouse, golf links and a full-service marina. They had designed the entire thing on napkins at Bruce's kitchen table; got investors and built Lake Haven Acres themselves, then sold it to a management company who built a large hotel and spa between the golf club and the marina. It had become a destination site for weekenders from Dallas and Houston.

"Jimmy Earl said we can use his boat today. It's got plenty of power to get us to the islands and back before dark."

The old man just nodded, as he stared straight ahead as the road snaked down the steep hill from the housing development toward the lake and the marina.

"He loves to fish. Or did," said Willie. "He hasn't been since ... well for a long time. Lee tried to take him maybe two or three years before he died. We missed you at the funeral. Everyone missed you. You would have thought you could have made it to your own brother's funeral."

"I didn't know he had passed." Clark said matter-of-factly, as his mother washed some dishes in the sink and he stood next to her, a dishtowel in hand ready to dry. His tall, lean frame towering over her.

"We hadn't heard from you. Didn't know where you were or what you were doing or if you were even alive or not."

"I had my reasons."

"I'm sure you did." Silence punctuated the end of her sentence.

They took care of the remaining dishes and then moved to the den. Lester Harvey was sound asleep in his overstuffed recliner. The TV set was playing an evening game show and Willie turned it down, then whispered to Clark. "He spends most of his time there. Asleep. I try to get him up and out. I drive him to the club to play dominoes with the guys. He loves his forty-two. But he is content just to sit there and nod off. Some nights I just throw a comforter over him and let him sleep there. He doesn't seem to mind. And I get a better night's rest that way. Otherwise he's tossing and turning."

"So what does the doctor say about his recovery?"

"It's up to him. He can recover as much as he wants to. But it's up to him. He doesn't like to be pushed. He fights it. I have to take it in baby steps with him. Like I'm sneaking in rehab inch by inch so he's not noticing."

"Obstinate as always."

"It's like getting a child to eat their veggies."

"Obstinate," he repeated.

"Cut him some slack, Clark."

"It's just that..."

"He provided quite well for this family and I won't have him talked about in a negative way."

Clark thought about her words then changed the subject. "And you? What do the doctors say about you?" They moved to a small sitting room off the den and both took a position on either end of a short divan. Willie drew a shawl around her shoulders. The windows were the old single pane type that got cold on the inside and sweated. The humidity perspired down the glass and onto paper towels that Willie had set out on the sills. A small gas fireplace crackled in the corner. It was on during the times Willie sat in the small den. "Summer or winter, I'm always cold," she told Clark. "It's the cancer."

"And the prognosis?" asked Clark.

She shook her head. "Not good."

"How bad is not good?"

"I won't beat it this time. They discovered its return too late."

"Have they given you a time line? And estimate?"

"You know how it is, Clark. Everybody's got to die sometime."

## Chapter Two

She wasn't going to do the chemo this time. It made her too ill. And the radiation was worse. "I'm going to let matters take their own direction. God's will." Willie sounded as defiant as ever.

"Well, I'm sure He's got a plan for you," Clark let it sound as sarcastic as he dared with his mother. He remembered how religious she was or at least had been. They weren't the kind of family that had gone to church every time the doors were open, but they did frequent it often enough to be called devout. For a short period during the trouble, they had stopped going altogether because of the wagging tongues and the constant stares. Willie hated it. The church had been a refuge for her and it had been taken away by gossip and innuendo.

Slowly as the gossipers died out and the rumors faded, she returned to the alter and worshiped her God. (Now as a Presbyterian instead of as a Baptist she had once been.) Lester never joined her in his days after the stroke. "God did this to me, so fuck him." He would say in the same rebellious way he lived his life. 'Damn the world, I am Lester Harvey. Damn the world.' Willie loved that about him. Even when it caused social awkwardness, she loved his stubborn insubordination and his belligerent attitude. They had grown up on that side of the tracks where a man and a woman had to claw their way to the top. Nothing was given to them, and heaven help those who tried to take it away.

His sweat and muscle had made them a life. He never shied away from hard work. Or a fight. Her determination had raised two boys to be good young men. Together, Lester and Willie had made a strong team: one that had risen far up the social ladder from their first steps in near poverty. They, together, had climbed and reached about as far as those above them would allow. Then a heavy boot came down and said – 'Far enough.'

The struggle had been worth it. They were not rich by any means, but the oil field had been good to them. It had provided them with a fine home, high on a hill above the lake and it gave them some sense of security – money can do that – not abundant amounts of it, but enough to insure their final days would not see them returning to the destitution they both had grown up in. They remembered those days. When an evening meal was a couple of soda crackers and a can of tuna shared between them; or sweltering in a hot, one-room house in August without enough money to pay for a fan.

Then one day, Lester answered an ad in the Tulsa newspaper. *Able bodied men looking for jobs in the East Texas Oil Field. Good pay. Benefits. Housing.* He left her with her folks in Oklahoma to seek out the sender of the ad. It was the Humble Oil and Refining Company. Lester had a job. He sent for Willie and together their life started over. They saw the ladder in front of them and they knew in which direction to climb.

"The doctors will give me pain meds and I'll be comfortable until close to the end."

"Then what?"

"We'll see. We'll just see."

"And what happens to him when you are gone?" Clark nodding to the other room where Lester rested.

"I thought that's why you were here?'

She had said it and it had surprised even him. Why was he here? Why had he broken his self-imposed exile, which he had promised himself never to break? What were his plans?

"I don't know," he said, as if answering himself.

"You don't know what?' Willie asked.

"I don't know why I'm here. Mrs. O'Brian found me and the next thing I know I'm back in Lincoln and here in this house and watching the two of you dissolve away."

"Well, I may be dissolving, but your father isn't. He is lingering and he might continue to do so for some time – years even."

"I see."

"And that's where you come in."

"Me?"

"Yes. Who is going to take care of him when I am gone?"

"That's a good question."

"It's one you'd better find an answer to very quickly."

"I don't even know him anymore. He's like a stranger to me. He has been ever since I left. Even before that. That's why I left. Why I went away."

"You did it in a hurry. Just gone one night and we never heard back from you."

"Not true. I wrote for a while."

"What, twice? Three times?"

"I needed a new start after..."

She placed her fingers over her lips to tell him to stop talking.

"We're not going there. Not back there ever again. Hear me?" She paused, and changing subjects said, "Take him fishing. He used to love to go fishing with you boys."

He studied her face. It was lined with shallow wrinkles. Her hair was short and the brown highlighted with streaks of silver – not white like his father's but rather a lustery silver, like Christmas tinsels strung throughout a fir tree. She had always, as long as he could remember, worn it shoulder length. But the last round of radiation, according to her, had thinned it back so there was nothing she could do with it and it would only grow so long, then stop. So she kept it cropped extremely short and combed over, like a boy's haircut. But photographs of her and her friends back from her days in Tulsa showed her with shoulder-length locks. She had a 40's Hollywood starlet style about her. And a figure of a dancer, always thin and light on her feet. She would float about the house doing her chores as if accompanied by some unseen orchestra fueling her feet to leave the confines of gravity and dance along some mystical pathway.

She loved to dance at the club. Lester was a so-so partner on the dance floor, if not a tad stiff. He claimed his bad back came from the oil field. She loved to play tennis, although the old man did not. Again his back. So she learned and endured golf, but they seldom played together. In fact, they seemed to do very little together, except they were now locked into an eternal dance to the death together. Who would lead? Who would follow?

"Fishing, huh?"

"Yeah. There's some old rods and reels in the garage and a tackle box. It's pretty rusty, but I bet it still has stuff in it you can use. Lee used to use it when he came up here."

The last time Clark had been on the lake was in the summer following his senior year of high school – just days after graduation. He and Lee had borrowed James Aldridge's old wooden fishing boat and spent the night out on Rock Island, which was a mound of crushed rock and debris from an old mining operation that had gone bust before the lake had flooded its deep chasm. Local yore said it was the best fishing hole in East Texas, but that night the boys were more interested in smoking weed and talking about girls.

"Jenny Albright...huh?" He said as Lee took a swig from the amber beer bottle.

"Yeah," said Lee.

"What about Missy?"

"No way. Not even close."

"You're telling me that you and Missy Rusk never did it?"

"Not even to second base. And you?" Asked Lee.

"Still a virgin." Clark lied, knowing his secret and the truth.

"Come on. A guy as good lookin' as you. An athlete? You've got to have the girls coming onto you like flies to meat."

"That certainly makes it sound romantic. But riding the bench on the basketball team doesn't make me an athlete. "

Lee laughed. "You know what I mean."

"Nobody has rung my bell yet."

"They don't have to ring it, just rub it." Lee chuckled and passed him a beer, followed immediately by a roach with a glowing ember on the end. Clark took a deep draw on the joint and then washed the acrid, burning smoke down his throat with the cold beer.

They were twins. But not identical. Fraternal. Although, they were as close as twins could get. They could finish each other's sentences and knew each other's thought and were inside each other's heads all the time. But they were different, too. Clark was tall and thin, and Lee was stocky and built solid like a linebacker, which he had played in high school and would play some more in junior college in Tyler, long after Clark had taken off out west.

"I'm thinking about going out west." Clark said aloud for the first time, as if to try the notion out on someone to see how the idea landed; like trying on a pair of trousers and looking at them in a mirror to see how they fit.

"Where out west? To school?" Asked Lee.

"Yeah maybe." He paused having not thought through his whole plan. "Yeah, maybe to school. Or I might just get a job and knock around some. I gotta get out of here."

"It's been hard on you ever since..."

"Yeah. And Dad acts like nothing happened. Like he didn't engineer the whole damn thing."

"Maybe he didn't maybe it was just an accident."

"Fat chance. No way. Don't you go and try and defend him now. It was bad enough the court let him off, but you and I were there – we both know what happened."

"Well, Clark, to tell you the truth, I'm fuzzy on it. That's what I told the D.A. and that's why they were reluctant to call me as a witness."

"But you knew. You still know. And I know and I can't just hang around here and live under his roof and act like I didn't know. I've got to get away and start my life over. I feel like I have a hundred pounds of shackles and weights pulling me down. And every day I see him he adds another weight."

"Think about mom."

"What about mom? She was there too and she lied bold-faced to that court. I was the only one who had the guts to stand up and tell them what really happened and then that stupid jury – his peers– they all voted for him. Go figure."

"That's a small town for you."

"Is that some kind of confession or absolution?"

"Neither. It is a small town and everybody knows everybody and his friends exonerated him. Old man Rusk, too. Period. Its over...let it go." Lee reached for the burning reefer and placed it to his lips. He drew in deeply.

The boys finished their fishing trip to Rock Island in an estranged silence and three days later, Clark took his gun-metal gray Rambler Rebel and drove away from Lincoln with a promise never to return.

It took almost twenty years for him to break that promise. And here he was with the old man sitting next to him in the old red and white Lincoln Drilling Company pick-up truck heading for the marina to go fishing.

"Want to go to Rock Island? Good fishing hole there," said Clark.

"No. Let's go to Pine Island. Fewer people about."

"Fishing's not as good."

"Pine Island, Clark. That's where I want to go." It was said as a command, not a request or even a bit of information being passed along. It was said as an order. 'Take me to Pine Island.'

Clark drank his way through the first manuscript. Then one day, he just threw it away. It was never published. To this day, he can barely recall what it was about. It took him two years to get sober enough to write another book. And if that wasn't bad enough, his first published novel was a bust. Few bought it and fewer than that finished it. And so he thought his career was over.

He wandered about in the Pacific Northwest living in cheap motels and earning a small wage in odd jobs – a day laborer mostly. One night he met a man named Harold Moss in a Spokane bar. Moss was about ten years older than Clark with the opposite temperament when it came to drinking. Moss could nurse a single cocktail all evening. Clark, on the other hand, was an empty bucket into which liquor seemed to constantly be pouring. Moss was a lawyer. "An entertainment lawyer specializing in Hollywood screen plays. I've had three hits recently. And I'm looking for more," he told Clark at the bar that night. Clark, to this day, can't remember why he was there – in Spokane or at that bar. But fate brought them together and Clark confessed to being a fledgling writer. "Books, huh? You ever write a screenplay?" Clark said he had not.

"Just books," he told the agent.

Little came of that first meeting other than Clark got the man's business card. He then promptly fell under the influence of the bottle even deeper for more than a year. But one day he awoke from his self-induced fog and began writing on a new novel.

He had taken a job in a hardware super store at a shopping center in Vancouver, Washington, across the river from Portland. He typed at night and stocked shelves by day. In reality, he had all but given up the notion of being a writer; but on a whim, he sent a nearly complete manuscript to the man he had met in the bar, along with a note to remind the agent of their chance meeting in Spokane. And a book deal arrived three months later. As reported, the book was a bust. However, a television producer thumbed through his first published work in a used bookstore, in Ohio of all places, and thought it had a made-for-the-small-screen idea buried within it. Clark received a three thousand dollar option and that was enough for him to live in a small cabin in Oregon, near Bend, and write his second novel: *The Tree Line*.

*The Tree Line* was a "smashing success," according to Moss to anyone who would listen. It became a Hollywood box office hit and Jack Lawrence's career was set. Royalties poured in. New York publishers beat a path to his door. (Well to be accurate, they beat a path to Moss's door.) Clark along with his nom de plume were crowned the next great thing to sit at a keyboard. Jack Lawrence was mentioned in the same breath as Faulkner, Hemingway and Steinbeck. He became the modern day equivalent to Fitzgerald or Salinger. His reputation flourished even more when he released the best-seller, *Men and Slaves*, his third book, which he followed closely with the semi-autobiographical *Angels and Whiskey*, considered by many critics to be his masterpiece. There were classes taught about his work at universities across Canada and the States. A woman in Australia wrote her Ph.D. dissertation on his depiction of women in his novels. (Her view was slightly biased and she did not have a very favorable opinion of Jack's male protagonists.) Moss told him not to be hung up over such intellectual arguments. "They are reading your works and writing about them;

that's all that matters." Hardly a week went by that he wasn't on some TV talk show, radio show or podcast somewhere. Alcoholic's Anonymous even used excerpts from the book for their curriculum. He never imagined that drying out could be so profitable.

Now his current project – *The Promised Land* – was being lauded as the next Pulitzer or Nobel Prize winner. Producers, directors and screen writers from southern California couldn't get to Oregon fast enough to throw money at his feet for a chance at the rights to the script.

His agent, Harold Moss, had to tell them that Jack was away for a few weeks. Family business. He would return their calls and offers soon. Soon he promised. Moss hoped it would be soon, because the fever was hot and so too were the offers. It was time to strike while the fire raged.

But he had gone fishing. With is father. On the very lake where the accident had happened over twenty years before.

It was about two weeks before the first trial was to commence. The house was empty and there were no lights on, except for the back den. Beams of pale yellow from the streetlights lazily drifted through the window sheers into the darkened living room and dining area, giving the rooms a shadowy, haunted feel, as the silhouettes of outside tree branches danced about the rooms like skeletons of ghostly figures. Clark sat on the back divan, not really engaged with anything, although there was a paperback book due for an English Lit class, resting in his lap. For the most part he was simply staring off into space. Wondering what he had gotten himself into.

A knock at the front door, then the doorbell, brought him back to Earth. He arose and walked in his sock feet to the entryway and opened the door. Standing all alone and with the light of the front porch shining down on her like a spotlight was Missy Rusk. She wore a blue jacket under which was a white silk blouse that was unbuttoned a few buttons too many to be a mistake and a very short, navy mini skirt. Her heels were not excessively tall, but they did add height to her slender frame and gave her beautiful legs definition. He spoke first. "I'm sorry, Missy. Lee is out. He went with mom and dad to dinner."

"You didn't go?" she asked.

He shook his head. "Didn't feel like it. I'm kind of an outcast just now."

"You're going to testify. Right?"

He nodded. Words wouldn't come out of his parched mouth. Had she been sent to talk him out of his legal obligation?

"Well, tell the truth, Clark. Just tell the truth. That's all anybody wants you to do."

"I will." He found his voice. "But I'm not too sure everybody sees the truth the same way I do. Anyway, like I say, Lee's out and they probably won't be back for some time."

"They go to the club?" She asked.

"No. To Longview. To the Rancher's Steak House."

"I see." She looked back at her car then at her watch. "May I come in?"

He nodded and stepped aside.

"How long do we have?" asking, as she brushed very close to him. She smelled of jasmine, he thought.

"For what?"

34

"Until they are home."

He looked at his watch. "Maybe an hour – hour and a half."

"Okay." She walked to the long floral sofa in the living room and placed her jacket across its deeply upholstered back and then she made a straight line for the light in the back den and as she did, she pulled her blouse out from the mini skirt and let it flow loosely around her slim hips. She eased onto the divan and kicked her shoes off.

She patted the divan, "Come sit by me, Clark."

"Listen, Missy, If you are trying to get me to change my ..."

"I'm not here to tell you what to say. I'm not here to tell you what you saw. I'm here to tell you something very important – at least to me it is."

"What?"

"Come sit." He did and she reached for him and pulled him to her. They had kissed before. It was while Lee was in the hospital having his leg operated on from the football injury. At first, it had been a quick kiss. In her car. In the hospital parking lot. She had been in tears. He assumed for Lee. And while trying to comfort her, they had come together and kissed. The first one was quick. In passing. But the second one was long and involved. It went on for several minutes. It was embarrassing. At least to him it was. But she had held on to him for a long time and then finally pushed him away and said she had to get home. She hurriedly drove off and he returned to Lee's room, very confused and very excited, after all she was Lee's girlfriend.

They had two other encounters, not counting the night of the dance. Again while Lee was convalescing at home. Clark had gone to the marina to check on his dad's old boat. Lester had sold it. His father was buying a giant party deck boat – a pontoon boat – with a cabin and huge outboard motors. He had asked Clark to go clean the old boat for the buyers who were coming to have a look at it on the following Saturday. As Clark was getting out of his car, Missy pulled up next to him in her Mustang. He stepped over to the passenger side window, which she had lowered.

"Get in. I want to show you something." She said it without emotion; just a matter of fact statement. They drove to the county parking lot above the cliffs that overlooked the east side of the lake. No one was around. She parked the car, turning off the engine and dousing the lights. She turned in her car seat and leaned into him. He knew what to do. They kissed. They groped and they kissed some more. It would have gone a lot further, but another car pulled in and made a giant circle around them, then sped off. Without saying a word, Missy started the Ford and drove him back to the marina.

"I hear you may be going away," he said.

She nodded with a tear running down her cheek. She tossed her long hair and its spiral curve out of her blue eyes, in a Rita Haywood motion. He reached for her, but she scooted away and grabbed tightly to the steering wheel. Then she turned and faced him. "I'm sorry, Clark. I am sorry it wasn't you."

All he could do was nod. He understood.

"I'm going away and we never had our chance."

"I know." He said it, rather pathetically, as he remembered it. "Where will he send you?"

"Europe. London first for finishing school A place called St. Mary's."

"Sounds like a school for nuns," he laughed trying to make a joke out of her banishment.

"Don't laugh. It will not be fun. Then I have a job lined up in Paris. With a modeling agency."

"Well, that seems glamorous."

"I am." She joked and this time they both laughed.

"I'm going to miss you," He whispered as he kissed her again.

"You'll leave here, find a girl, get married and have about a thousand kids. You won't think twice about me."

"That's not true. You are all I ever think about."

"That's what Lee says, but I bet he forgets about me before you do."

"May I write you?"

"Yes. But I don't promise to read your letters."

"Why?" He asked, feeling let down at the prospects of her ignoring his letters.

"It would hurt too much to hear from you. I want to remember you just as you are. And again, I am sorry we never got our chance."

But now they were on the divan together and she lay back and he was on her and before they knew it, they had made their union once more. It was not like the evening of the dance. It was nothing of great and lasting art. Hot and steamy, rushed teenage sex, at best. If someone had been keeping tally, they wouldn't have been impressed with the score. But it was satisfying to both of them. So she held him tightly, not wanting the moment to leave her. She had him in her arms at last. He smelled her deeply and thought that if he died just then, his life would have been fulfilled – silly high school romantic notions. And then just as quickly as she had shown up, she dressed and headed for the door.

"Oh no you don't. You don't make love to me and then run out like that. What the hell is going on, Missy?"

"I love you Clark. I have loved you for years and years. I have dreamed of having you. And, I don't know. Somehow I thought I could get to you through Lee. And I guess I have and now it is too late. I am going away and ..."

"Missy." He said her name over and over as he pulled on his pants. "Missy, don't go. Stay."

"No, Clark. I have to go. We had our time, as short as it was. Now it is over. But at least we had it. It is ours." She stopped her advance on the doorway and turned back to him. "...I want you to never, never, never tell Lee."

"I wouldn't. You know I wouldn't."

"Swear to me."

"Oh, I swear. Missy, I have loved you for a long time, but I couldn't tell you because of my brother..."

She placed her finger over his lips, then she kissed him one last time and turned to leave. He grabbed for her, but she pulled her slim wrist away from his grasp. "No. I have to go, Clark. You have to let me go. It's over."

She gathered her jacket, stuffed her blouse back inside the blue mini skirt and exited the front door leaving Clark in a cold, dark house, all alone.

It would be almost twenty years before they laid eyes on one another again. But when they did, they both knew that nothing between them had changed.

The studio lights shown on his face, and he felt as if he was squinting. He asked the host, before the cameras were turned on, if he was squinting, and the host, Tanner Brooks, said not to worry, "Everyone feels that way under these bright lights. Just try and forget they are there. Forget there is a camera. Just you and me, lad, having a wee conversation. Two blokes talking about books."

He nodded.

The floor director pointed to Tanner and did a countdown with his fingers from five.

"Good evening ladies and gentlemen and welcome to this edition of The Written Word on BBC. It is our distinct pleasure and honor to introduce you to Jack Lawrence, author of several critically acclaimed novels, including *The Tree Line, Men and Slaves* and a new book, just out from Simpson House, *Angels and Whiskey*. Jack, welcome."

"Thank you, Tanner. Good to be here." Clark said.

"Your first time with us, I believe?'

"Yes. First time in England, as well."

Well, on behalf of the queen and her realm, welcome." They both laughed. "Let's begin with *Men and Slaves*. A rather caustic look at life wouldn't you say?"

"Yes. I would. But the whole reason for its biting attitude is that many men today are wandering – loose – adrift with nothing to guide them and they end up in the bottle."

"Men alone?"

"I said men, but really I should have said persons, because it applies to the female gender as much as the male version of the species. It's just that I am male and I write it from that perspective."

"Much like your latest offering, *Angels and Whiskey*, believed by more than a few to be autobiographical."

"Perhaps."

"You're not saying?"

"I suppose everything I write has a touch of me in it. It would be almost impossible not to have. In *Men and Slaves*, the protagonist certainly isn't me. I have never killed anyone. Thought about it, but never carried it out."

"You have thought about killing someone?"

"Well, not like I planned a murder, but there have been times when I was so angry with a person that I could visualize them dead."

"A product of your own bout with the bottle?"

"To be sure." Clark paused wondering how much he should offer of himself on TV. "I am..." He paused and then plowed ahead, "...I have never hidden from the fact that I went through some rather dark days thanks to my dependence on alcohol. It was my liquid depression."

"Did you write during those times?"

"I tried," said Clark. "But more often than not what came out was gibberish. Nonsense. But I will also confess, that part of *Men and Slaves* was written under the influence. It was a test to myself – to see if I could swim up through the murkiness of being a drunk and create something coherent."

"I would say you passed the test."

"Only partially. Much of the section written while I was under the influence, had to be reworked. Heavy editing."

"What did Hemingway say – 'Write drunk-edit sober?'" Tanner raised his thick brushy eyebrows.

Clark nodded, "Yes, but I have never actually found the attribution of him saying that. He is credited with it, but I'm not sure it was his or certainly not originally his. But the sentiment is there: be overly creative, washed in the spirit of the muse, if you will, when writing; then be brutally honest and fastidiously sober when editing. Writing takes spontaneity and an explosion of ideas. Editing takes a brutal and sharp knife. You can't be in love with your words when you edit."

"And did you then wait until you were sober to continue writing?"

"Yes. Only because I discovered that writing sober is so much more rewarding. You have so much more control. Plus you're not wasting valuable time always looking for the next drink. There is a true freedom to sobriety."

"Losing control seems to be a theme, which weaves through your collection of work. Why is this so vital to you?" the host leaned back, with his long legs crossed in his neatly pressed suit pants, as if he expected Jack to go off on some personal story. His posture said 'go ahead and tell us something about yourself. We're waiting. We're all ears.'

"I lost someone every close to me a long time ago. Over something that was," Clark stopped, remembering – then continued, "...that was for the most part, out of my control. I realized that no matter what I said or did, the act of her being removed from my life was beyond my power. It created in me the emptiest feeling I have ever suffered through. It was, in no small way, the reason my life spiraled down and into a bottle."

"So, do you write to warn others of the same fate?"

"No. I write to exercise the demons still within me. If someone gets a lesson from it, so be it. But it is written for me. And I write for her. Wherever she might be, whatever she might be doing. I write to let her know that even though she is no longer in my life – I still care for her."

"Your latest book is already getting rave appraisals from critics and reviewers; and it is being whispered, rather loudly I might add, that it is autobiographical. True?"

Clark was a bit perturbed because Tanner had circled back to this theme; one of which Clark had tried to avoid. "Perhaps more than others books I have written before it. But still only symbolically. The characters are friends of mine from inside my own brain. Some share the same faults that I have. Other are purely witnesses to the acts that my imagination conjures. But in this great gumbo that I mix, the true ingredients – the stress and the conflict – are all things I have endured at some level. So to that degree, I suppose it is autobiographical. But just."

"Have you heard from this lost love?" Asked Tanner. "Has there been communication?"

"No. I have no idea where she is." It was a lie. He had seen her on almost every magazine cover she had posed for and had a good feeling she lived either in the South of France or in Italy. But he wasn't about to say that on the BBC.

"If you could reach out and speak to her – if she happened to catch this show, what would you tell her?"

"Read my books. Buy them. I need the money." The host and Clark both laughed. He had made a joke and turned the interview away from the deep scar that constantly reopened and bled profusely inside of him. He had turned the attention away from her. No need to drag her into this moment.

"Sober these days, are we, Jack?"

"Yes. Thankfully."

"How did you break away from your addiction?"

"My manger and agent, Harold Moss was the one who got me dried out, propped up and writing again. I owe much to his persistence and devotion."

"Does he appear in any of your work?"

"No. He just gets a percentage from it." Again laugher from the host.

"So, what's next? A new book in the works?"

"I am always noodling. Always jotting notes and sketching scenes. Always looking for the next venue in which to set a novel. But so far, nothing."

"And the characters you develop...any new ones floating about in that gray matter of yours?"

"Always. I never stop meeting new people in my mind. It's as if I was holding a continuous casting session of potential characters to write about."

"Therapy might help that," joked Tanner.

"Then my pool of talent would dry up and I would fear not being able to produce another book."

"Well, I can speak for a lot of readers, myself included, stay off the counselor's settee. We're counting on you to thrill us some more. Would you be so kind as to read a passage from your wonderful book *Men and Salves*?"

He handed Jack the paperback version of the best-selling novel. It was marked to the selection the host wanted shared with his audience.

"The main character in this book," explained Clark as background for the episode he was about to read, "...is a day laborer who has fallen in love with the daughter of the wealthy landowner for whom he works. It is a love affair that will never last – at least powers beyond his control will see to it that it never lasts. This scene is the young man and the woman, at a river on the father's property. He has observed her bathing and has moved to her and taken her into his arms. It is their last meeting." He began to read:

"The lazy river wandered past them almost unnoticed. The wind, which had wrestled with the cottonwood branches earlier, eased its tormenting and nestled softly to watch as the two lovers fell into each other's arms. The sun, shown softly to warm them from the coolness of the early autumn afternoon, its shadows growing long on the lush banks of the stream. She pushed her damp body back from him and sat, as he placed his hands, wrapped in a towel, on her head. Slowly he began to dry her hair. Massaging her scalp, then her neck, next he ran his fingers along the contours of her soft cheeks and finally, placing a single finger beneath her chin, he lifted her face upwards and bent to deliver to her, a soft, moist kiss. She wrapped her fragile hands around the back of his thick neck and interlocked her fingers and pulled him to her. They lay down in the soft, matted reeds at the river's edge. In the distance a bird sang out. It was answered by another, then another, until an entire chorus of birds filled the air with some melody of a song that only they knew. But they knew it well. And then as suddenly as the song started, it was quiet.

"'This will not go on. My father has already warned me. He has said that I can't see you anymore.'

"'I know. He has warned me as much, as well. In fact, he has even threatened me,' the young man said.

"'What are we going to do?'

"He didn't have an answer for her. Yet, in his heart he knew this would be their last time together. He would be exiled from the farm and sent away – far away – to work somewhere else for some other master growing some other crop. He was no more than a slave. His shackles were not of iron but rather of poverty. He was no more than a number on an accounting ledger – number two hundred and ten. Easy to erase and even easier to replace.

"He would receive a day's wage and then be sent down a long, dusty road away from the farm that stretched the length of the valley beside the meandering river. He would have to walk to the distant rise, to the highway, which led to Salinas. Everything he owned would be neatly folded into a single cloth bag. There at the highway, he would catch a ride with some long-haul trucker who would drive him away from her. They would cross the river at the bridge over the gorge, leaving the farm to their south and he would be out of her life. But not out of her heart.

"He held her tightly. There was a rustling in the leaves across the river and they saw a deer emerge from the shadows of the trees. The doe spotted them and froze. Slowly, carefully it moved to the edge of the river, bending down it lapped the water gently then quickly returned to the shadows of the trees and was gone. That would be his life – tasting her one last time, then he, too, would slowly disappear into the shadows of the future, whatever it held.

"The afternoon passed. The sky darkened. He kissed her and stood to dress. She was still on her back where she had accepted him. He looked down on her, wishing to apologize for not being of wealth and means to provide for her – at least in the measure of her father's eyes. He would have asked for forgiveness for his poverty, he would have asked for forgiveness for not being of the right social status to deserve her. But no words would come. He simply nodded and blew her a kiss.

"Looking to the west he saw the storm clouds growing tall and dark. There was lightning in the distance past the ridge and a muted drum of thunder. 'Weather's coming. You'd better go.'

"'She pulled at him to return to her, but he resisted. 'I must go. You must go. It is over.' As he said it, he knew in his heart that he had just sealed any chance he might have her. They would separate and go their own ways. Each following a path prescribed for them by others. Each moving away from the one thing they shared– their love for one another.

"'It would be the last time he saw her in the flesh, although she visited him, everyday for the rest of his life.

"She even shared a cell with him in the prison. Shared it to his dying days."

Applause. A small studio audience had enjoyed his reading.

"Jack, it is such a sad and forlorn passage, considering all the things that it leads to in the young man's life. He truly became a slave to his love for her, as well."

"Yes. It was his fate and he, instead of fighting for her or even facing the situation and the struggles it meant, he turned and walked away and that one act tormented him for the rest of his life."

"Well written. *Men and Slaves*, by Jack Lawrence. Find it at a bookseller near you soon ... and enjoy it...and the rest of this fine author's work.

"Ladies and gentlemen, Jack Lawrence."

More applause.

"Next week on The Written Word, we have another American author, James Commer. If sci-fi and westerns are your cup of tea, do tune in, because James takes us along a spooky, dusty labyrinth filled with rattlesnakes, aliens and supernatural wonders. Until next week, I'm Tanner Brooks and this has been The Written Word on BBC."

The lights faded and the floor crew became instantly busy tearing down the set and moving chairs. A production assistant removed the microphone attached to Clark's coat "You know James Commer?" asked Tanner.

"Met him at a writer's conference in Austin, once. I think it was during South by Southwest. Before Covid."

"I love his mixture of the fantasy and the old west."

"Yes. He's rather inventive at that," said Clark. And for some unknown reason, at just that moment, Clark thought of her. Clearly seeing her in his mind's eye. She came and went in his life like that: not a thought about her for a day or two, then suddenly a barrage of images as clear as if she were standing right next to him. At times he could even smell her.

Maybe it was the reading of that passage. He never knew.

At that moment, she was in the British Airways lounge at Heathrow. They were less than five miles apart. She was heading for a week-long shoot, staged on some beautiful Indian Ocean island– an oasis for the super rich to congregate and relax. There would be a camera crew, make-up artists, hair stylists, the clients and scores of hangers-on, all staring at her bikini-clad body, basted in coconut oil and glistening in the tropical sun. And the only thing she had to do was look like Missy Rusk. That is, after all, what they wanted – what they paid for.

She walked to the bar and ordered a glass of white wine and looked up at the TV monitor. On the screen was a BBC show called The Written Word, hosted by Tanner Brooks, a man she knew ever so briefly from a drunken party over a New Year's weekend several years ago. He was a bit of an ass if she remembered. He wanted sex and she wanted to go home.

But the other man – the guest was a writer from the States. A man Tanner kept calling Jack Lawrence. But she knew who he really was.

He was Clark Harvey.

She had not seen him since high school. But it was Clark. She asked the bartender to turn the volume up so she could hear what they were saying. His voice sent shivers down her spine. Her heart raced for a moment. She breathed deeply as he read the selection from the book, which poured off his tongue as poetry to her ears and heart. It had been so long ago. But there he was. His moppish hair was longer than she remembered. His face, narrowed and pale. His thin nose was framed with wire-rim specs that he continually pushed upwards. It occurred to her that it was more a nervous action than a correction of gravity on the glasses. He seemed to squint – the lights, she guessed.

But it was him. It was her Clark.

She stopped at a newsstand on the way to her gate and bought three of his books. He was going to accompany her to Asia, so it would not be such a long and lonely flight after all.

## Chapter three

Miles Pennington recognized him one day at the grocery store. Willie had sent him into town for some milk and bread. "And pick me up some of those good Spanish olives, if they have 'em. Sometimes they have 'em and sometimes not. If they have 'em get me a jar. They're the ones with the green and yellow label." And so, while he was walking the aisles hunting for Willie's Spanish olives, Miles Pennington, who was roaming the aisles searching for empty holes in the inventory on the shelves, came upon him.

"Clark. Clark Harvey, as I live and breathe. Here in the flesh in Lincoln."

"Miles. Good to see you." He extended his hand and Miles shuffled the notebook computer in his hands and they shook.

"What brings you back here after all these years?" Asked Miles.

"Mom and dad."

"Yeah I heard. Tough going there with Willie. She is a great lady."

"Yeah. I'm afraid cancer's gonna win this round." He said it, but felt no emotion to his pre-announcing his mother's demise. All have to die, and Willie, like the rest of humanity would die, too. That's how Clark felt.

"Hell of a fight she's given it," said Miles.

"She's a tough old bird."

"I'll say. Hey, how long you in town for?"

"Not real sure."

"Maybe I can scare some of the old gang up and we can go have a drink or grab some barbeque. We got a new place here called Angry Bob's. Really, really good ribs. And the sauce is made by the devil himself. You remember Bob Armstead?"

"The quarterback from high school?"

"Yep. It's his place. It's his second shot at running his own restaurant. This one seems to have the magic."

"Sounds good. Why don't you give me a shout in a day or two. I'm taking dad fishing tomorrow."

"How's the old man doing?"

"There some of the time. Someplace else the other times. Never quite here. I'd call it dementia, but the doctors say it isn't. Who the hell knows?"

"Well, he did have a pretty good kick in the head with that stroke."

"Yeah. So I heard."

"Where you been keeping yourself?"

"I live up in the Pacific Northwest."

"That's a long way from Lincoln."

"Yeah." He wanted to say more but he refrained.

"Say, I was sure sorry about Lee and all. I mean what a guy! What a guy!"

"Yeah. Lee was the best."

"Sorry we missed you at his services."

"Yeah, nobody could reach me so I didn't know anything about it. Say, do you know where the Spanish olives are?"

"That Willie. She is always after me about keeping them stocked." He checked his computer. "I'm out now, but I'll put an order in from Shreveport; they'll be here tomorrow for sure. Got to be on our toes. National chains are on there way here. And folks will drive up to Marshall for that new big Wal-Mart. I gotta do everything I can to compete. Know what I mean?""

"Yep. Thanks Miles. And call me about that barbeque."

"You can count on it."

Clark hoped that Miles would forget about it and it would not come to pass. He really didn't care about reliving old days with high school friends.

The boat had a gray hull with maroon pinstripes running along each side from stern to bow. A Johnson outboard was pushing it from behind. It made a purring sound, not the big guttural grunt of an Evinrude, but a more gentle, almost silent hum. It was just as powerful but quieter. "Johnson's a lot quieter than the Evinrude. I know you used to like Evinrudes on your boats back in the day." His father just nodded, looking blankly straight ahead.

They made their way along the eastern shore of the lake, leaving the marina behind them while passing the road up to Lincoln, before it made its wandering turn at the park into the club. He could make out a few trucks and cars driving down the road, heading toward the giant body of water. "Glad we got out early to beat the crowds."

It was a Friday. The weekenders would be flocking to the lake soon and the waterway would get crowded with other fishermen and skiers. Drunks would be the real danger.

Lester nodded and looked out across the still lake'. "I like Evinrude motors best of all."

Clark took a quick look at his father, nodded then returned to scanning the lake for the peninsula with its protruding rocks, guarding its eastern most flank. There they would go either north or west. North would lead them up to Rock Island, while heading west would put them on a trajectory to reach Pine Island.

Pine Island wasn't truly an island but rather a long strip of sand, clay, pine and oak jutting out into the lake almost surrounded on all sides by water. Except for a thin wisp of land where Cotter's Creek and Newsome's Creek emptied into the lake; one on either side of that sole stitch of land that for a few hundred yards clawed into the mainland holding the peninsula to the landmass and kept it locked forever as a part of the shore. But still most people called it Pine Island.

"You know it's not really an island, don't you?"

Lester nodded. "Yes. Everyone knows that."

"Why did you like Evinrudes better?"

"They looked and sounded meaner."

"Like Ford and Chevy? You're either a Ford or Chevy guy, right?"

"Nope. Company owned both. I'd trade with Lowery's and Carr every other year. Kept my business going between them. Chevys some years. Fords other years. Even bought a couple of Dodges once from a guy over in Henderson. Our big trucks, the ones we had rigs on, were International Harvesters. They come from Kilgore. Didn't have favorites. Just the best deal. It was business.

But boats ..." Lester paused. "... but boats were show. Boats were sport."

It was the most that Lester had said to him in twenty plus years. Then he slipped back into his fog.

The boat glided smoothly along the slowly undulating waves, which ran slightly north and south. Ripples basically, because the day was still and little wind was present to stir the great body of water. Not like the night of the accident.

"You ever eaten at Angry Bob's?" He asked his father.

Lester shook his head. "That's the Armstead fellow's place? Yeah. They brought it into the club one night. You know, for us to try out. Pretty good if I remember right. But it's a new place and I don't get out much anymore. Especially at night."

"But you've tried it?'

"I said I had. I said I thought it was good. Okay?"

"Got it." Clark paused then said, "Let's go to the railroad bridge and work our way back along the north shore of Pine Island."

His father nodded. Then after quite a spell said, "Whatever."

Miles recruited about six old high school chums to gather at Angry Bob's. The beer was cold, the ribs hot and the sauce even hotter. "I'd say Lincoln has a winner when it comes to barbeque," said Clark, as he sipped a cola while the others swigged beer after ice-cold beer.

"So what'cha been doing with yourself, Clark?" Asked Beth Rollings, who used to be Beth Towns. Her dad had been a pharmacist until he was caught sticking needles in his arm to get a kick every now and then. Only every now and then had become something of a habit and was more like all the time. One day the FBI or DEA or somebody from the government with a bunch of initials came in and drove him away. That was Clark's junior year of high school. He always felt bad for Beth because of that. They had dated once but it had gotten no further than a quick French kiss. She had braces back then and they cut his tongue. Besides the braces souring his romance with Beth, Clark was interested in another girl – a girl a year younger. Her name was Missy Rusk. She lived twelve miles away. In Kilgore.

"I'm a writer." His answer was quick and cryptic. He liked it better that way. Maybe they wouldn't ask too many questions. He suddenly felt it had been a mistake to come to the gathering. He preferred the solitude of his cabin in Oregon. He missed it and the ability to become a hermit and hide away from questioning strangers or even more – nosy old friends.

"My mom says you had a hit movie." It came from Andy Reynolds. His dad had been district judge and had presided over both of the trials. Clark remembered Andy's father to be fair – tough but fair. He was a man who didn't like people twisting or bending the truth. And he didn't give lawyers much room to badger witnesses.

"Not me. A screenwriter who used one of my novels as a platform did. I don't write for movies."

"Why not? There's a lot of money in that, so I hear." Andy said.

"Well, we all make a few bucks in the process here and there."

"What was your movie?" Asked Miles. "Say pass me another rib and some sauce."

"Well I didn't write the movie but my book was called – is called – *The Tree Line*."

"Jesus Christ of Cleveland. You wrote that?" Said Andy.

"Not the movie. The novel it was based on."

"My God, that was big. Who was that blonde who played Margo?" asked Miles.

"GeeGee Phillips," answered Beth before he had a chance to tell them. "And she co-starred opposite Phil Rice. What a heartthrob. Did you ever get to meet them?"

"Ah yes. A few times. The producers would fly me down to L.A. and have me on location while certain scenes were being filmed, so I could pass my ideas over to the writers. It's a tough novel to turn into a motion picture. The dialog and the narration. It kind of runs together – stream of consciousness. It has to be done in balance...well, listen to me go on and on. Enough about me, what have you guys been up to?"

"Fuck us. You got to meet GeeGee Phillips?" Miles was frothing at the mouth to know more.

He nodded. "Yes."

"What's she like?" asked Andy. "She is so hot. Did you write the part with her in mind – I mean at the outset?"

"No. No. Nothing like that. I didn't even have much say in her being cast. The studio does all of that. The producer and the director get together and make those kind of decisions. Way above my pay grade."

"But you got to talk with her?" Andy asked hopefully. "Right?"

"Yeah we went out on her boat one night and partied. Fun girl. Great hostess. And we even got Phil Rice drunk and made him dive overboard into the harbor." They all laughed.

"You were on her boat? Asked Miles in disbelief.

"Yeah it was awesome. Big cabin cruiser with about five staterooms. And a kitchen bigger than my mom's kitchen. "

"I thought she was married." It came from Beth.

"She is. Her husband was there with us."

A collective moan came from the group. They had visions of their friend, the writer, and movie star cohabiting on a party boat. He had to inform them that no such intermingling happened. Not then anyway. Later, at a Hollywood party and under the influence of a lot of booze and dope, he and GeeGee had managed to comingle. There were photographs, but GeeGee's agent had paid a lot of money to suppress them. He didn't really remember much of it, partly because of the chemical-induced fog he was swimming in during those days. He still would be in that dark cloud, had it not been for Harold Moss, who fished him out of the blackness and got his feet planted on solid ground and headed back in the right direction.

"So what does a writer get for a screenplay like that?" asked Andy.

"Don't know. I just wrote the novel."

"Why didn't you write the screenplay as well?" asked Debra Howell, a friend of Beth's who seemed to be there at Angry Bob's with Andy, who was married to Judy Brooks. He had forgotten how incestuous small town romances and trysts could be.

"I don't write screenplays. I write novels. Once I've struggled through five or six hundred pages, I don't want anymore to do with those characters. I wish them off onto somebody else, take my money and go back under my rock." As the words left his lips, he thought they painted a rather apt picture of his life in Lincoln. He was truly through with these characters and wished to leave and go back under his rock in Oregon and write.

"I'm hung up on a rock." His father was struggling with the rod. He didn't have enough strength to free the lure and line from the submerged foe. Something under water was holding taught to his line. "It's a rock, I tell you. I'm hung up on a damn rock."

Clark took the rod and reel from his father's trembling hand and eased the boat forward to take the pressure off the line. Suddenly the line went slack and he began to reel in the lure. He handed the rod back to his father. "Here. It's fixed now. Try again."

"I don't like this lure," the old man sounded pouty.

"There's a whole box of them behind you. Help yourself," said Clark. Then he added, "If you can."

The old man didn't seem to pay the dig any mind. He turned the tackle box toward him, opened its hinged top and selected a shiny silver lure. He replaced his old lure in the drawer of the box and closed the lid and returned to fishing. "We got any beer?"

"Yes we do. But it isn't even ten in the morning."

"So who gives a damn? We're fishing. You drink beer when you fish."

Clark produced a bottle of ice-cold beer from the cooler in the front of the boat and handed it to his father. The old man took a long swig from the amber bottle then stared off into space. "You drink beer when you go fishing. You drink from brown bottles not green ones. Green ones taste like skunk. Know what I mean? You drink beer when you go fishing... from brown bottles."

"Or when you go boating with a problem on board." Clark let his words linger in the gentle breeze, which was freshening. His father either didn't hear it or ignored it.

They were not from Lincoln originally. They lived first in Oklahoma, then they moved to Kilgore, some twelve miles to the west of Lincoln. His parents had moved there in '50. Well, actually Lester came in '49 and left Willie in Ardmore with her folks – the Crows – until he got his feet firmly planted in the oil patch. He did, thanks to a good-paying job with the Humble Oil and Refining Company. For four years he worked with the big oil company until one day a man named Rusk, as in Howard Rusk, one of the wealthiest families of Kilgore, came to him and offered him a job. "I need a driller to run my operations. I hear you're pretty good." That was the same year the twins were born.

"I'm better than pretty good," bragged Lester. "I'm the best one you'll interview."

"You may be the only one I interview." The two struck a friendship that would last the next sixteen years. It would see them drill well after well and strike more riches underground that just about any outfit in the East Texas field.

Howard Rusk had been born in the county that bore his family name. It was a stretch of land south of Gregg County – south of the Kilgore oil field, and for the most part, was populated by day farmers – cotton people and people who worked in the giant brick factory or at the commercial feed lot. Even with the family name enshrined on that corner of Texas, his side of the clan was by no means wealthy or powerful. His father was little more than a sharecropper who had eked out enough savings during the depression to buy some land west of Henderson, the county seat. Howard only left East Texas long enough to go to school in Austin, earn a petroleum engineering degree then go to Houston to chase and marry Ruth Paramour and then return with her to East Texas. This time, he drove eighteen miles north of Henderson to Kilgore. The oil boom was in full swing. He hired two rigs and set them up on his dad's property and began drilling. Somewhere around 3,500 feet below the muddy service of the bottomlands, in the strata known as the Woodbine, they hit pay dirt. Oil. Lots of it.

Rusk tore down a two-story house and built a huge mansion for Ruth and his two daughters, Ellie and Missy. The girls would grow into beautiful women, Ellie going to New York to dabble in fine art, real estate and exciting men, while Missy ventured to Paris to become a very sexy fashion model.

"Let's troll the far bank. More brush than rocks there. I think the fish will be more likely there."

The old man nodded. He didn't say anything but just nodded. He let out some line to allow the lure to flow away from the boat and dive under a bit. Clark eased the boat slowly toward the bank and then slowed it to a crawl, as he too cast toward the waiting shallows, with downed trees and scrub brush. "They like it in the dark shallows over there," Clark said. He pointed to a pine tree that had uprooted in an earlier storm and lay partially in the water, its ball of twisted roots thrust out of the red clay into the air toward the island, looking like an explosion caught on a frame of film.

The old man slowly reeled in his line. Suddenly there was a flurry of activity below the water's surface and a fish began to tug at the unseen lure. "Got one," said his father in a very calm manner. "Got one." He began to crank the reel and the fish responded with a quick jerk then everything went still. The line went limp in the water. "Lost it."

His father reeled the line in and the lure was missing. "Took my damn lure." Lester laughed. "He'll live a long time with that hook stuck in his fuckin' mouth." The old man reached into the tackle box and produced another artificial bait. He tied it onto a swivel and tossed it into the water, letting the line out slowly to match the speed of the drifting boat. Inch by inch, the silver reflection of the lure disappeared beneath the murky waters until it was out of sight. They both waited.

Clark thought of the fish, swimming away, fear and adrenalin rushing though its veins after the brief fight. He thought of the hook lodged in its mouth. It was the same feeling he had for his father everyday he was away from Lincoln. His father still had a painful sharp hook into Clark. It wasn't connected so as to pull him back, but it was a painful reminder of what had transpired on that lake. The pain was always there. He couldn't get loose from it.

Willie got up from the small sofa to fetch a box of tissues. Her nose had begun to bleed. She coughed a few times and he could tell she was bringing up bloody mucus.

60

It was a sad sight for him to see his mother like this, but she didn't seem to notice his staring, or if she did, she certainly didn't say anything about it. No reason to cause any more attention to be paid to her than already had been. That's how Willie lived her life.

She turned the conversation back to her husband. "You're going to have to decide what to do with him. I mean, you two can live here. He knows the place. He's comfortable here. No sense putting him in some home where they'll let him wilt away to nothing."

"And who's going to watch after him here? I mean when you're gone."

"You will. Of course."

"No, way, Mom. No way. I'm here for a few days then I'm back home."

"This is your home, Clark."

"No. It hasn't been my home for a long time. Not since that night..."

"We're not going there. Not under this roof. Not ever again. That day, those days, are gone. If you want to talk about that stuff, you take him out on the boat and discuss it with him out on the lake. But not under my roof. You hear me?"

He nodded, but inside Clark was steaming mad. It was as if nobody would recognize the truth. At least not recognize his version of the truth and of what happened that night.

"Someday you're going to have to face this, Mom."

"No. I'm going to die soon and I'll be rid of it and this whole mess. It has torn my family apart and just about ruined my marriage. Compared to that, cancer is a blessing, Clark. It truly is."

## Chapter four

When an oil well is drilled, a rotary bit is sunk into the ground that is attached to a stem of drill pipe. On each end of the pipe are threads, and as the bit goes deeper and deeper into the ground, sections of pipe are screwed together to form what the drillers call a string. Think of it as a long straw sinking into a deep, thick malt. The weight of the pipe, as it forms its string, helps push the rotating bit deeper into the sediments below.

To cool the drill bit, to lubricate it and to lift crushings and sediment out of the path of the bit, a watery paste called 'mud' is pumped into the center of the hole and it flows back up-stream from the pressures below.

Down, down the drill bit rotates and more and more pressure is applied to the mud at the surface to get the lubricant to the bottom of the hole to flush debris back to the topside. The drilling goes further and further down, until somewhere along the way the drill bit gets dull and has to be backed out and replaced and the operation is repeated. The crew call it a trip. Fresh bit and stem after stem of pipe, cutting into rock, shale and sand. It is long, hard and gruelingly dirty work.

Now an astute driller will know that if he applies a bit of weight and pressure at an angle to the top of the incoming drill stems, he can slowly turn the bit far below the surface to a direction that suits his needs. Next he adds a device called a whipstock, which sets the course of the drilling into the new direction at a more acute angle. It is professionally referred to as horizontal drilling, but crudely referred to as slant-hole drilling. And it is very rewarding if say the property one is drilling on is barren of any subterranean oil deposits, but the neighboring section of land has oil beneath it. One simply turns the drilling toward the neighboring oil pool and begins to sip oil from someone else's lease.

A little at a time and no one knows. A lot at a time and everyone knows. Cheating in the oil patch is a fine art. A slight of hand played thousands of feet underground. Some have likened it to playing poker with hands held under the table – cards unseen by the participants. Crafty watchers of the dark art can spot the illicit wells by the amount of drill pipe they use, or by the pressure their wells gain while neighboring wells begin to loose pressure.

It is a game of directional degrees and inches of pressure. It is measured in gallons of mud and feet of cast iron pipe and steel casing.

Regardless of how it is discovered, it is a crime. A huge crime. And beginning in 1960 the crime started to unravel. Rumors ran wild around Gregg and Rusk counties. Kilgore and Longview suddenly played host to all sorts of lawmen and investigators. Speculation grew that there were cheats syphoning off oil from unsuspecting victims. A Shell Oil Company well – toward the western edge of the Gregg County field was being worked on and a drilling engineer alerted a Texas Ranger who noticed that drilling mud from a well a few thousand feet away was coming up in the Shell Oil well's pipe. Impossible, unless the two wells were intersecting in and near the same pay zone.

One by one, the house of cards began to fall.

380 wells across East Texas were shut down. Hundreds of oilmen were arraigned and dragged into court. Suit after suit and trial after trial occurred and nobody was ever convicted. Juries knew better than to throw the book at fellow East Texans. It was the little guy versus the oil giants.

And this is how the biggest unsolved crime in the history of American business came to pass. But after all the lawyers were paid and all the cases and all the indictments were over and all the legal dust had settled, there were those who believed even in the late '60's and early '70's that the art of slant-hole drilling was not dead, but rather had been so perfected that it was once again in full swing and no one was the wiser.

Except Howard Rusk.

"So tell me about Franklin Scroggins."

"Why would you ever want to know about that man?" She said looking at Clark as she daubed the blood from under her nose. She then placed an ice pack over her face that he had retrieved from the freezer for her.

"Maybe I'll put him in a book I'm writing."

"Well, you'd better make him the antagonist. He's the devil in a shiny suit, I'll tell ya."

"Why do you say that?"

"Your father and Howard Rusk had a very good business. They made a lot of money together. A lot. And Scroggins came along and tried to ruin it."

"How?"

"Ask your father."

"Will he talk about it?'

"Some days he will, others he won't. It just depends on his frame of mind; but I can tell you this: If it hadn't been for Scroggins, none of this other stuff would have ever happened and you wouldn't have ever had to take the witness stand. You would have never had to run away and leave home."

"I didn't run away. I left on my own accord."

"Fine. If that's what you want to call it. But I'm here to say that Franklin Scroggins was the root of our problems. Plain and simple."

"And greed didn't raise its ugly head somewhere on our side?"

She turned and faced Clark, removing the ice bag, "You listen to me, son. Your father is many things but he was never a crook nor did he do what he was accused doing. If anyone should have fallen victim to all of this it should have been Scroggins. Franklin Scroggins. But no, he goes Scott free and is living high off the land somewhere."

"I bet he's dead by now."

"Serves him good if he is."

"Tell me about the three of them. Howard, Franklin and dad."

"What do you want to know?"

"How they met. What they did."

"Your father was in a partnership with Howard Rusk. He ran Rusk's drilling operation. He was very good at it. Your father I mean. And Howard had a nose for finding oil. It was uncanny. Many people thought he was a cheat. He was siphoning oil from others, but he was never dragged into any of the slant-hole mess.

"Oh, they were investigated all right. We had Texas Rangers and FBI and all manner of Federal marshals coming and going and searching our books and bank accounts. But we were squeaky clean. Your father told me a man without sin doesn't have to fear the law."

"Sounds rather Baptist for a Presbyterian oil man."

She ignored his jab, knowing full well that Lester Harvey wasn't religious in the least bit. In fact, there were days when he was at full-scale war with the Creator. "After a while the whole slant-hole thing died down and everything and everybody went back to normal."

"No one went to jail?"

"Not a single person. Then Franklin Scroggins showed up and our world turned upside down."

"How so?"

"Ask him. When you're out on the boat and he can't get away or hide from the truth. Ask him." She got up and left the room, leaving Clark with a million unanswered questions about the family's past he knew little about.

"Andy, did your father know Franklin Scroggins?"

"Yeah. I heard him talk about him one or two times. Why?"

Clark shrugged, "Just wondering."

"You gonna write a book about him? He's a crook you know." It was Beth, expressing a common held belief. She wiped barbeque sauce from her thin lips.

"Of course he knows. His old man was in bed with him," said Miles, trying to make the indictment sound as if he were joking, but everyone around the table at Angry Bob's knew that it was true. They also knew of the rift between Clark and his father, so saying something negative about Lester was not seen as a breech of protocol. Most around the table that night knew that Franklin Scroggins and Clark's dad, Lester, had been in partnership secretly for years. But then again, nobody ever really proved it. Certainly not Howard Rusk.

"Isn't that why your folks moved over here to Lincoln to begin with? To get away from that asshole?"

"I suppose."

"You suppose? Hell, you know its true." Miles protested a bit too loudly and Beth hushed him up.

"What year did you and Lee start school over here?" asked Andy.

"Third grade."

"So that was what? About '66. Slant-hole trials were over and done with by then. A thing of the past. A lot of people who had disappeared out to California or God knows where, had returned." It was Andy putting the timeline together for all to think about. "The feds and the Texas Rangers had cleared town. Everything was back to normal."

"Then Scroggins came to town," said Miles.

"Ever wonder why he settled in Lincoln and not Kilgore. Kilgore was the hub of the oil field. Then. Lincoln was just a bump in the road," said Miles

"Easier to hide here." It was a guy named Allen Lowery. He was a hanger-on and in the background most of the time. In fact, it was one of the few times Clark ever remembered Allen speaking up at all.

"I guess," said Clark, not remembering the past as well as his friends seemed to. Most of them had moved from Kilgore or Longview at about the same time. Families wanting to start over in a new locale with new schools and without all the baggage that the oil field had wrought on so many. But the oil field found them in Lincoln as well. 1970 – A major strike between the railroad, which ran through the town center and the lake on the west side. Big play as the locals called it and Lincoln took off and became the next oil center. And with the newfound prestige and wealth came Franklin Scroggins.

"Next time reel it in slower. Give the fish some time to really dig into the bait."

The old man nodded and continued to watch the still lake surface.

"So how did you and Franklin Scroggins get together?"

Lester turned toward Clark and frowned. "Why the hell would you want to know about that SOB?"

"Curious."

"Well, get curious about something else."

"Okay, Let's talk about Howard Rusk."

"Why don't you mind your own goddamn business?"

"It is my business. It involves my life and this family's life."

"It's got nothing to do with you. Not a damn thing. Nothing. Neither one of them men do. They are in the past and they will stay in the past. You understand me?"

"They still both torment you, don't they?"

"No, Clark. You do. You torment me. I could go fishing with Lee and we'd spend a nice day out here by the island and never bring anything up like this. Just fishing and drinking beer and going home in peace and quiet. But you come here from California and bring all kinds of questions and stirring up things."

"Oregon, I came from Oregon."

"Whatever." He spat into the lake as if to put an exclamation on his thoughts and to end the conversation. Which he did.

At a little past three in the afternoon, as they drifted past Long's Sound, for the second time that day, Clark's phone went off. It was Jimmy Earl Jackson at the marina. "Clark, you guys better get back here ASAP. Willie's been taken to the hospital."

## Chapter five

They parked in the emergency lot at the hospital in Longview. A helicopter's giant blade was still slowly rotating; as the orange and blue bird sat on the landing pad a few hundred feet away. Clark wondered if it was the one that had brought his mother from Lincoln.

Inside they found the cool green tile walls filled with notices of employment and federal directives about keeping one's mouth covered when coughing and getting all the vaccinations mandated by law. There were signs admonishing staff to wash their hands as often as needed to keep the spread of communicable diseases down. Covid and its dreadful pandemic were still fresh on everyone's mind.

Clark hurried to the nurses' station. "Willie Harvey. We're family."

"She's been moved upstairs to ICU. Take the green elevator."

At just that moment the green elevator door opened and out stepped Judy Jackson, Jimmy Earl's mother. She had been the one to find Willie spread eagle on her kitchen floor, all but unconscious. Mrs. Jackson, a former nurse in Vietnam, immediately called 911 and started CPR. She followed Willie's ambulance to the hospital.

"I stopped by to bring her a cake. I baked her a cake. Knew you were home and she'd like serving you a cake. I knew she didn't feel like baking it herself. Then I found her out on the floor. I started CPR and she came to. They say she became somewhat lucid half way here," said Judy. "I called an ambulance then I called Jimmy Earl to get you two off the lake and over here. She was as pale as a ghost." While she was spilling her guts, Clark was patting her shoulders to calm her down. Tears were flowing down Judy's face.

Lester pushed past Clark and Judy and entered the elevator and said, "Let's go."

Judy joined them and they rode to the fifth floor. Stepping off the elevator, a nurse recognized Judy and came to them. "They are her family, Christine."

"Where is she?" Lester wanted to know.

"She is in ICU with the doctors just now. She's very, very sick. But I'm sure you knew that.'

"Cancer. Damn cancer again." said Lester as he moved to a chair that was on the edge of the nurses' station. "Goddamn cancer."

"I'm going to move my car," said Judy.

"Mrs. Jackson, thank you for all you did, but if you need to get home, we've got it from here," said Clark.

She grabbed Clark's arm and squeezed it and said, "I'll check back in with you. If you two need anything call me or Jimmy Earl. We'll be here in a flash." With that she disappeared behind the green elevator door and the ward became suddenly very quiet.

"Dr. Grant is her oncologist," said Lester to the nurse.

"Yes. He is in with her just now. Give me a moment and let him finish and I'll let you speak with him." She motioned to a set of chairs in a small waiting area. "Wait over there and I'll come and get you."

Clark and his father sat down on opposite sides of the small space; his father looking down the hallway towards Willie's room. "What's keeping them?" He asked rather impatiently.

"Give him time Dad. They're examining her. It takes time."

Lester continued to stare down the hall and a nurses' assistant came by and offered them some coffee and juice. Neither took anything. Suddenly Lester shot up out of his chair and stood as erect as he could make his weathered frame. A doctor in a long white coat entered the area and nodded to Lester. "Mr. Harvey."

"Dr. Grant. How is she?"

The doctor shook his head. "I'd gather the family as soon as I could, Lester."

"This is us. All we got left," said his father, as he nodded toward Clark, who was at the doctor's back. Grant turned and introduced himself to the writer. "Paul Grant. I've been seeing your mom for several years now. Several rounds sparring with this old bug. It is going to beat her this time I'm afraid. Nothing we can do."

"So she tells me," said Clark. "How bad is it?"

"She has internal bleeding. From where we are not sure and her T cell count is very bad." He shook his head. "We're close."

"Can I see her?" asked Lester as he moved away from the doctor and Clark.

"Yes. She's resting. But she is alert again." Lester left them and the doctor motioned to a chair and sat facing Clark, as he too took a seat.

"Your mother is tough. She has fought a good fight but she has little left to give. She has made it very clear she doesn't want us to extend her life in any way. Painkillers are fine, but nothing to prolong her life. I'm afraid today we were lucky that Mrs. Jackson found her when she did and knew CPR. We might not get a next time."

"If she could be talked into chemo...I mean... would it help?"

The doctor shrugged. "I would like to say yes. Science winning out and all, but I'm afraid her time is up. Nothing we can really do but make her as comfortable as possible. I'm going to move her to our oncology wing tomorrow and we'll watch her there for a few days. But..." he paused searching for the right word. "... I'd say we're real close."

"A day? A week? A month?"

Again a shrug. "Your guess now is as good as mine. To be quite honest with you, I didn't expect her to get this far. I'd go spend some time with her. I can't promise you how much more time she has in her."

The doctor rose from the chair and shook Clark's hand. "I'll be around and my nurse is Eugenia Crawford. She'll check in on you." Grant walked away and Clark noticed a slight limp to his gate. If he had been a character in one of Jack Lawrence's novels he would have made something of it. A war wound or an injury from growing up on a farm. Or an ex-wife stabbing him with a kitchen knife.

Clark returned to his chair and waited. He wanted to give his mom and dad a few minutes alone.

Five days passed like a century. Each hour was a decade unto itself. They moved Willie to the third floor with other oncology patients. Soon Lester was worn out, so Clark drove him home and put the old man to bed and returned to the hospital with a promise that should her condition change he would call his father and come and get him.

He sat next to her and watched as her labored breathing raised and lowered the graph on the bedside monitors. Her pulse was steady – slow but steady. The oxygen content – what the nurse called the O2 reading – was lower than they liked, so she had an oxygen tube inserted into her nostrils and Clark could hear the gentle flow of gasses into her.

She awoke one afternoon and was disoriented and asked for Lee, but fell back into a deep sleep. Then an hour later she awoke crisp and alert. She turned her head and saw Clark and smiled. "Clark, when did you get home?"

"Mom. You made it."

"I did? Where?"

"Jimmy Earl's mom found you and got you to the hospital. You've been here for days."

"Oh my. How's Lester? Is your father holding up?'

"Yes. Yes. He's fine. He's been here... right beside you most of the time. You've talked with him once or twice. He got tired this afternoon so I took him home so he could rest."

"Good. That's good. He needs his rest."

"Dr. Grant says we were close to losing you."

She made a face. "Those doctors are always such alarmists."

"No, mother. It was close. Very close. They moved you here to the oncology ward. Out of ICU."

"Goodness. A lot of trouble for me."

"You need to rest. I'm right over here if you need anything."

She closed her eyes and a smile played across her parched, dry lips. Without looking at him she whispered, "I'm glad you came home."

He didn't respond. Not then anyway but later that night, when her biological clock had awakened her and told her it was morning, he sat up with her and they carried on a conversation that to him was like trying to follow a road map written in code. Left was right and up was down. He didn't know what was going on. He tried as best he could to keep up with her, but soon he sat back and just let her ramble. Around two in the morning she drifted back into slumber again.

After breakfast the next morning, he got up and told her he was going to the house to check on his father.

"You be nice to him, Clark. He was a good father. A good husband You treat him with respect. You hear me?"

"I hear you." He said it, but he didn't feel it. Before he could get out of the door Dr. Grant emerged for his morning rounds. Clark stayed behind while the doctor checked his mother's vital signs and the charts from the night nurses.

"Not sleeping well?" The doctor asked looking over a pair of half lens spectacles.

"Oh this old body of mine likes to get up late in the night and pretend it is morning. It's nothing really."

"I can give you a sleeping pill that will help you through the nights. Gets your circadian rhythms back in line."

"Don't trouble yourself doctor. I'm an old lady who sleeps in the afternoon and worries at night. Done it all my adult life."

"Well, if you want, I'll have it in the orders. You just ask the nurse and they'll get you a sedative." He turned to Clark. "How about you? You holding up okay?"

Clark nodded. "Yeah. I was about to drive out to the lake and pick up dad and bring him here."

"Say, my wife is headed in. We live about a half-mile from your folk's house at the lake. Let me tell her to get him so you can stay and visit with your mom. No sense driving all over the place playing taxi." Grant pulled out a cell phone and before either Willie or Clark could object had placed his order with his wife to stop by the house and get Lester. "Call him first and let him know you're coming."

The doctor hung up his phone and walked up close to Willie in her bed. "You rest young lady. Your body needs the rest."

"I'm gonna get plenty of rest where I'm going. Just as soon as I let go. Only thing holding me back is to get Clark here to make arrangements for his father."

Grant nodded and exited the room.

Clark returned to the chair where he had spent the night. He folded the white sheet the nurse had left for him and placed it over his mother's feet. "We really do need to have a talk about dad."

"You need to stay with him at the house. He knows the house. It is comfortable to him. If you put him in some kind of home somewhere – among strangers – he won't make it, Clark. He won't."

"And what am I supposed to do with my life? Put it on hold until he decides to die? Hell, as ornery as he is, he'll try to live forever."

That brought a chuckle to Willie's face. "You be nice now, you hear?"

"Mom, I tried to get him to talk while we were out on the boat. I wanted to know about Franklin Scroggins and Howard Rusk."

"You know Howard. He was like an uncle to you."

"So what happened?"

"Business stuff. Things got sideways."

"How?"

"It happens. One partner wants to go right and the other wants to go left and they split up and neither ends up going where they wanted to be in the first place."

"But Dad came back and worked for Howard after the first split. Right?"

She nodded and reached for a cup of water with a straw. Clark got up and handed it to her and she took a long slow drink and then handed it back. He noticed her lips were raw and parched. "Two years. Your father worked away from Rusk for two years."

"Did he work for Scroggins during that time."

"With. Not for. Your father started the drilling company then. And we moved to Lincoln."

"Lincoln Drilling Company?"

"Yep."

"Did either of those men have money in it?"

"Like ownership?"

He nodded.

She shook her head. "No way. Lincoln was all your father's. His idea and his capital and his blood sweat and tears. Then we went through a bust. You know how the patch will do – up and down – bust and boom. Feast and famine. Well, we hit a dry spell. Very dry and our savings were just about to play out. Your father had leaned his crews down to just a few men and Betty Whiteside in the office. When Howard came to him with a proposition. 'Drill one well for me and I'll finance one well for you.' That was his deal with your father. It was enough to get him back on his feet and before long Lincoln Drilling Company was back in the black."

"Then what happened?"

She paused. "Clark. Why do you want to go over all of this stuff? It is ancient history. Very ancient. Way in the past. Most folks have forgotten about it. It is gone, let it go."

"Scroggins came and made Dad a better deal didn't he?"

She turned away. "I don't remember."

"Oh you're good at saying that. Like on the witness stand 'I can't recall your honor. I can't seem to remember what happened.'" He mocked her voice with a high falsetto version of his own. She glared at him.

Pointing a long, thin finger at him, "Don't you ever bring that up to me again. Ever. I don't have long left here on this Earth, but what time I do have, I never want to be reminded of that again, you understand me?"

"Sure if that's the way you want to play it. Sure."

"I swear, Clark, even Lee left it alone. He was there and he never brought it up. And you come back here after being gone – what was it nineteen years or so – and you want to rub our faces back in all this. I won't have it. And don't you go and get your father all worked up about it either."

"If there is nothing to hide, I don't understand why no one will talk about it or what happened that night. It's all related, Mom. I know it is."

78

"You go on now. You've got my blood pressure worked up. I need to rest. You heard the doctor. I need my rest."

Lester spent the night at the hospital that night with Willie. He slept in a chair pulled up next to her bed where he could reach out and touch her arm and where he could hear her labored breathing. He wanted to be next to her. To reassure her and himself that they had more time ahead of them. It was an unsaid promise.

Clark, however, was alone. So he drove into Marshall about thirty minutes away, to a steak house there in the county seat of Harrison County and ordered dinner. And before he knew it, he had two old friends sitting next to him. Andy and Miles.

"We seen you come in and thought you look like shit, man. Heard about Willie. Bad news huh? She gonna be okay? Good thing Jimmy Earl's mom was there, right?" Miles was a talker. A free ranger – free association talker. His next sentence might have been about men landing on the moon or the splitting of an atom or the stock market or something that disjointed, had it not been for Andy interrupting him.

"What's gonna become of your old man when Willie goes?" Asked Andy.

The question hung in the air like the restaurant's smoke from the charcoal grill. Clark studied his two friends. "I don't know. Don't even have a clue."

"Nursing home, if it were me," offered Miles quickly. "Park his ass in Whispering Pines, throw them a wad of cash and tell 'em to take care of him. Then I'd take that lake house of his and your mom's and I'd sell it. Turn the cash into a nest egg for him to live his days out playing dominoes or drinking beer."

"Well, that is an idea, Miles. And one that has crossed my mind a time or two."

"You're not thinking about taking him back with you to California are you?" Asked Andy.

"Oregon. And no. I mean I have thought about it, but the answer always comes up – no."

Miles yelled out, "Mary Ash, three more beers over here. And some raisin pie. You ever eat their raisin pie?" Clark shook his head. "You're gonna love it...

"I dunno...but no beer for me. I'll have a cola."

"Make one of those beers a cola. And you, Mr. Clark are going to love this pie. Can't get it anywhere on Earth. Swear to God that's the truth." Even Andy nodded. "Trust me. You'll love it."

Clark, who had barely started his steak surrendered. Miles and Andy were going to take over the evening.

The diner was long and narrow, as if it had been built on the side of an easement without enough room to expand, so it kept going back and back and further back. The walls were pine– knotty pine – and they were weathered old and stained deep brown, at one time yellow, but now brown from the smoke of the grill and the aging of the years. The floor was a black and white checkerboard tile floor with a few tiny pieces missing here and there, from traffic over the decades. A wooden counter with a glass top ran toward the front door and an old cash register – the kind that rang a bell at every entry- standing as a sentinel to the comings and goings of the eatery.

The waitress wore a white, starched outfit that was too tight for her. The bun in the back of her hair seemed too tight, as well. She seemed quite acquainted with both Miles and Andy.

"Say, Clark, how come you write about all that dark family stuff in your novels? My old lady says it's got something to do with your family's past. The legal stuff and all. Any truth to that?" Miles was picking his front teeth with a wooden toothpick as he spoke.

Clark shrugged. "I suppose. But I still don't know what happened. I mean the real inside stuff, the real gooey stuff."

"You don't?" asked Andy incredulously. "Well hell, the rest of Lincoln and Kilgore sure do." Andy said.

"Yeah." Added Miles.

"Like what?" asked Clark.

"Like how your dad was jerked around by old man Scroggins and caught up in the fight between him and Howard Rusk," said Miles.

"I guess I was too young when all that went down to appreciate what was happening. I was too busy playing basketball or doing homework. Something...just not paying attention to Dad's business affairs. We never discussed it much around the dinner table."

"Yeah, but I bet your old man remembers. And I bet he's not talking," again it was Miles offering his commentary.

"That's for sure. He won't say a word about any of it," said Clark.

"Well, I guess not. Rusk paid him off." Andy had said it. Then he waited.

Silence descended over the table. The three friends studied each other. "What do you mean?" asked Clark.

"Well, the way I hear it, is that Scroggins got loose with his tongue and was tellin' everyone who would listen how Rusk was stealing oil out from under them and it was Scroggins, all along, who was doing the slant hole drilling, along with the help of your old man." Miles said.

"Then Rusk goes to him and threatens him..."

"Him? Scroggins or my dad?"

"Scroggins. Tells him if he doesn't shut it up, Rusk is gonna come after his ass." Miles was at full sail in his story when Andy reached over and touched his arm to quiet his buddy.

"It's hearsay, Clark. All of it. No one knows for sure what went down, but everyone believes that Rusk shut the talk down. With money and with a little muscle."

"Muscle?" Asked Clark.

"You know, had him run out of town. Threatened him and his family." Again it was Miles and he was wound up now. Andy spoke up, trying to turn the conversation, which he could tell was making Clark most uncomfortable.

"Lot of hearsay in all of this. No facts, just hearsay. And then there were the trials and all. You know..." He let his voice drift off without finishing the thought.

"You seen Missy since you got back?" Asked Miles out of the blue as he was apt to do.

"Missy? Missy Rusk? No." said Clark.

"Yeah. She's back in town. In Kilgore. Lives in the old man's mansion out on the Henderson highway. Brought a French guy back with her to live with her. I don't think they're married, but they live together. He doesn't speak a word of English from what I hear," said Andy.

"Wasn't Lee sweet on Missy at one time?" Asked Miles.

"He might have been. But it was a fast whirlwind romance that crashed and burned rather quickly."

"Ever wonder why?" Miles again.

"No. Boys and girls date then break up and that's life. It wasn't like they were going to get married or anything."

"Don't be too sure. From what I hear they were hot and heavy until old man Rusk put an end to it. She went away to model right after that. Overseas."

"Yeah. I knew that. Howard Rusk broke up Lee and Missy's romance." Clark had believed this to be the case, "Sent both daughters away."

"News flash from outer space, Kilroy. Your old man and Rusk were at odds something big time right about then and your brother and Missy got caught in the crossfire. Plain and simple."

"He's right. The Scroggins' thing was in full swing and I hear that your old man took Scroggins' side in all the mess and Rusk blew a lid."

"But Rusk bankrolled my dad's company to get it back on its feet."

"That's precisely why he was so peeved at him. And then here was his flesh and blood snooping around with his youngest daughter and he put an end to that. Sent her ass away to Paris. Even going to send Mrs. Rusk off with her to chaperone her for a year or so. Some folks around these parts will tell you that fling with Lee got Missy exiled to Paris by her old man, just to spite your dad. Just to show him that he or his offspring were off limits to your family. Y'all couldn't have anything to do with the Rusk family for betraying him with Scroggins. Suddenly your family was beneath them. They were too good for you. Missy was too good for Lee. And he up and moved her cute ass to France."

"That seems petty to me," said Clark.

"Petty? Lot of money tied up in that squabble. Millions." Andy spoke from some authority. His own father had been presiding judge over several of the slant-hole civil trials that sprang up after the Federal indictments were processed in Tyler, not to mention the trials that sent Clark packing west himself.

"So how much did Scroggins steal from Rusk?" Asked Clark as his cell phone went off.

"You get that and I'll tell you when you get back," said Andy.

Clark inched out of the booth its faux red, leather seat sticking to his long legs that were sheathed in khaki Bermuda shorts. He walked outside, the night air was punctuated by sounds of the nearby highway with its big rig trucks and speeding cars heading east to Shreveport and west to Dallas. Clark looked at the number ringing on his phone. It was Harold Moss his agent in Los Angeles. "Jack here."

"Jackson, my boy, we've got three solid offers on the book. Three. They all want an answer ASAP. How soon can you give me some time to talk? This is big time, bro."

"Mom's in the hospital and I'm playing nursemaid to my old man. Can you fly here?"

"Where is here? Bumfuck, Texas?"

"I'm staying at the lake house. Fly to Dallas. I'll pick you up."

"See you tomorrow afternoon." Clark nodded but didn't verbally respond. "Jack? Did you hear me? Tomorrow afternoon?"

"Yeah. Yeah. I'll be there."

He hung up the phone and returned to the diner.

"Everything okay?" asked Andy.

"Yeah. My agent. Business. Where were we?"

"I was going to tell you how much Scroggins stole from old man Rusk."

"Before you do, tell me about Missy. What's she like now?"

"She's like us. More mature. Just as pretty, but older and wiser. Doesn't have that freshman face anymore. It's a sexy face, but not that *I just got out of bed and put on skin cream face.*" Miles was on another of his rolls. "Hell, we've all aged. Put on a pound or two..."

"Which she doesn't seem to have," added Andy.

"No. She looks good. Like the day she left, but now she's a woman. Not a girl. That's all I was trying to say. A good looking woman at that," said Miles, as he continued to ramble.

"Five or six million," said Andy interrupting Miles.

"What?" asked Clark.

"Scroggins, it is said, stole five or six million dollars worth of oil out from under old man Rusk. That's in 1970 dollars mind you. Today it would be a much larger fortune, but even then, that was a hell of a lot of money and enough to go to war over."

"War?"

"The two fought off and on for five years. It was during this time your dad got involved. Tried to be a peacemaker and got his ass kicked and his nuts cut off in the process." Miles' description of the events bothered Clark.

"What'd you mean?" asked Clark.

"He means that when Lester Harvey tried to get in between the two giants of the oil field he got squished. And when he picked himself up off the ground and dusted off his overalls, he sided with Scroggins. Big mistake. Chose the wrong side."

"How come?"

"He made an enemy out of Howard Rusk. A lifetime enemy. And you didn't want to do that."

Suddenly, a piece that had been missing for so long fell into place in Clark's mind. It was just one piece, but it fit perfectly. And he began to understand things he hadn't known before. True, he had suspected, but never knew.

"But hey, don't take my word on all this. Go talk with Missy. She'll tell you. She knows what went on." Andy's encouragement registered with Clark. He finished his steak and his raisin pie and left his two friends in Marshall, as a lone guitar player took the small stage at the back of the diner to play some folk music. Clark sat in his car in the parking lot for some time letting his mind work freely. Then he started his car and drove home to the lake house.

Clark got to the hospital at eight o'clock on the dot. He brought his dad a fresh change of clothes and told his parents he was heading to Dallas. "My agent is coming into town. I've got to go to the airport to pick him up."

"Why didn't he fly into our airport?" asked Lester.

"Don't know. He had a ticket to Dallas. I'm going there to get him."

"He could have flown here. Saved you a trip." Again Lester – pushing a tad bit harder now, as if to prove some point.

"Trip will do us good. We got things to talk about. The car will be a quiet place to discuss business."

"Where's he gonna stay?" asked Willie, sounding rather hoarse from the drying oxygen that was being forced into her nose.

"He'll stay at the house."

"Oh dear lord, it's a mess," said Willie.

"No mom. I cleaned it up. It's fine. Plus, Moss wouldn't know a clean house if one bit him in the ass."

"Just the same, I'm not there to welcome a guest."

"You've got more important things to take care of right now, Mom. Moss will be here just a day maybe one more, then he'll be gone."

"Les, why don't you ride to Dallas with Clark to pick up his agent?"

Lester was about to speak when Clark intervened. "No. That won't be necessary. Moss and I have business to discuss. And besides, dad needs to be here with you."

"Please, he's gonna take care of me?" She grinned at her husband.

"I've done a pretty good job of that for close to fifty years, now," said Lester.

She smiled and reached for his hand. "Yes you have dear, yes you have."

Clark left and drove south from Longview, but at the exchange for the Interstate to Dallas, he kept going. Instead of west toward Dallas he drove south through the neighboring town of Kilgore. He moved past its crowded downtown lots of oil derricks left over from another time – a time when the oil field erected iron statuary at every hole it drilled. Monuments to the progress man and petroleum were making – monuments to phenomenal wealth and gains captured and retained by a few proud families. Past the oil derricks and down the Henderson highway he traveled, to have a look at the Rusk mansion. It was overgrown with weeds and brambles in the long, sloping front lawn that at one time had been as manicured as a formal golf course. In its hay day, its green pitch had been as smooth as any carpet ever laid, attended to by an army of lawn workers. The shrubbery had become matted and angry looking – gnawing at the front porch of the three-story southern-style brick manse – whose rising columns were dulled white with peeling strips of paint hanging down in the summer sun. Up the long driveway, which rose according to the measure of a slight hill, he could see a red sports car parked under the portico on the east side of the house – the side lined with loblolly pine trees and two giant oaks. He figured it belonged to Missy or her boyfriend. He drove past the house and turned around at Mason's Gulf station about a half mile to the south, then continued on his way to Dallas.

Along the Interstate to Dallas, he turned on the radio to listen to music, but his mind took him back to that night – back to the events that had created such turmoil in the family – and in some small degree – in the community itself. He thought of the players in that small performance, acted out on the deck of his father's new pontoon party boat: a cool, windy spring evening, with loud country music playing and whiskey flowing. He thought of the conversation that grew into accusations and then into shouting and then the fight itself. Screaming followed by shouts of distress and finally silence.

Deathly silence.

Clark came out of his memories as he turned into the large expanse of the Dallas/Ft Worth airport. He drove to the terminal and gate where Moss had said he would be. Clark was a few minutes early. So he stopped in one of the 'do not park zones' and sat; waiting for his agent to emerge into the heat of a Texas afternoon. He lowered the audio on the radio and watched as people appeared from the glass doors of the air-conditioned terminal to be attacked by the onslaught of summer in Texas. Withering was the word that came to his mind, as he watched them first shield their eyes from the brilliant yellow glare, then try and turn their heads from the on-rushing heat wave.

Moss saw him first and waved. One small carry-on bag and a brief case. The Lawyer/agent was traveling light. He didn't plan to stay long. Just to get a decision. Get a signature. And he would be on his way back to California. Back to a fortune that was growing under the care of his watchful eye and the creativity of his best client, Jack Lawrence.

"Jackson, my man. You are looking, well..." He paused studying his client, "...you are looking a tad bit tired to tell you the truth."

"Lots to do over here. Mom's in the hospital and my father is a load to care for."

"Sorry to hear that. You been writing?"

"No."

"No? How am I supposed to feed and clothe my young infants if you are going to sit on your thumbs all day?" He laughed. It was an on-going joke between them. Besides, his young infants were not toddlers; they were teenagers now. And were as wild as some of Clark's characters. "I take it old times aren't what you thought they'd be?"

"Oh no. They are exactly what I thought they'd be. Everyone denying anything ever happened. And my reappearing after all these years, it was like everyone was seeing a ghost."

"I knew it. I told you not to come."

"I had no choice."

"So, if it is this strong a pull on you, you need to write about it. " Moss waved his hands in front of his face as though he were seeing an image, "The Great American Novel by Jack Lawrence – Going Home."

"How about going to hell in a hand basket."

"That bad, really?"

"Yep." He drove on for a few miles and let the silence rest in the car. "So why is it you are here in Texas with something that can't wait a few weeks?'

"Money, my boy. Lots and lots of it. Lots of money to be made. Right now. Even as we speak. There are people waiting back in California, sitting by their phones – sitting on pins and needles waiting for your word. Go or no-go. Yes or no. Sign the contract and let's get rich."

"What are the offers?"

"There are four. Well, really three. One is just a courtesy for your old friend, Bill Moffitt. He wants to buy the rights to your novel and direct the film himself. But he's way out of his league on this one. Lots of studio money vying for this property, Jackie my boy. Lots and lots of hot greenbacks. I'm telling you, *The Promised Land* is going to be our promised land. I can't remember a time when Tinsel Town was so alive with gossip about a property. Every actor worth his or her salt is trying to elbow their way to the front of the casting line. Every director who has ever yelled 'action' is waving at the movie moguls trying to catch a lucky break on this one. And the studios themselves are hot after it. Deals are being made. Partnership forged. Stocks split and boardrooms locked into late night negotiating to get the right money and the right people together to come after you."

"Who else besides Moffitt?"

The Big three. In a package deal. Can you even fathom that? The three biggies together on one movie. The SEC might be called in to investigate collusion. Ten million, that's their bid. Ten fucking million. Wall Street is going nuts over the rumors. Then the cartoon guys. It's their live action division. Eight million, but they've got Ray Donavon lined up to shoot it and rumor has it they have an inside track on GeeGee Phillips and Phil Rice to reprise their roles. Have them under contract already and they don't even own the rights."

"Who else?" Clark slowed for a farm truck pulling off the highway and then sped around him. He looked into his rear view mirror and all he could see was a giant orange ball in the western horizon.

"Studio Nine teamed with a Canadian outfit. Out of Vancouver. The Film Factory. Solid money and great credentials. Paul Ridley for director and Bruce Miller for cinematographer. They are opting for two unknowns to take the lead roles. To make it more authentic. They have a whole write-up on their vision for the film. They even have Gene Diller and Ruth Crisp doing the screenplay. Already under contract."

"They're top notch."

"I'll say. Wait 'till you see everybody's pitch. I mean this thing is huge."

At the lake house, Clark took the roll-on bag and Moss followed closely behind with his briefcase, which appeared to Clark to be slightly overstuffed. "Let me call the hospital and check in on my folks. You can spread things out on the dining room table. There's beer and soft drinks in the fridge and if you want, I'll make some fresh coffee."

"Go make your call. I'll get set up. A beer will do."

"Help yourself. Fridge is in there." He pointed to the kitchen. Clark dialed the number to his mother's room and to his surprise she answered. "Clark? Are you back?'

"Yes. Where's dad?"

"He's in the chair over by the window. Sound asleep. Is your friend there with you?"

"Yes. We're going over some paperwork. Can I bring you two anything?"

"No. But you make sure the house is clean. I can't believe we have company and I'm not there to straighten things out. Put him in the front guest room. That bed is better."

"Lee's old room?"

"Yes. And get fresh towels for that bathroom from your bathroom. They are newer and not so ragged."

"Mom, relax. Moss lives in a house with three wild kids and a hippie wife. He'll do fine."

"Your father told me you had words over..." She paused looking for her way into the conversation. "...over what happened before. He said you were prying. I've really got to ask you Clark to let it be. Let him rest. Let him have his final time in peace."

"Hell, Mom, you said it yourself, he's liable to live for a long time yet. He needs to clear his conscious."

"No. Maybe some of us do, but not your father. And I want you to leave him alone on this business. You hear me?"

"Yes ma'am." Clark hung up aggravated that his parents were discussing the issue around the issue and leaving him in the dark, picking at crumbs.

On the dining room table, Moss had three stacks of papers. "Here's the deals." He said.

"I thought there were four."

"Well, I mean come on – Moffitt isn't a real contender."

"Does he have a prospectus?"

"Of sorts. Two pages. His vision for the film, who he sees starring in it and how he wants to stage it. I mean the studios have close to a hundred pages here. Details upon details."

"Where does the money fall out?"

Moss smiled. That was his good boy. Let the money lead you. "Jackson, my man, the Studios want to make you rich. And they have enlisted the powers of Wall Street to make sure it happens."

The two sat down and began to sift through the offers one at a time. They didn't stop until well after midnight.

Clark rose and stretched as he yawned. "Enough for one night. Your bedroom is up there to the left. Front room. It used to belong to my brother Lee. It's not haunted or anything, but some of his paraphernalia is still in there. Mom's way of keeping her boys close."

"You leaning on any direction right now?' asked Moss looking at the table that was a sea of paperwork spread out in all directions.

Clark shook his head. "Nope. Can't say that I am."

"Oh, I did want to pass along one thing. Simpson House says they are already on the third printing of the hardback. Paperback options should sell soon. And we need to negotiate international rights with them. I thought we'd hold both until a Hollywood announcement was made. Big news and big numbers might drive the book future prices upwards yet again."

"How much is Simpson House offering?"

"Package deal- two mill. We could break it apart and bid it out and double that. What do you think?'

"Let me sleep on it. I don't want to get greedy. There may come a day when I can't write anything good anymore."

"My children are surely going to starve." Clark laughed and slapped his agent on the back as he wandered up the hall toward his room.

"Fresh towels on the sink. You and my mom's favorite color – green..." he called after Moss.


Clark had barely laid his head on to his pillow when sleep came over him. And just as quickly, he was awakened with a jolt. His cell phone was going off.

"Clark. It's your mother. She's passed." His father's voice was trembling.

"What time is it?" Clark asked.

"Three in the morning."

"I'm on my way."

"Bring me my dark suit would you? I don't want to see people dressed like a pauper. White shirt, thin navy tie and I'll wear these black shoes I have."

"You need a belt?" He asked.

"No. The one I have on will do."

"I'll be there in an hour." Clark was trying to swim up from the deep sleep that he had succumbed to hours earlier. He eased down the hall and tapped on Moss's door. A sleepy voice said to enter and Clark went in and told his friend the news and that he would be back in a few hours. "Make yourself at home. There's tons to eat in the fridge. The club delivers. Our number is 2020. Just sign for it. If anyone asks any questions tell them you want to speak to Ray. He'll know what to do."

"You go man. I'll wait here for you. And gosh, I'm so sorry, Jack."

He nodded and reminded his agent that people in these parts knew him as Clark.

Clark finally returned to the lake house at three that afternoon. His face was long and tired, his eyes were puffy and his curly hair matted down. He needed a shower. The old man with him looked much worse, in an ill-fitting black suit. Moss reasoned it was Clark's father.

Moss had cleared the dining room table because, by ten that morning, ladies were knocking on the door dropping off food. Cakes, casseroles, breads, pies and one even brought a spiral-cut ham. Moss made room in the refrigerator for the perishables and helped himself to a piece of the best peach pie he had ever tasted.

The home phone rang non-stop until finally Moss took the handset off the cradle and gave the house a reprieve from the constant bombardment of calls. He even lay down on the sofa in the small den off the living room and waited for Clark to clear his schedule long enough to finish their conversation. It didn't occur until well past nine that night, as a few of the straggling visitors had left with promises to do anything they could – 'just give us a shout.' The front of the house was still filled with the old guard who were visiting and reminiscing.

Lester fell asleep in his recliner. Clark covered him with a light blanket. He motioned to Moss to follow him to the back of the house. There they found their way to a small study with a card table. Moss pulled out all of his paper work and began the analysis once again.

"Big studios. Big bucks. No control. You know how that game is played. But we're talking multi-multi million. We'll opt for a producer's cut. If all goes well, we should clear five or six million easy. The mouse folks are about the same. A tad less upfront, a pinch more on the backend. The real sleeper in this whole thing is Studio Nine and the Film Factory. Big Canadian bucks. They'll give you some creative license and four or five points – that's negotiable. Could be a big deal. Not as big as the big studios, but you'd have more control."

"And what about Moffitt?"

"Jack...or should I call you Clark? No way. The deal there is... well, there is nothing there. A mill at the most. The most. Your book deal overseas will be bigger than that...if..."

"If I go with one of the big offers?"

"Right on sir. Right fucking on. Money begets money."

"The Tree Line did how much?" Clark asked.

"Net? Three million."

"What did I see out of that?"

"A cool mill and a half. But I know what you're thinking. You want to replicate the magic there and what Moffitt can do especially with GeeGee and Rice, but I'm telling you the studios have them locked up. If they don't get the deal, then Phillips and Rice are off the table."

"And Studio Nine?"

"Good people. Solid money behind them – the Film Factory is well financed. Canadians with deep pockets. Made it in American Real Estate. Now they want to ply it back in celluloid."

"Track record?"

"Studio Nine is well versed in films and TV. The Film Factory is known for art films, but ones that seem to always make a fair amount of bucks. Cutting edge kind of stuff. Cannes loves them."

"What about the mouse people?"

96

"Like I said, it's their live action branch. The Thompson boys as producers. Good writers to boot and Ray Donavon is their director. I've known Ray for years. USC together. The guy is a genius. Great credentials. They too have the cash to bankroll this thing."

"Shortcomings?" asked Clark.

"The big three are going to block you from having any or little creative input. The cartoon people, as well; although, I might be able to leverage some space for you with Donavon – but not much. Studio Nine will give you a bit more say and are more flexible in you helping mold the story.

"Moffitt is Moffitt. He'll make a beautiful picture. It may take a decade, but it will be incredible. And it will lose a fortune."

"Moffitt is out?"

"In my books he is."

Clark took the Moffitt pages and placed them on the floor. "What's your vote?"

Moss studied the table and said," I'd normally tell you to go with the big three and screw the creative control, but this book is going skyward and I think you're going to want to see it through on the big screen. No one gives you more control over that than Studio Nine. Not quite as much money, but again, you'll drive the ship."

"Call them. Tell them if they can come up with another million, it is theirs. Otherwise, we'll go with the mouse patrol. Now I'm going to take a shower and put on some fresh clothes.

At just that moment the doorbell rang and Clark Harvey's life changed.

# Book Two

## Chapter six

The first drill crew had left the Winston Well No. 3 and the second shift was underway when Franklin Scroggins drove up, got out of his yellow Cadillac convertible and walked over to the driller's hut at the edge of the well site. He told E.C. Humphries to start directional drilling to the west. Shouting over the noise of the heavy equipment and the large industrial diesels running the pumps and the drilling rig, "Hard right-hand turn, E.C. Hard right."

Lester Harvey heard the command and came out of the mobile home-turned office, to see what was going on.

"Time to deviate, Les. We'll do it on your second crew. Put the whipstock in on the next trip down and we'll gauge the pressures as we go. Take it slow and no one will be the wiser."

E.C. Humphries looked to his boss, Lester Harvey of Lincoln Drilling Company and asked, "Les? Watchca want me to do?"

Lester shrugged. "Make a hard right-hand turn, I suppose. Mr. Scroggins here is paying the bills."

The Winston Well No. 3 sat in a small shallow glen surrounded by pine trees and an occasional pin oak. But mostly the rolling valley was scrub grass and coastal Bermuda in the lower regions, as well as wild Johnson grass straddling along the marshes. To the far north of the glen, before it dove deep into the Piney Woods, a blackberry thicket spread out and rambled north and south away from the dirt road, which had been plowed and grated to allow the heavy drilling equipment access to E.O. Beckham's land – land that had been surveyed and leased by Franklin Scroggins. He was insistent on this very location for a well, even though his own geologist told him there was a minimum chance of pay dirt deposits beneath the old farm site.

Scroggins claimed the valley held riches yet discovered. The valley ran north and south between Kilgore and Lincoln, and if one were to point a compass at the well from behind it, say on the south side, one's compass needle would draw a line straight through Longview fifteen miles to the north.

To the west, away from the Winston No. 3 was a tree line and a creek – Potter's Creek, which was a muddy, soft banked waterway that flowed between two low-lying, flat marshes, eventually finding its way to Turkey Creek and then on to the Sabine River. Further west, past the tree line and up a slight rise, sat an oil well named Rusk-Humble No 12, and another one further up the rise that over looked Potter's Creek called Rusk-Sawgrass No. 6. Both of these wells were producing wells and had been completed at a shallow depth by the Humble Oil and Refining Company in the late 1930's, then sold to Howard Rusk who reworked and deepened them with the assistance of the Lincoln Drilling Company. The reworking had occurred sometime between 1967 and 1969.

The second crew began the painstakingly slow process of turning the bit, now fifteen hundred feet underground towards the west and under Potter's Creek. Day by day, supply trucks would bring more and more drill pipe and casing to the site, with the foreman saying only that they were going deeper than ever to find oil for old man Scroggins. By some calculations a mile and a half of pipe went into The Winston Well No. 3. That would have made it bottom out at somewhere around 7500 to 8,000 feet. A deep well in the Woodbine section of the East Texas field for sure. But in reality, the well never went deeper than 2500 feet. But it went straight to the producing sands owned by Howard Rusk.

Pressure at the Rusk well began to fall. Not totally unrealistic for a work-over well. It was felt by Rusk's engineers that the drop in pressure could be relieved by a new fracking and cementing job at a depth of 1200 to 1500 feet. What the engineers didn't know, was that by cementing a fresh frack zone at that level, they all but sealed out their own production and caused most of the oil to flow into the pipe laid by The Lincoln Drilling Company under the direction of Franklin Scroggins. "He's paying the bills, boys. Lets drill west and keep our mouths shut."

And so they did.

And they did it again further north at the Rusk-Sawgrass No. 6. And again on the far side of Gregg County, right on the Smith County line. This time the victim wasn't Rusk, but rather Western Reserve Oil Company. Again on the western side of Gregg County near the Smith County line – a well owned by Magnolia Oil and Refining became the target of Franklin Scroggins and his deviating pipe.

And each time, at the controls was none other than Lester Harvey's chief driller, E.C. Humphries.

In early 1973, Scroggins approached Lester Harvey with a plan. Since Harvey had drilled the Rusk wells, and knew their depths and locations, he would pay Lincoln Drilling Company a small fortune to tap into five more Rusk owned and operated wells. At first Harvey declined. Balked was a better term. He didn't outright say he wouldn't do it. In fact, as soon as the cash deal got sweet enough, Harvey swallowed hard, agreed to a trio of wells, and told his crew they had three more bores to drill. Interestingly, during this time there was a downturn in activity in the East Texas field, so the men who wore the overalls with the Lincoln Drilling logo on them, were more than happy to work. And no one bothered counting the feet upon hundreds of feet of excess pipe that was delivered to the drilling sites and was being laid underground. Lincoln Drilling Company wanted to go deep. They'd drill deep. Work was work.

And nobody found it strange that Franklin Scroggins never drilled a dry hole. Nobody except Howard Rusk.

It was a spring day – April if memory serves the historians correctly, that Howard Rusk came upon the plot. And he did it not by geology or engineering, but by good old-fashioned accounting. His office manager had run the numbers three times. Each time the same answer showed up.

If Rusk had a well and a Scroggins well was within a mile of it, then the Rusk well began to underperform. Not all at once, but gradually. It's flow would slow until just a trickle of the black gold was oozing though its steel veins. It would make it seem as though the well had reached the end of its performance and was ready to be shut in. To be sure, Rusk called for fracking and re-drilling along with new down-hole pumps and all manner of procedures to bring life back to his wells. He flushed them with salt water under tremendous pressure and he perforated the pay zones to open up new passages for the oil to flow; but each time, the process was the same. The Rusk well would spurt back to life for a month or two, then begin to ebb downward again until it was back to a mere dribble.

And if one checked the state's logs, the Scroggins wells would be humming along with little to no interruptions.

"He has drilled five straight aces. Goddamn him, he's cheating. I can smell it," said Rusk to his old buddy Lester Harvey, as they sat in Rusk's office atop the First National Bank tower in downtown Kilgore. "Five straight. No dry holes. Just oil. One right after the other. Next to my leases. Next to Magnolia's. Next to Shell and across from City Services. And no excess salt water either. I've checked that out. Just drill and go to the bank. I'm telling you the guy's got a scam going."

"You thinking slant-hole?" asked Lester.

"You're damn right I am."

"Well, I drilled those wells. Most of them. And I can tell you they are as straight as a Baptist minister's morals."

"I have known me some Baptist ministers with some very crooked morals, Les. But if you say they are true, then I've got to think it's something else. How can a guy be so fucking lucky? Five straight. And that doesn't count the ones he did over near Lincoln."

"Have you checked your logs? I mean maybe you've had some equipment problems."

Rusk got up from his deep leather chair, which sat behind an acre of teak called a desk and lit a cigar. "No way. Show me an operator who has that much breakdown on that organized a schedule and I'll show you an idiot. And I am not an idiot, Les. Now am I?"

"Howard as long as I have known you, you don't seem like an idiot."

"Think you could get me the logs for some of Scroggins' wells?"

"I could try. Sure."

Rusk opened a map of the county with dots all over it. Each dot represented a working well in the Gregg County field. "This one." He pointed to a blue dot. "It's the Moody No. 3. And over here. The Hendricks-Griffin no. 8. And if you can get it I'd like the records for his wells near the Winston Well No. 3 and the Rusk-Sawgrass No.6."

Les was busy jotting notes down in his ubiquitous brown pocket notebook with a pen that Willie had given him for his birthday. "Any others?" He asked.

"Yeah. Let's do the Shell-Hamilton No. 12. It seems to be having sporadic troubles. Shell's been trying to pawn it off to me for months now."

"You got the geology reports on these wells? Prior to production?" Asked Les.

"Sure I do. And I've got core samples and analysis of pay zone and seismic depth zone charts. I'm telling you, a well like Sawgrass doesn't go dry overnight. No way. No how."

Give me a few days and let me see what I can dig up. Sniffing around Scroggins is like sticking your nose in a skunk's ass."

"You're telling me."

Lester Harvey rose from his chair and then stopped. His blue shirt and khaki pants were starched stiff and creased to perfection. "Just remember, Howard, we had a string of six in a row. Then one dry and then four more strikes. It can be done."

"That guy is a fucking cheat, Les. I'll prove it. With your help I'll prove it.

## Chapter seven

She looked exactly the same as the year they graduated from high school – well almost. Her shoulder-length auburn hair was still wavy and fell across her right eye and she was constantly tossing her head back to the side to free her vision from the wayward locks. Her features weren't as soft and rounded as when she was seventeen, but she was every bit as beautiful. Tall and erect and with a look that would melt most mortal men's souls and corrupt their mores in the process. And those legs. They went from the ground in her skimpy leather Italian sandals, until they disappeared beneath the skimpier white short shorts she was cuddled into, inside of which was tucked a red and white horizontally striped cotton top. She looked like an ad for a nautical fashion brand.

She smiled and reached for him. "Clark. Clark. They said you were here. I am so sorry. So terribly sorry. We heard the news about Willie and had to come out and see your father. On our way to the lake, we ran into Andy and he told us you were back in town. Oh Clark, my dear, dear

Clark." An actual tear vacated her left eye and plunged down her cheek as gravity pulled it toward her breasts. She hugged him again and he could feel the warmth of her chest reside next to him. He found his arms folding around her back and slightly squeezing her as if to return the favor.

Suddenly she pulled back and revealed a handsome dark-skinned man with a full mustache to match his equally dark and thick hair standing in the wings. "Clark, this is Roberto Guchillini."

"Italian? I was told you had a Frenchman with you."

"Ha. Roberto is Canadian. He speaks French because he does business in Quebec, but he lives in London and is originally from Brooklyn and from Naples in the off season."

"What is the off season in Naples?" asked Clark playfully.

"Anytime I am not working," she said with a wry smile both on her lips and in her voice.

Clark reached out and took the hand of the handsome young man who was dressed somewhat formally in a dark suit that resembled a tux ensemble and a white shirt, but with no tie. Clark immediately noticed he wasn't wearing socks with his expensive tan loafers. Willie had always scolded Clark for wearing tan shoes with a blue or black suit. "Not appropriate," she would say.

"Pleased to meet you, Roberto." He said, trying to sound sincere.

"And likewise. Missy tells me you are a novelist."

Clark looked back at his old friend. "And how did you know this? Andy no doubt?"

"No. I saw you when I was in England and you were on the BBC. What did you go by then? She paused trying to remember.

"Jack Lawrence."

"Yes. Yes that's it. But I knew it was you, Clark Harvey. None of this Jack Lawrence stuff for me." She was thirty-seven now, but didn't look a day over twenty, while Clark found himself feeling ancient and worn out.

"And who is talking about Jack, my Jackie boy?"

It was Moss, who had ventured to the front door to meet the guests.

"Missy, Roberto, this is my manager and agent, Harold Moss."

"Pleased to meet both of you. Clark, why don't you step out of the threshold and allow them to come in out of the night air, although I do see they arrived without a top on that red spider."

The three entered the house and Moss closed the door behind them. From the living room a voice cried out and Missy hurried off to give Lester a hug about the neck as the old man struggled to arise from his recliner.

It seemed so surreal to Clark. Not a notion of the past and what had happened. Nothing. It was like there was a clean slate. The only change was that now Willie was gone. It was just them – Missy, Clark and his father. True there were others in the wings. A man from Brooklyn and an agent from California and a kitchen full of gray-haired women and old men from the club who were helping themselves to some of the enormous amounts of food that were stockpiling by the minute.

Clark stuck his head into the kitchen to be polite. One old guy grabbed him, "These deviled eggs are divine. Who made them?'

Clark frowned. "No idea."

"I did you silly geezer." It was the man's wife.

"Why of course you did Molly. Of course you did." He winked knowingly at Clark who moved beyond the two and through the crowd at the refrigerator into the den.

Missy was sitting on the arm of Lester's recliner and they were deep in story and catch-up time. Roberto stood attentively to one side, occasionally smiling and nodding like a man lost in the translation of two foreigners. Moss slipped to the front door as the bell went off to announce yet more visitors. He heard his name called, "Jack...Clark. Clark."

He looked and there were two men in dark suits with ashen-looking faces standing there. He approached them and Moss said, "Mr. Wilkes from Wilkes-Chapman Funeral Home and Reverend..." He had already misplaced the preacher's name.

"Rev. Tom Cavanaugh. First Presbyterian." Both men shook Clark's hand and offered their deepest condolences.

"Might we find a quiet place to chat?" Asked Wilkes.

Clark nodded and Moss said his room was tidy, to use it. Just then another carload of well-wishers showed up and Moss smoothly guided traffic – those with casserole dishes were directed to the kitchen and those with cakes, pies and cookies were sent to the dining room table. "Jack, we're going to need some chairs."

"In the garage. Over behind the ping-pong table. They'll be dirty."

Moss headed for the garage, as Roberto, unasked, took off his dark coat, draped it over the living room sofa, and joined Moss in retrieving chairs for the guests. After dusting them with a dry, red cloth from the kitchen, the two set up a line of the folding metal chairs as neatly as any reception at Buckingham Palace. "We're going to need to get these folks something to drink," observed Moss.

The two men opened the wet bar at the far end of the den, turned on a neon Budweiser bar light that had a constant buzz to it, and began to take orders for beer, wine and cocktails. The gathered wasted no time in filling the bartenders' to-make list. Roberto looked relieved to have a chore to do; something to keep from having to stand and pretend he understood all the stories being told and the backlog of friends. A Scotch and soda was an easy order to fill. Knowing when to laugh and when to frown at a passing tale from twenty years ago was far more difficult.

Soon friends other than the country club set were filtering in. Andy came and so too did Miles. Jimmy Earl Jackson and his mother were walking up the driveway. Beth was about two minutes behind them. They all made a big deal about seeing Missy and were very pleased to meet her new beau Roberto. And each time, Missy had to explain he wasn't French but did work in Quebec, therefore knew how to speak the Gallic tongue.

In Moss's bedroom, Mr. Wilkes spelled out the requests Willie had already left behind. She had picked out and paid for a casket many weeks earlier. She had decided on a church service and that's why Rev. Tom Cavanaugh was there. Cavanaugh was a recent arrival to Lincoln. As in the last month, so most of the faces and names of the people were new to him. He barely knew who Lester was and was a bit confused at the presence of Clark, until Mr. Wilkes, who had lived in Lincoln his entire life, explained the relationship. "And Clark here, is an author. He's just returned from California"

"Oregon," corrected Clark.

"Is that so?" Asked the minister sitting very erect and proper. "...have I heard of your work?'

"I am sure you've passed it in your favorite bookstore." Clark then named a few titles and the minster was a bit in awe at sitting in the presence of such a famous and gifted author. At just that moment, Clark felt somebody ease onto the bed next to where he sat facing the two somber-looking gentlemen. It was Missy.

"Gentlemen, Missy ..." He paused not knowing for sure what her last name was or of it was still Rusk.

"Missy Rusk," she said as explanation that she was still unattached. "Still Rusk," she said it again, with a slight emphasis, staring right at Clark.

Both gentlemen rose slightly and offered a perfunctory nod of their heads as if to say hello. It was a southern thing to do.

Wilkes began, "Now, Clark, we need to make arrangements for the service. Who do you want to speak? Who will sing, and what scriptures do you wish us to read? Did your mother have any favorite passages?"

"You bet. The one that says I'm going straight to hell, she used that one a lot." They all laughed. Missy gave him a gentle jab in the ribs. "To tell you the truth, I'm not sure what passages to have you read."

"Why don't we let Miles sing? He's got a beautiful voice." It came from Missy, taking over in the awkwardness created by Clark's inability to make a decision. "He was in a band in high school...What were they called?"

"The melon eaters." Clark said

"Yeah. Something like that. Two keyboardist. One piano– one organ and two guitars, a bass and drums. And Miles on tenor sax."

"He was all-state in the marching band. Tenor sax," said Clark, as if to remind everyone in the room, himself included, of Miles' accomplishments.

"I remember. And his voice was like heaven. He could sound like Sinatra..."She was interrupted by Clark.

"Or Paul McCartney..."

"So mellow. So smooth. He is a Methodist, so you will have to sprinkle some holy water over him or something." She laughed.

"We're fresh out," said Cavanaugh, making an awkward comeback to her joke.

"Yes. Miles Pennington," said Clark.

"From the green grocer?" asked Wilkes

"Yes. And Andy Reynolds," continued Missy, "can read the scripture. He used to have a radio show over in Longview. Great voice. And father..."

"I'm not a father," said Cavanaugh, "...well not that kind of father. Just call me Tom."

"Well, Tom, you could pick out some great verses, Miles will sing and Andy will read the verses and then we'll all gather for prayer and your final words. Then it's off to the cemetery. Pretty easy." Missy had in a single sweep of her hand solved the entire funeral planning. "I'll even give you the names of some old classmates that would be honored to be Willie's pallbearers. Any number of them were at Lee's funeral." She said, as if she were making a commentary on Clark's absence from his twin's final service; but if she were, no one paid it any mind, except for Clark, who was rather sensitive to such admonitions, especially since they were all seated in Lee's old bedroom.

The minister rose, nodding and Wilkes was also standing, "Clark you should come by and approve your mother's outfit and her hair and make up."

"No. I wouldn't be any good at that. Let your people handle it. Mom left you a dress to use, did she?"

"I'll drop by and take a look," volunteered Missy.

Wilkes nodded. "Very well, that's enough for me." The two gentlemen strolled back into the den and locals saw them and came to shake their hands and press the flesh. "She was so wonderful....A great lady... What a woman..." the words followed them out the front door into the cool evening air.

"Thanks for that," Clark said to Missy.

She hugged him again and nudged him toward his old buddies. "Go get drunk. It'll do you good."

"The last thing I need is a drink," he said.

"That sounds like a confession." She studied him.

"Let's just say I became very friendly with the bottle after I left Texas." He paused. "Too friendly."

"You dry now?"

"Right this minute? Yes. But one never knows how long that will last."

"Well, go get a tea and mingle. It will still do you some good." She walked away grabbing Beth by the arms and hugged her old friend. They drifted away heavy in a sudden conversation, like two boats catching the same billow of wind and sailing off side-by-side.

By ten thirty, the crowd had left, leaving only Missy, Roberto, Moss, Clark, and a sleeping Lester. Moss and Roberto, having closed up the bar, were in the kitchen washing dishes. Anything to keep their hands busy and their minds occupied and away from the sadness, which was easing back into the house. Moss was going on and on about Clark's latest work, having spent an equal amount of time explaining why his client went by so many different names. "Jack Lawrence, is like Mark Twain or Lewis Carroll or George Orwell. All belonging to another named individual. Like John le Carre'...the spy novelist. That wasn't his real name. I suppose they each had their own reason. I think Jack's – that is Clark's– was to simply leave his past behind him. Anonymity. You see?" Roberto nodded.

"An alias?" asked Roberto.

"Yes. Of sorts.'"

Clark stepped onto the back porch and looked at the clear sky overhead. It was so dark, that from the backyard, one could make out a portion of the Milky Way. Missy eased up next to him and placed her arm inside of his, at first to get warm, then to simply be near.

"So why are you in town?" Clark asked.

"Family business. Ellie was named executor of Dad's estate, but she dropped the ball. Didn't want to have anything to do with all that paperwork and lawyers and courts. She handed off to me and as soon as I could, I got here to clear up the mess."

"A lot of mess?"

"To tell you the truth, I don't know. A lot of unfinished business, that's for sure. Or so Roberto tells me."

"Roberto?"

"He's a kind of accountant. Specializes in forensic auditing. We met in Paris a few years ago. I had no idea what he did for work. Just that he was fun and knew his wines. We hit it off really well. Then he showed up at Cannes and then to my place in Naples. And before you knew it, Roberto and I were..." she stopped to search for the right word. "... a thing. Not an official thing, but a thing just the same."

"More than friends?"

"Some. More like friends and business partners."

"How so?" Clark asked staring down at her.

"At first he was my financial manager. Not a full-time job, but there were side benefits." She grinned and Clark felt a pang of jealousy cross his heart. "When Ellie dropped the ball on the estate, I was devastated. The last thing in the world I wanted to do was come home to East

114

Texas and go through tax records and oil and gas receipts and lease contracts. But Dad had left cryptic instructions to trust no one. I mentioned this to Roberto and he formulated a plan. Let him weed through the briars and thorns of the accounting underbrush and what he could salvage, we would split 80—20."

"I take it twenty is his end?"

"Of course. Howard Rusk didn't raise any fools. Besides, if he found enough, Ellie and I could get by with forty percent each. Don't you think?"

"Sure."

"I balked at first. Wasn't sure I wanted this charismatic beautiful man, slogging though my father's financials and finding God knows what. But again, he does it for a living and he offered. So we came this week for him to begin his audit."

"Find anything so far?"

She shook her head. "Boxes and boxes of paper. Enough to stretch from here to Dallas and back. Contracts, plans, offerings and well maps. Not to mention check stubs – my father was a pack rat when it came to keeping financial things. And tax receipts. Oh my God, they are as deep as the ocean. Roberto said it could take him the rest of August to go through it all just to get it organized."

"Is that his red Fiat?"

"No. We rented it. He loves Italian sports cars. So, we thought what a lark. Let the estate afford us a fun car while we are here on business."

"Smart."

"You have to be set pretty well – what with the movies and books..."

"I've done all right, I guess. Wasted some on booze, but kept some, too."

"I missed seeing you at Lee's funeral." She paused and looked down. Pain played across her face. "I had hoped you'd be there. I had seen you on BBC and was looking forward to catching up on old times."

"Yeah, well, I left here while you were away in Paris. Changed my name and started living inside a bottle. Things got pretty dark. Darker than I ever want to see again." He hesitated remembering. "When that dried up, I thought I'd try a spell as a writer. Slowly it worked out. I still prefer the bottle, but the pen pays better and it's not as lethal." He had to get out of this morose confessional. "You'll never guess who found me and got me back to Lincoln?"

"Who?" She asked.

"Mrs. O'Brien."

"No way." She laughed. "Old Ironsides?"

"Yeah. At a book signing of all places."

"Get out."

"It's true. She walks right up to me like it's last period and we had just spoken ten minutes earlier and says that Willie is real sick and I'd better get home."

"And here you are."

"And here I am. Here we are."

There was an awkward silence. Something along the fence line rustled some dry leaves then quieted, as if to pay respect and show reverence. She squeezed his arm again, real tight then said, "I'd better get back inside and see if I can help out Roberto and your agent with the kitchen."

"Tell 'em to leave it. I'll get it tomorrow."

"You have too much to do to worry about the kitchen, Clark. Let us do it." She started to leave and suddenly turned back to him and kissed him on the lips. A long and lingering kiss. "That's for not telling anybody back then."

## Chapter eight

Willie's service was an event to behold. Flowers galore and Miles sang like an angel. Andy read a few passages, with tears flowing down his face. There wasn't a dry eye in the church. Even the new Presbyterian minister, who didn't even know Willie or her husband, had tears in his eyes.

At the graveside, the pallbearers, high school buddies of Clark and Lee all pitched in their white boutonnieres into the open grave. There were only two Harveys at the service – Clark and his father; but the Crows came in rather large numbers from Oklahoma. Each family member dropped a long-stem red rose in Willie's grave. Andy read the 23rd Psalm and Rev. Cavanaugh left with these words:

Willie is gone. But not forgotten.
She is not dead, but alive in Christ.
Her spirit is and will be with us until we all return to the dust and
ash of our land.
Lester. Clark. It hurts just now.

Her shadow no longer spread before the Texas sun.
She no longer walks beside you or holds you or
whispers to you...
But she is well and she is watching down on you.
'Live on.' She says.
'Prosper and live on.'
We will miss Willma Crow Harvey.
We will miss her laugh.
Her stories.
And her deep devotion.
We will miss a wife...
A mother
A sister...an aunt
And a friend.
But today's loss is ours.
Not hers.
Today Willie is at home.
At peace.
She finally beat cancer.
She lives on....
She lives on.

Amen.

And with that the fried chicken feast began in
earnest at the clubhouse, sponsored by Lester's old golf
buddies and his forty-two pals. More fried chicken than a
whole town could consume. And mashed potatoes and
green beans and buttered corn and rolls and cherry pie. It
was all washed down with iced tea, almost frozen-cold beer
and soft drinks for the young ones. A man on the grand
piano played some of her favorite tunes, and Clark could
still see her dancing in the den, all alone, listening to a
silent orchestra deep in her head, hearing every note and

floating to the tune one fluid step at a time. Andy came and sat next to him.

"You did a hell of a job today, son," said Clark.

"Thanks. Anything for your mom."

"She was the best." It was Miles coming up to them from behind, a plate of chicken still ready to be inhaled.

"And you my baritone wonder, you were awesome."

"My pleasure, Clark. Sincerely it was."

"No, I mean it guys, you made the service. Without you it would have been dreadfully dull. And mom never liked dull funerals."

"Your mom never liked dull anything," laughed Miles.

"You can say that again," it came from Missy who walked up to the three friends and at once had a trio of chairs offered to her. Roberto was nowhere to be seen and Clark mentioned the fact. "He stayed at the house. Working today. Besides, he never knew your mother and this would be a glob of poop for him. Let him run numbers and account for something." She grinned, liking her own joke.

"A glob of poop...is that a French term?" asked Andy

"He's Canadian...and no it's a family expression. My mom used to say that. My father would simply say shit, but mother wouldn't ever let that word cross her lips. A glob of poop was her expression." Missy sat next to Clark and the other two slowly made their way back to wives, families and more food.

"Lovely service, Clark."

"Yes. Thanks to you."

"Me?"

"Yes you. You organized it."

"I made a suggestion or two. That's all."

"Whatever. It still feels like you pulled it out of your ass and wah-lah, we had a service that Willie would have been proud to call her own. Wait...it was her own." They both laughed and she hugged him again. This time he didn't let her move away, but instead brought her closer to him.

Missy slowly wiggled free from his caress and said, "Not here. Let's go somewhere. Somewhere there's not a thousand eyes staring at us."

"Let me get Lester home and in his chair."

"I'll follow you and give you a hand. We can go on the back porch. It doesn't have to be any place far. Just to be alone with you. Again. Like old times."

By late afternoon, Lester was sound asleep in his recliner, worn out from the activities at the church and the clubhouse. Clark covered him with a light comforter and showed Missy out to the back den. They sat next to each other on Willie's favorite divan, Clark's arm around her. She nestled closely next to him and placed her head on his chest. There were no words passed between them for the longest time. Just silence. The sounds of the house – a grandfather clock in the dining room, the icemaker in the kitchen and another at the wet bar, dropping their wares into freezing trays was all the noise the sleepy, tired house produced. It was as if it too were paying last respects to the woman who had wandered its halls and rooms, to the lady who had entertained guests there, who had danced to her imaginary orchestra throughout its confines. The house was quiet for Willie –may she rest in peace.

"How did Howard die?" He asked the question somewhat out of the blue. It felt abrupt to him, but Missy didn't seem to notice.

"Bad heart. Went quickly. He had gone to Houston for his annual check-up, stayed with his brother, Joel and then returned home and the next night passed away. In his sleep."

"I'm so sorry."

"At least, he finally got some peace."

Clark studied her. She hadn't said it as an indictment or even an acknowledgement of things past, but rather just a comment about her father's death. "Big funeral. Filled the Methodist church and had a spilling out into the streets of hundreds of folks. Many oil field workers who used to roustabout for him were there. It was on a Thursday afternoon, and many of them stood outside in their dirty, oilfield overalls and boots having come straight to the church from the rigs on which they were working, just to have a chance to pay their respects. Inside were bankers, lawyers and oil company executives in their three-piece suits and silk ties and their wives in their jewels and fine dresses; but outside the working folk were there. The men and women who really made dad his fortune. They were on the sidewalk just to say 'We're gonna miss you, Howard.' It was something to see."

"Was there a big wake?'

"No actually. We came back to the house, had a small lunch and it was all over. A big public to do and then nothing. He was buried before the memorial service, so there was no graveside service. Just a big to do at the church and then we drove home and ate some pimento cheese sandwiches and drank lemonade."

"Simple."

"Yeah. Just the way Howard Rusk would want it."

"Howard would have wanted the lemonade to have some extra ingredients, I suppose?" said Clark.

Missy smiled. "A lot extra. In fact, to him, who needs the damn lemonade? Just pour the extras in a tumbler and drink away." They both laughed remembering the bigger than life man that Howard Rusk had been.

"Did Miles sing at the memorial service?"

She shook her head. "No. Some woman from the Dallas Opera was flown in and she did several numbers and a small string ensemble from Centenary College in Shreveport accompanied her. I have no idea who arranged that. But like I said, one moment the town was there to celebrate him and the next minute we were alone in the house. All by ourselves."

"Did Roberto come home with you then?"

"No. He was in Canada on some business trip. It was just me and Ellie and Uncle Joel from Houston. And his two kids. They are from his third marriage and let me just say, they were brats. But Joel is an excellent cook and he fed us that night and then returned home the next morning. It was a blessing to get those two kids out of the house. So by the weekend it was quiet. That's when Ellie and I went into Dad's study and started finding all the paperwork that faced her in the closing out of the estate. Boxes and boxes, file cabinet after file cabinet. I don't think he ever owned a PC.

"I think she was overwhelmed even then. She just didn't want to say anything on the account it would scare me."

"Scare you?" asked Clark.

"You know, like I was going to have to do her job and she could see that it was a major undertaking. She was going to try, but she wasn't up to it. Not emotionally."

"Didn't your dad have accountants and lawyers who could help?"

"Sure he did, but remember he left us that cryptic note that said not to trust anyone. And anyone was underlined."

"That seems weird to me."

"Yeah me, too. Seems now it's kind of up to Roberto to piece all the parts together. To see what's what."

"And you trust Roberto?'

"Why not? He's got skin in the game."

"That could make him greedy- you know- maybe wanting more."

"I don't think so. When it comes to accounting stuff he's a pretty straight-laced guy. By the numbers. No fooling around. Plus the more he finds for himself, the more he finds for Ellie and me."

"Did you miss your deadline for probate?" He asked.

"I think we got an extension."

"You think?"

"I don't know about those things. All I know is that there is a tangled mess that Roberto is working his way through to figure how much Dad had and how much he was worth. In his last days, he acted like a real old man. Stuffing every piece of paper he could lay his hands on into boxes and drawers. He trusted no one with his secrets."

"Reminds me of stories about Howard Hughes."

"We all want to keep our secrets very hush, hush."

"Every family has their secrets," said Clark and as soon as the words had left his mouth he hoped it would not conjure up past, bad times.

She raised up and kissed him squarely on the lips. For a long time the embrace lingered and they did not push away or try to stop the moment. Finally she let her lips slowly leave his – but just so – and she said, "We too have our secret, now don't we Clark?"

## Chapter nine

It was late fall in their senior year of high school and Lee had a limp from a football injury that had occurred in the Gladewater game just the week before. Truth be known, he had hurt it the week before that against Gilmer, but he brushed that off as a light sprain. But in the Gladewater game, he had twisted his ankle while covering a kick-off in the first half. There had been a big hit and suddenly he couldn't put weight on his leg. He sat down on the damp turf and thought his football career might be finished.

Andy saw it happen through the lens of his camera. He was a reporter for the student newspaper and the yearbook staff. He gave the photograph to Lee who put it on the cork bulletin board in his bedroom. The moment of impact as a black and orange clad Gladewater player hit him just below the knee. 'It was a wonder the leg wasn't broken' – that's what the doctor had thought as he examined Clark's brother after the game. "You'll live, but you're going to limp for a while. No heavy lifting and make that no-good brother of yours mow the yard." Clark and Lee laughed. Clark was there in the examination room with his twin. He, too had witnessed the hit, although not through a camera lens.

So, when the team's trainer loaded him into a car to transport Lee to the hospital at halftime, Clark jumped in and rode along as well, with Willie calling after him from the stands, "...you call us if it's bad."

Lee had a limp a week later and was concerned it wasn't getting better. It actually hurt him to put any pressure on it. So he revisited the doctor and together they decided it would be best that they put a brace on it for support. "No dancing, now Lee. You hear me. You tell those girls they'll have to wait until you heal." Lee laughed, but realized that the fall Senior Officer's Dance was close at hand and he would not be able to take Missy.

"You take her." Lee said to Clark.

"What?" exclaimed Clark, sitting on the floor in Lee's room as his brother struggled to prop his heavily bandaged leg up in pillows.

"No. You take her to the dance for me. I can't go. I've got to stay off this leg for a week. Otherwise I'll be on crutches until Christmas. I'll miss the playoffs."

"But I can't dance..."

"She can. She'll show you what to do. Just let it flow. Hell, you take lessons from Mom; she's always dancing through the house. Just let her teach you some fancy moves."

"Lee?"

"It's settled. I'll call Missy and arrange it and that's enough said. I'll even buy her flowers for you, since I know you don't have any skin in this game. It's a favor, bro. For me."

"Well, okay. If you insist."

"I do." He did and that was that. Clark was taking Missy Rusk to the Senior Officer's Dance at the country club. "It is settled. And Clark, one thing more…"

"Yeah what?"

"No funny business. She's my girl. Okay?"

Clark nodded. He felt a strange pang of guilt cross his consciousness as Lee uttered those words because he had lusted after Missy from afar, but what boy at Lincoln High or Kilgore High hadn't had at least one fantasy about doing it with Missy Rusk or with Ellie for that matter? But Clark's lust was deeper than a passing thought of a fling in the hay with Missy. And that bothered him. She was, after all, his twin brother's girlfriend. There were boundaries. Boundaries you just didn't cross.

But they did.

Funny thing about boundaries, sometimes they are easy to cross, other times, they are an impassable obstacle. In the case of Lee's claim on Missy, Clark ignored it. His logical side warned him that he was on shaky ground, tantamount to family betrayal, but his imaginative side suggested he dive headfirst into the matter and let his heart lead him. Missy wanted him. She had said as much. And that was all he needed.

Regardless what people will say, Clark didn't break up Missy and Lee. That was the work of Howard Rusk. And in some small way, Clark's own father played a role in the fast-dissolved high school relationship. One might also add the name of Harold Scroggins to the list of participants in the demise of the budding romance between Missy and Lee.

126

But deep inside Clark, he knew that there was another lover who was abruptly separated from his love the afternoon Howard Rusk sent his daughter away to boarding school and on to Paris to become a top fashion model. And that was him – Clark. He would not be able to finish what they had started that night at the Officer's Dance.

And he never told a soul. Just endured the fate as a sad state of affairs that surrounded his brother and his ex-girlfriend, in which Clark happened to be a very silent player – at least in the deepest, darkest parts of his heart.

The history of the events are somewhat blurred with time, but the best remembrance says it happened when Rusk's lawyers found a contract that was written between Scroggins and Lincoln Drilling Company ordering them to drill wells on as many as six adjacent leases to Rusk wells. Other operators were targeted as well, but Rusk was only concerned with his leases.

Howard Rusk blew up. He created a huge drunken scene, first at home and then at the marina. He simply called his daughter into his home office along with Lee who was there that afternoon and told them their days of courtship were over. He sent Lee out of the house and limping to his home and Missy upstairs in tears. Next, he faced off against Lester telling him what his investigators had uncovered and accusing his former partner of betraying his trust.

That was the night of the infamous boat ride.

But before the incident, before the boat ride, there was a dance. The dance Lee could not attend, but rather sent his twin as his stand in: trusting him with Missy. At the dance, Clark and Missy giggled like strangers at first –

not like the friends they had become. They were a bit uncomfortable with each other at first. But that only lasted for a few moments. Several songs passed as they whirled in socks across the ballroom's hardwood floor, keeping plenty of distance between themselves, as well as the other gyrating couples. She teased him and he laughed back at her. He twirled her around and caught her on a fast revolution in his arms, and she spun herself free to begin dancing again, but he could tell she was enjoying herself. Then the band played a Joe South tune, slow and mournful, and they came together in a gentle entanglement of arms and sweaty torsos; and as if by magic, the night changed. The world stop spinning the way it was supposed to and the stars realigned. History rewrote a chapter that very instant.

She looked up at him and smiled. It wasn't a friendly smile, but rather a knowing smile that said, 'let's try this.'

Missy's folks were in Dallas that night and Ellie, the older sister, was God knows where with God knows who. The big house was all theirs. He parked his Rambler behind the house, past the portico, so it could not be seen from the road down the hill. Racing up the stairs to her room their clothes flying in all directions, he caught her on the landing and removed her last vestiges of material. Her body was lean and taught. Her skin was soft and smooth. Her breast and her face was aglow with light from a lone lamp in the hallway. She turned on music and they danced in the flesh, holding each other tighter and tighter. Sex came after eleven at night and lasted briefly. Neither was very good at it, but they enjoyed the experience. So, after about an hour they tried it again, with better luck the second time. Holding each other in the cool of the night air, they lay in her bed, surrounded by a pile of comforters and her big stuffed animals.

"I never thought I'd make love to a bear." He joked pushing the giant stuffed panda away from them."

"Careful. He's been in the family for years. Daddy won him for me at the State Fair when I was a little girl."

"Speaking of family, what are we going to do? I mean with Lee and all."

She rolled away from him. "It's you and me now, Clark."

"But I can't do that to Lee."

"You just did."

"You know what I mean." He said as if trying to enlist her as an admitted partner in his crime. "I can't tell him its over between the two of you. Its now me."

"If you want me, you'll have to."

He thought about it, swallowed hard, while bringing her next to him. They kissed deeply and soon he was inside her again and this time they consummated the act in extraordinary pleasure.

"My God we're getting good at this," she said.

He agreed and kissed her again.

"Promise me this, Clark. You'll break it to him gently. Lee is special to me. But you are my lover now. I belong in your arms and in your heart."

"And how do you suggest I tell him?"

"I dunno. He's your twin."

"Yes, Lee, I just made love to your girlfriend and now she's mine."

She took a pillow and struck him over the head, "You'd better be more sensitive than that or this will be a one night stand."

It almost was anyway.


Clark never had to worry about how he would tell Lee. Mr. Rusk did that for him. Sending Lee away and separating his daughter from Lester's offspring. The dating was done. Over. His daughter was soon to be moving on, out of town to a girl's boarding school and then onto the fashion runways and photography studios of Europe. Rusk had arranged it, to get Missy and her sister away from the wagging tongues and peering eyes of East Texas – away from the shallow, small town minds that loved to make stories up and to spread gossip.

It happened something like this. Howard Rusk had just finished his third cocktail in the early afternoon. He should, by all accounts have been feeling victorious and proud. A judgment had been handed down in his favor over the Scroggins Estate. After years and years of court battles, it was finally settled: they owed him a great deal of money. Now, whether he saw any of it or not, would be up to the lawyers and the judge, but at least he had a modicum of justice. He and Lester Harvey–he had to include Lester in this, as much as he hated to.

The phone rang. It was a lawyer from Dallas and his personal attorney from Kilgore. They had uncovered something and wanted to talk with him about it. He excused Ruth from the room, and behind closed doors he took their call. He took another drink. Then another. Then his blood boiled over.

Rusk came busting out of his office and into the den where Missy and Lee sat watching TV and playing cribbage.

"Out. Out. Get out of this house. He yelled at Lee. "Go. Go now. Get out and do not come back."

Missy wailed and grabbed at Lee who was ducking and weaving trying to escape the lunging Rusk who was about to wrestle the young man to the ground if he could have put his hands on him. "Leave my daughter alone. Never come back in this house again."

Lee, hobbling on his one good leg and dragging the other behind him, fled out the side door and to his car, which was parked on the edge of the portico. Rusk chasing after him shouting and waving his fists. "Get out and stay out."

After the commotion the house was suddenly quiet. The only sound that could be heard was Missy crying upstairs.

She was sobbing. Her heart crushed, her feelings trampled upon and there was at once an offended feeling along with anger in her heart. Perhaps a bit of hatred, as well. Her father had betrayed her.

Howard Rusk opened his young daughter's door and stepped in. She yelled at him to go away, then buried her face into the pile of pillows in her bed. Tears sobbed down her face. Ruth Rusk, stepped in next, but Howard nodded to his wife to let him handle this alone. It was between he and his younger daughter.

"Missy, roll over."

"Go away," she cried.

"Missy, I'm not leaving until we talk. I can wait you out. So let's get this over with right now." Slowly, begrudgingly, she tilted her hips enough to see him through reddened eyes. Her face wet from the tears she had just shed. "I know you are mad at me. I know your heart hurts because I sent that boy away. I get it. But you have to listen to me and listen good." He waited for her to sit up and pay attention. Her sister started in the door, passing Ruth in the threshold, but Howard held up his hand, "Not now, Ellie, this is for Missy." Missy's older sister slipped back out of the room and slinked down the hallway. The entire house was quiet after the explosion of emotions that had just rocked the mansion.

"Just leave me alone. You have ruined my life."

"No dear. I have just saved your life. Saved it from a grave mistake."

Missy sniffed, "What do you mean?"

"That boy..."

"His name is Lee..." More tears.

"Okay, Lee ... he's not right for you. Your mother and I have grander visions for your life. We don't want to see you tied down to something here in East Texas that will limit you. Lee would limit you. He is not like us, honey. He is..." Rusk hesitated searching for the right phrase. "...he is less than you. He is not up to your standards. Don't settle for a Lee. Reach higher. Reach for a grander future."

She rolled back over and began to cry harder. "You don't understand, daddy."

"Oh, I do. But what you can't see at your young age is the limits a boy like Lee would put on you. He could never give you the life you deserve. And his family comes saddled with a dark side. A very dark side.

"I am sending you and your sister to London's St. Mary's Prep to finish school. Just like we talked about before. A year away from Texas in London. Your mother will accompany you two. You'll get a great education and get to see Europe and all that it has to offer.

"And a friend of mine, Mr. Calloway– who I believe you have met on numerous occasions – is married to a wonderful woman who is editor of a fashion magazine in New York. She is a very powerful player in the world of fashion and the world of models. And he assures me she can find you work after schooling, in New York as an intern and perhaps with a bit of luck and persuasion, a modeling career there or even in Europe. Imagine that. Being a fashion model in Italy. The glamour. The fun. The excitement. It is what you have talked about for so long and now it is within reach – it is about to happen. But it would not happen if you were weighted down with Lee and his family.

"Trust me and my judgment on this. In the days to come, there will be many dark things discussed here in Kilgore and Lincoln and in Longview in the courthouse. Accusations and innuendo and charges and countercharges – falsehoods thrown about as fact. Many lawyers and many courtroom antics and I don't want you or Ellie to be a part of that circus. It all arises from my business dealings with Lee's father and another man. And there is no reason you two should have to endure the gossip that will surround the hearings.

"So off to boarding school you will go and then to Europe and to a world of high-fashion and glamour. If that is still what you want."

"I want..."

"You want someone to pay attention to you like Lee did. But you don't want him. Don't settle for him. You may hate me right now. You may despise me, but hear me when I say, your life will be far better off without Lee and his family than it ever could be with them. You will see. One day you will understand." He started to leave then he retraced his steps and sat on the edge of her bed.

"You remember two years ago, how I made you stop riding that motorcycle with the Peters kid? What was his name? Tommy? Remember what I said? I told you it was too dangerous. He was too dangerous. And you cried like a baby and called me names then, too. I tried to tell you it was for your own good, but you wouldn't listen. And what happened a few weeks later? Do you remember?" He shook her feet and she rolled over again.

"He got killed on the motorcycle," Missy said it between sobs.

"That's right, Missy. He died acting like a fool on the highway. And you could have been right there with him and you too would be dead. So sometimes, I know what I'm talking about. Sometimes you have to just trust me – even though it makes you mad as hell and it breaks your heart. Sometimes I am right. And I do things for your own good. This kid and his family are no good for you. And you're going to have to trust me on this."

She buried her face in the pillows and began to sob again. Rusk stepped out into the hall closing the door.

He looked at Ruth who had stood there hearing the entire thing. "So I'm going to finishing school as well, huh? You are banishing me, too?"

"Get serious woman. The girls need a chaperone and it will be for just a few months until they are settled in. Now go get dressed, we have a victory party of sorts. The court in Longview has announced we are victorious over Scroggins in the first round. We don't know by how much yet, but we do know we have won and that there is justice somewhere."

"They will be there?"

"Of course they will. We have to put on a game face for this. Even if they are scoundrels."

"I don't want to go, Howard," she said.

"To the boat or to St, Mary's?"

"Both," said Ruth. I do not have a good feeling about either."

"Very well for your feelings. Now go put on a party dress and prepare to leave. I am going to have another cocktail. I plan on telling Lester Harvey off tonight. Plan on settling a few scores. We may have won a round in court today, but his legal problems have just begun. You can mark my words on that."

After her parents had driven away from the house, Ellie came to Missy's room. "Come on. Let's get out of here."

"Ellie..."

"I know. I know. Come with me." The sisters got into Ellie's car and headed away from the mansion.

"Where are we going?' asked Missy.

"The lake," said Ellie.

"He has no right to treat us this way," said Missy.

"Of course he doesn't. But he has and we have to make the most out of it. I happen to agree with him about getting out of this small town with its small-minded people. London will be grand. And Europe for you – wow. What a wonderful experience that could be. And you have always said you wanted to model. Now's your chance. A chance at a life away from here. Don't get so flustered over a boy. I know your heart breaks for him right now, but soon, you will find another."

"It's not Lee, Ellie."

"What do you mean?" her sister asked steeling a glance at her sister as she navigated the road toward the lake.

"It's Clark. His brother. I am in love with Clark Harvey."

"Jesus, girl," Ellie flashed another look at her younger sister.

"I know. I know. It's complicated. It's crazy."

"How far has it gone?"

Missy simply nodded her head. She said nothing but just nodded her head.

"Does Lee know? Does he even suspect?"

"No. And you can't say a word. To anyone."

Ellie pulled a joint out of her purse as she parked the car on the far side of the country club's outer parking lot away from anyone else. They sat there and got stoned. Trading secrets and sharing their deepest thoughts about moving away from home and friends. As the afternoon turned to evening, they started to leave. "Let's go to the marina, and see if Clark and Lee are there," said Missy. "And not a word about this to anyone. Promise?"

"Cross my heart," said Ellie.

At the marina, Missy saw Lee and his brother Clark. They got onto the boat with them. Lee coming to Missy and holding her and commiserating about the afternoon's events, while Ellie ventured to the back of the large pontoon party boat and sat across from Clark who watched his brother and Missy in the front of the boat. "Weird afternoon at the Rusk house," was all he said.

"Yeah. Really weird," said Ellie, not taking her eyes off of Clark.

Within an hour both girls had been driven home and the pontoon boat was heading out onto the lake. Darkness falling over it as the sun set.

## Chapter ten

"Do you remember that night. The dance. My parents' house?" she asked as she lay in his arms on the back den sofa. Lester was sound asleep in the other room and Moss was somewhere in the house, he didn't know where. Probably on a phone making deals, thought Clark.

"I have thought of that night everyday since we departed," answered Clark.

"I felt bad for Lee."

"Don't. He had a new girlfriend within weeks."

"And you?"

"You were always there in my heart. In my brain. I could not get rid of you."

"You had to have others– women?" She said it but it was asked more as a question. As if he was being cross-examined by a sharp attorney.

"I was engaged a few years back. A woman from Oregon. She was well,..." He paused. "...she didn't stand up to my standard."

"Me?"

"Yes you. And she didn't know if she could be married to a writer. A drunk writer at that. There are very moody times when I am creating. Quiet times when I am thinking and rowdy times when I've finished, before I start the editorial process," he said and waited for her to react. She did not.

"And?"

"She moved out. If I am honest about it, the bottle played a big role in the breakup. Bigger role than I imagined at the time. I blamed her, but really, I wasn't sober much in those days. Not that I was a mean drunk. But I was a drunk, just the same. She wanted something more – something concrete – more solid and stable. I promised to reform...To be honest, I was just about ending my bottle days – trying anyway– and starting to get very serious about writing and she was in the way. Sorry to say."

"Too bad for her."

"Yes." He paused and then switching the subject he moved ahead, "You didn't come back for the trial."

"No. After mom's funeral that was all I could stand. I immediately left for London. To finish school."

"I remember seeing you there. At her funeral." he said.

"You were there?"

"In the back. Alone."

"No one else from your family came?'

"No. Already too many babbling tongues. Too much hearsay. It was already uncomfortable. Both in Kilgore and in Lincoln."

"Why didn't Lee come?"

He shrugged. "Can't tell you. I don't know."

"I didn't see you or I would have spoken to you."

"That's okay. Things got weird very quickly after that."

"You mean the trial?"

"Yes."

"Dad kept me away from it. Ellie, too," she said.

"Why?"

"Who wants their kids messed up in all of that?" She asked. She sat up and wrapped her arms around him and kissed him. "That was a million years ago, Clark. I want us to forget about it. It would do us both good to just forget about it."

"What about Roberto?"

"Business. Just business, if I say so. And I will say so."

At that moment, Lester stirred in the other room and called out for Willie. Clark stood and walked into the other room where his father was wrestling with the comforter and trying to arise from his nap.

"Willie's gone now, Dad. Remember? We buried her today. You need to rest."

"I need my oxygen. Would you get it for me?"

"Tell you what, let's get you to bed for a while, out of this old recliner and into your bed. There's an oxygen bottle next to your bed. Come on." Clark lifted his father up and helped him straighten. The old man noticed Missy for the first time. "I'm glad you came back around. He is a lonely boy."

"Come on, Dad, let's put you to bed." Lester ambled into his bedroom and Clark followed, helping him into the bed and covering him with a floral comforter from Willie's side.

"It smells like her, Clark. I can smell her. I never want this blanket washed. You hear me?" Clark nodded as he connected the oxygen tubing to Lester's nose. "Never wash it. I don't want her to leave this house."

Almost as soon as Lester's head touched the pillow he was asleep. Clark checked the flow of oxygen and made a note on the pad next to the bed as to the time and the flow rate. The nurse had asked him to do this so they could keep track on Lester's breathing.

"He asleep?" asked Missy.

"Yeah. Out like a light." He took her hand and led her back to the den. They sat, but now, Missy moved to the opposite end of the divan.

"Where were we?" asked Clark.

"Me and Roberto."

"Yeah. What about that?"

"There is nothing between us at this moment. In the past sure. Now it is business. That is how both of us want it."

"I feel a big but coming."

"No. No buts...Well yes. The but is we might be together, but he is married."

"Married?"

"Yes. I didn't know it at first. But I found out. His wife tracked us down in the south of France and made a scene. I'm talking huge scene. He left for a few days and when he returned he suggested that our relationship should just be business. Strictly business."

"And how did you feel about this arrangement – this new arrangement."

"I was fine with it. I suppose."

"Suppose? Like you're not sure?"

"No. Suppose like I'm not totally sure I trust someone who kept something as important as the fact that he is married away from me."

"Yet he's here. With you."

"Working for me."

"But is that all?"

"You're digging."

"I just would like to know where I stand."

"You stand nineteen years removed from me. I hate that, but it is the truth. A lot of water under that bridge. For you and for me."

"But you told me you loved me."

" I was seventeen."

"So you don't love me?"

"I don't know you anymore. I want to. I want to get it back to the way it was, but..." she stopped.

"But you're not sure."

"I'm not a lot of things, Clark. And one of them is that I don't want to be the girlfriend from the past. If we have a future it needs to be grounded in the present, not some romantic outing of kids fucking in a great big empty house and cheating on a brother and doing it on a lake the week before I was sent away."

He started to speak and she moved close to him, placing finger across his lips for quiet. "You and I had something very special. It was very volatile. I think that is what made it so special. That it was so volatile. We knew it could explode at any moment. That was the dark fun of it. The sheer excitement of getting away with it and not letting the world know."

"Our secret?"

"Yes. Our secret. That is what made it so very special. Once it sees the light of day, I'm not sure it is as special."

"You might be wrong."

"I could be. But its been hidden away a long time. This secret I speak of. Nineteen years. And to bring it to life now, I don't know."

"We could keep it a secret for a while longer." He grinned.

"You just want inside me again, don't you?"

He did. And she wanted it, too. And as Lester slept in his bed under the blanket with Willie's aroma, Missy and Clark returned to their secret once again.

She left after midnight. He checked on his father and the old man was snoring soundly. Clark wandered into the den, opened the wet bar and took out a bottle. He stared at it for some time, then replaced it. No sense getting two bad habits going at once. He had to think clearly about what he was going to do with Lester and what he was going to try and do with Missy. He wandered up the hall and noticed the light in Moss's room was on.

"When did you get back?" Clark asked his agent.

"Somewhere between the third and fourth act I think," said Moss as Clark blushed.

"Sorry you had to see that."

"No. It was fine. She is a lovely person. Makes me homesick. And speaking of home, which is in southern California and near some very big and powerful studios, have you made up your mind?"

"Studio Nine."

"Great, I'll get their paperwork out first thing in the morning, we can sign it and I'll be on my way."

"Moss, I can't tell you how much help you've been during all of this. I mean it. You didn't have to do what you did. You were a godsend."

"Well, you do help me pay my bills." He grinned. "Seriously, Clark. You are like family. I never knew your parents until now, but I love their son like a brother. It was the least I could do. Plus I learned something about you I didn't know."

"What was that?"

"Your middle name. Your real middle name, Mr. Clark Anderson Harvey."

The next morning, papers were signed and deals made on the phone and Studio Nine promised to increase the take, not by a million that both Moss and Clark wanted, but by 750,000 U.S. dollars. Good enough. The contract was official and announcement would be made in Hollywood the next week. Writers were on it getting a screenplay ready and the head of the studio wanted Clark to take a peek at the first draft as early as possible.

At eleven, the phone in the house rang and it was Missy. She said that Roberto was heading back to Canada on business and if Moss wanted a ride to Dallas to catch his flight, the two could share the red spider.

So by noon, Moss was gone. Roberto was gone and Missy was alone in her big mansion.

"Want to come play house with me?" she asked.

"Think it's okay to leave Dad alone for a few hours?" he wondered aloud.

"Sure. He's fine. Leave him a note and some food and a phone number how to reach you. Lester is a survivor. He'll do fine."

By three o'clock he was parked under the giant portico. He didn't give a damn who saw his car that day. He had found his way upstairs to Missy's room. It had not changed in nineteen years.

She lay uncovered in the comforters that floated atop the tall, four-posted bed. It was as if she was being sucked into a giant vortex of quilts and blankets and duvets. She reached for Clark who was sitting at the side of the bed gazing out the window as the afternoon sun drifted in.

"A penny for your thoughts," she said

"You are cheap."

"Okay a nickel."

"That's more like it. You and Moss negotiate for top dollar," said Clark

"I like him," she said, sitting up, covering her breast with a sheet. "Moss I mean. He seems very nice."

"The nicest. But don't let that fool you. Cross him and he's a beast."

"But at least the beast is on your side."

Clark nodded. "To be sure. He has scratched and clawed to get me a contract that earns a living wage."

"A living wage? I thought you were worth millions."

"I didn't say who's living wage," laughed Clark.

"No really. Moss seems like he genuinely cares for you."

"He should. I feed his family. Those kids of his are going to hang around his fortress in Montrose until he is an old, withered man, just to suckle the riches his royalties – my royalties – bring in. He'd better care for me."

"I mean it. Be serious for a minute. He is special to you apart from being your agent. Isn't he?" She asked. "Well?"

Clark turned toward her and lay down with his head nestled on her legs. "Moss saved my life."

She pushed him back into an upright position. Sitting there staring at her, she wanted the entire story. "Tell me."

"Book one was a bomb. I had found Moss quite by accident. Kept his card and called him when I had written a new draft. I thought it was good. He did as well. No one else in America agreed with us. It was a bust. Except for this guy in Hollywood, who saw it as a made-for-TV script. That eked a few pennies out of the moviemaker's coffers and enough to afford me a place to go and write. Moss didn't take a dime for commission. As he said, it wasn't big enough for the both of us to live on, so I might as well take it and invest it into another project.

"I did. It was called the whiskey bottle."

"This is when you became a drunk?"

"Well, that's when I became an official drunk. I had dabbled in the mystic beverages before – off and on again. Thought I had it under control, but now I was swimming in them. No, I was treading up-stream in them – in the liquors, and wines and beers and anything I could get my hands on and down my throat. And back in L.A., Moss was waiting on the next script. And waiting. And waiting.

"One day he calls me. It wasn't one of my more coherent days. He could tell over the phone that I wasn't my usual glib self. Something was wrong. He gets a plane ticket to Bend – which getting there from L.A. isn't an easy task in itself – rents a car then drives up the mountain to the cabin and finds me passed out on the sofa with enough empty beer cans and whiskey bottles to build a bridge over Niagara Falls.

"First thing he does is pour me into his car and drives me to an inn outside of Eugene. Quaint spot. Cabins on the edge of the forest. Quiet. And we had room service. We stayed there for six weeks. Me, drying out, and him watching over me, making sure I didn't backslide. He had the mini bar cleaned out and had warned the housekeepers within an inch of their lives that I was not to even see a mini bottle of vodka or rum or whiskey.

"I was on an ice water and coffee only beverage diet. I couldn't even have iced tea. It looked too much like whiskey.

"Slowly I come up for air. Fresh air. Then he pushes a goddamn P.C. under my nose and tells me to start writing. He commands me to.

"'Write about being drunk. Write about losing control. Write about anything. Just type damn it; just type.' That's what he said.

"So, I did. I began a book called *The Tree Line*."

"That was a biggie." She said, her eyes growing big with the excitement of his tale.

He nodded. "Yeah. Huge for me. Breakthrough. And every few hours he would come and get a page or two from the printer, proof it, make some notes on it and then we'd discuss the day's work over dinner.

"This went on for one solid month. Day-in, day-out. 24-7. Until one day he looked at me and smiled. 'You did it. You just finished a masterpiece.'"

"It was spectacular. I read it." She confessed. "Once I knew who the author was – who he really was – I read it and realized it was about us."

"Us and my battle with the bottle because you were no longer in my life. You had disappeared along the tree line that was this frontier between warring countries that people couldn't enter and I didn't know where you had gone. So liquor took your place. Just as it had done in my real life.

"And the critics loved it – no?"

"Hell, everybody loved it. It made a hit movie and I was on a roll. And thanks to Moss – my best friend in the whole word – I was sober."

"Had it been bad?" she asked.

"My drinking?"

She nodded.

"Oh God, yes, Missy. Yes. Yes. Yes. I was the worst. Fights. Strange women. And I mean strange. Real strange. All ages. Some maybe even minors." Missy frowned. "Lots of promises. Lost cars. Hell, lost weeks at a time, not knowing where I was or who I was with or where I was supposed to be. Drunk tanks all along the west coast. Seattle – a court date for some crime I don't remember committing. Charges were dropped with my promise to do community service and to dry out. That lasted about a day. L.A., a huge fight at some rally a young actress took me to – to speak on the behalf of whales or walruses or something. I ended up telling the crowd there that they were all butt fucks and cowards. And a guard came to take me off the stage and I hit him and all hell broke loose. It took Moss spending a lot of his own money to get me out of that one.

"I wrecked three cars. One mine and two belonged to Mr. Avis. Moss again, paid for the damages.

"And sometime during all of this I met Anna and we lived together. I guess we were going to get married, but I was such a lousy partner she left."

"Did you ever beat her up?" Missy asked.

"No. I wasn't that kind of drunk. Not toward her anyway. I did steal from her to get money for booze."

"But you had money." She said sounding confused.

"I was a drunk. I didn't know where my money was. And Moss had cut back my allowance – that's what we jokingly called my draw. Then one day she catches me digging through her purse. Well, that was all she could take. She walks out and I go to the cabin above Bend and the next thing you know, Moss is there picking me up off the floor, dusting me off and setting my feet back on the straight and narrow."

"Did you ever try and harm yourself?" She asked.

"Like kill myself?"

She nodded.

"No. I'm too big a coward to take my own life. At least with a gun or something with a sharp, pointed edge. But I was willing to drown my life in alcohol. And if that killed me, so be it."

"Have you ever wavered since then?" She asked.

He paused and breathed in hard. He shook his head. "No. Because while I could do it myself, I could backslide and enjoy a shot or two or two hundred; I couldn't do that to Moss after all he has done for me. Do you understand? Do you know what I mean?"

She sat up and the sheet hiding her breast fell away and she brought him into her chest and hugged him tightly. "Yes. I do."

"I feel a story coming on." He said, rolling over and staring up at her.

"I was in my hey day in Europe. Photo shoots every week, a new cover ever month, deals and more deals and endorsements and ads and never enough time for yourself. Never enough time for me." She touched her heart. "The real me inside here."

"Got it." He said and she continued.

"I started to lose touch with who I was. At first, Roberto had a pill or two to relax me. You know, to take the edge off. To help me find a bit of peace. But they made me gain weight. Retain water, the doctors said. So they prescribed me some drug that helped me slim down and to stay slim. But the more I took them, the more my body wanted them. I craved them. The doses weren't enough. So I went looking for more of them. Anything to stay slim.

Anything to keep the cameras pointed at me. Me. Me. Me. It was all so vain. Soon I had switched over to harder pills. Much harder. I would get high and do a shoot and they would have to have a handler there for me. Someone who could control me during the shoot. It wasn't unusual in the business. Models strung out and the handlers were there to bring us down with a blue pill or send us back up with a red or pink pill. Some girls were shooting up."

"You could stick a needle in your arm?" He asked.

"No. But I came close. Besides the models don't use their arms. It would leave tell-tail marks. They do it between their toes, so no one can see."

"Heroin?"

"Oh sure. And crack. And meth. You name it and we could get it and in any supply our bank accounts would pay for. Really easily, too. Snap my fingers and I was high. Snap them again and I was higher still. Roberto had been in Canada on a big project for the government there and came to Naples and found me strung out and sick. He called Ellie and told her she had to drop whatever she was doing in New York and get her ass to Europe, to Italy and to help me. He couldn't because his wife was so jealous of us, but he had the good sense to call my sister and she came."

"And you beat it?"

"Just as you wrestled the bottle to the ground and put it away, I did the same with the drugs. Gone. Thanks to Roberto and Ellie. It is one of the reasons I keep him around. Business. Only. But he saved my life. Just as Moss saved yours. There's a trust built in that. It's implied on a daily basis. We don't plaster it on posters or billboards – we don't even put it into words in our conversations – but we know – Roberto and I know. Moss and you know. It is that implication of 'you saved me and I owe you. I owe you with my loyalty.'"

"Yeah. I get it."

"I knew you would."

"So I have nothing to fear about Roberto? I mean in the future department?'

She shook her head. "As long as I don't get strung out again."

He laughed. "So here's the deal. You catch me drinking and you can smash the bottle over my head. I catch you with drugs and I will..." He paused.

"You will what?" She asked.

"I will be the one who disappears in the tree line."

## Chapter eleven

"Dad we need to have a talk." Clark said, as the old man ate cereal in the morning. Clark got up to get hot coffee. He poured both of them a fresh cup. "We need to talk about where you're going to live."

"Your mother promised me I could stay in this house. You would take care of me." He slurped his words with milk and cereal drooling down the white stubble on his chin. He looked in his bowl, not at Clark.

"She didn't have authority to tell you that," said Clark, a tad angry at his departed mother for having promised things she could not have influence over.

"Well, she did. And I'm staying."

"Dad."

"I don't want to go to some damn nursing home."

"No one is talking about a nursing home. There is an assisted living place not far from here. You can still come over to the club and play dominoes and eat lunch and see your old pals."

"What is assisted living, but a step up from the nursing care."

"True, they do have nursing care facilities there, but the assisted living is like having your own apartment. Come and go as you'd like. Have your meals in a central cafeteria, or cook for yourself. You can have cereal in the morning alone, if you'd like, or go get scrambled eggs and bacon with people down stairs in the main lodge. There is complete freedom; yet someone is close to keep an eye on you if you need it."

"I don't need it."

"You do."

"I don't want a tiny apartment. I want my house."

"Dad, all you do is sit in that recliner and come into the kitchen to get a beer and in the late part of the night go and get in bed in there. You don't need a lot of room."

"That was our bed. I still share it with her."

"Fine you can take the bed with you. No one cares. It is whatever you want, but you'd be taken care of at the assisted living facility."

The old man grunted and took a mouthful of cereal and milk and Clark watched as a good portion of it dribbled out of his father's mouth and onto the plastic mat on the table beneath him. He wondered if his condition was worsening. He made a mental note to get him in front of his doctor soon. Let him evaluate his father.

"Dad, would you at least come with me. Come see the place?"

"What's it called?"

"Whispering Pines. It's on the Henderson highway. Charlotte Reynolds, Andy's mom, lives there. He says she loves it. She plays bridge, knits and is in an aerobics class. She looks and feels great."

"Good for her, I want to stay right here."

"Would you at least go and see the place?"

The old man stopped eating and looked at his son. "Why don't you want to have anything to do with me? I raised you, now you could spend a little goddamn time with me in my twilight years."

"Dad, this has nothing to do with me. It's about getting you the best place to live."

"I've got the best place to live. This lake house was the pride of your mom's. We bought it and she decorated it and we loved it. Still do. Don't need to move and start over some place new. Don't want to live with a bunch of strangers."

"Will you at least ride with me over there to see the place?"

"You haven't seen it?"

"Not in person. I've driven by it and Andy showed me a brochure."

"He get a cut out of this?"

"No. Now will you go?"

"Okay. If it'll shut you up, I'll go. Let me finish my cereal and coffee in peace. I'll get dressed and we can go." With that, his father returned to his breakfast, his right hand trembling slightly.

Whispering Pines was just short of a resort. Very little expense had been spared in its construction or in its accommodations. It resembled a posh country club. There was a main lodge that could have been at any five-star hotel anywhere in the world. The chandelier in the domed entryway alone was worth several hundred thousand dollars. And five smaller cottages surrounded the main lodge. A patio and swimming pool sat beside the main house and a set of tennis courts and the new sport, pickle ball, was on campus, as well. Behind the pool was a putting green and a chipping lawn manicured with impeccable care. There were tables spaced out along a meandering walkway. Some were designed for chess or checkers, others had lines for games that Clark didn't recognize or understand.

On the north side of the community was a thick forest of pine trees. To the south was a slight elevation and atop a red clay hill, sat a lone pine tree. There were lighted walking paths all along the contour of the property and every so often a cedar pole with a box on it. Inside each box was an emergency phone. "If you need it while you're out, you open the box and pick up the phone. Our staff can see exactly where you are and can either come and get you or send emergency people to you. On top of each pole is a blue light. It will go off when you call, so people on patrol can locate you rather quickly." The woman, dressed in a fashionable gray silk dress with red high heels was conducting the tour. She spoke directly to Lester, leaving Clark as an outsider. A common practice thought the observant writer. Let the prospective patient feel he or she has an ally in Mrs. Parker and the staff. It's us versus them.

Each cabin contained four separate apartments. They reminded Clark of condos he had seen in Miami. Luxury had not been overlooked in the accommodations. Each apartment had its own door and a hallway inside leading to a rather spacious den and kitchen. There was space on the wall for built-in hook ups fitting a large-screen TV. The apartment was wired with satellite radio and a control unit on the wall allowed the residents to select their favorite type of music or news. The same box allowed for complete environmental control of the A/C and heat. One knob just to adjust the humidity in the apartment. And if the resident requested, the entire device could be programmed to be voice activated. Speak and it shall be done.

The bedroom was huge and had a walk-in closet on one side and a deep bathroom on the other side. Inside the bathroom was a long marble vanity and full width, lighted mirror. The bathtub was a tub-shower combination with a low step-in doorway. "We don't want any falls, now do we, Lester?" asked Mrs. Parker, sounding a bit condescending to Clark. This was a man who built an empire in the oil and gas industry. He didn't need to be coddled. In fact, the less hand holding Lester got, the more apt he was to make up his mind. Don't force him, thought Clark.

The kitchen and the dining room in the main lodge were spotless. The dining room featured tall oak walls with deep carved recesses and oak beams overhead with smaller copies of the chandelier that had greeted them when they first entered the facility. The tables were round, four-seaters, much like the gentleman's card room at the country club with thick, high backed leather chairs. The hardwood floors were spotless. A full bar was in the back, which he was told would be open most days from three p.m. until seven at night "Cocktails every night." She smiled. "Except on Sundays."

"What? People don't drink on Sunday here?" Lester asked.

Clark thought he could use a drink at that moment.

Out front, under a tall portico was a black SUV, as well as a black van. Whispering Pines logo was stenciled on the doors of both vehicles. "We can take you anywhere you'd need to go, Lester. Kilgore. Henderson. Lincoln.

Longview. We even have guests who go over to Tyler a few times a week. Just let the front desk concierge know and a ride will be waiting for you. To and from. Special trips to Shreveport and Dallas may be arranged as well, but there is a slight charge for them."

Lester nodded and turned to Clark and said, "Time to go. I'm tired."

And with that they drove back toward the lake, only Lester wanted to go to the clubhouse and play dominoes with his friends. Clark promised to pick him up at six, but Lester said not to bother; he'd get a ride with Sam Daly.

As Clark pulled out of the country club's lot and headed out the tree lined driveway toward the street that would lead him back up the hill toward his parent's house, his cell rang.

"Clark?"

"Missy. What's up?"

"Did you show your father Whispering Pines?"

"Yes. We just got back. He's at the club now. Beering away over forty two."

"Want to swing by. I'm lonely."

"Sure. Be there in thirty minutes.

She had a small dinner ready for him when he arrived. A Salisbury Steak, mashed potatoes and green beans. Clark never knew Missy to be a cook, so when she stepped out of the room he peeked into the trash bin in the kitchen pantry. There were no frozen food carton inside, so he guessed she had done this all on her own. She came back into the room as he was closing the pantry door. "Checking up on me?" She asked with a smile.

"I never knew you to be a cook."

"I'm not. I threw the packages out earlier because I knew you'd look."

They both laughed. She sat down across from him at a small breakfast nook table. "No dining room service tonight," he joked.

"I wanted it to be more intimate," she said and they ate for a few minutes in silence.

"This is actually not bad," he said. She told him the brand and he made a mental note that when he returned to Oregon to look for it in his local grocery store. "Miles directed me to it. Said they were delicious."

"Miles should know."

"Any odds on Lester taking the apartment at Whispering Pines?"

"Who knows? He was liking it, then suddenly it was time to leave."

"Maybe he had dominoes on his mind."

"Maybe."

"Come with me," she said pushing back from the table. Clark wiped his mouth with an aqua linen napkin that matched the paint in the room and placemats under the white china. He noticed that in blue – a faint blue at the rim edge of each plate and saucer – were the initials of HAR. Howard Adolph Rusk. "You might consider getting new china, you know." He teased, but she either didn't hear him or ignored him. He hurried after her. She walked down a wide marble hallway and into a giant downstairs bedroom. A huge four-poster bed with a pile of covers and blankets was inside. A bathroom was off to the right and a walk-in closet filled the left hand wall. "Think he'd move in here?" Could he be happy here?"

"What?"

"Better put, would you be happy here?"

"Missy, what are you talking about?"

"I've been thinking. We've been apart most of our lives. Longer apart than together. But we still share some spark. I admit it. I am willing to re-kindle that spark. Or at least try, if you are."

He paused before he spoke. "There is no way in hell Lester Harvey is going to live under Howard Rusk's roof. Not today – not tomorrow."

"What about his son? Would his son?"

"Yes, well..."

"You'd be damn close to take care of him. Either here or Whispering Pines or the lake house. And you can have an office upstairs to write. It will be quiet and ...and I need an answer because I am dying inside."

He took her hands and laughed. "Are you proposing to me?"

"In a way I am. Now get over your male silliness and pride and decide. Do you want me or not?"

Clark looked around the house. He looked at Missy. He nodded. "I could get by here. Might need some fresh paint and new plates and stuff, but I just might get by."

She flew into his arms and they kissed. He felt them grow together and before he knew it, they were immersed in the giant bed surrounded by quilts and pillows.

"We have nineteen years to make up, Clark. Let's start right now."

The Salisbury steak and green beans got very cold, sitting all alone in the kitchen.

## Chapter twelve

Lester opted for Whispering Pines. It was a real battle. It raged off and on for weeks, but finally the old man succumbed and granted his son the right to move him and to sell the lake house. For months, he wasn't happy. Twice he wandered off the property at night. Once Clark found him many miles south on the Henderson highway, going the wrong direction – away from the lake and away from his old homestead.

It was a chilly late October night.

"Dad. Get in this car. What are you doing?" Clark stopped the car, got out and helped his father into the front seat.

"Where were you going?"

"I was just out for a stroll."

"Dad you're five miles from Whispering Pines. They've got the police out looking for you."

"I don't like it there. I just don't." Clark saw his father was shaking all over. He couldn't tell if it was cold or fear or rage, but his father was very upset. Clark called the office at Whispering Pines and told them he had found Lester and was taking him to his home that night. He'd return him in the morning.

When Clark pulled up under the portico, Missy stepped out with a sweater wrapped around her slender shoulders. "Lester," she said," Oh Lester we were so worried."

"I was okay, Missy. Just out for a walk. That's all."

"Let's get you in here and warm and to bed."

"I need a beer."

"I'll get you one," said Clark who left his father and Missy on the side porch. He returned in a moment to find Missy holding his father in a hug and rubbing his shoulders like someone would do to warm a freezing person. The shakes had returned to his father's frail body. Trembling, Missy would recall later. "He was trembling in my arms. I looked up at Clark and said, 'We can't do this.' He has to move in here with us.'"

By this time, the lake house had sold and was in the possession of a couple from Bangor, Maine who had moved to Texas to escape the frigid winters up north, so moving back to the lake was no longer an option.

"I'll go to the Pines tomorrow and get him some clothes, he can stay here a few days until we figure things out."

She nodded and led the old man to the den where he could sip his beer and get relaxed enough to go to bed. Instead, he asked to be covered with a light throw and he chose to sleep in an overstuffed chair across from the fireplace, which was not active. Missy walked across the room and turned on a light switch and a fire roared to life in the fireplace. Lester smiled and nodded his head. That was more like it. "I gotta get me one of those things." He said with a grin.

Missy placed the alarm system on, in case Lester got up and tried to wander off again. She crawled back into bed with Clark and rolled over and placed her head on his chest. "This is going to take time, Clark. We need to show him some patience and give him time."

"I suppose," said Clark who was feeling trapped in the knowledge that his father was now a burden to him. "I always feared this day," he said. "Always thought it would come to this."

"What do you mean?" asked Missy.

"I feel like I'm going to have to commit him or something."

"Clark, don't you think that. Not for a moment. He is old. He misses Willie and his old home and he is a bit confused. He is not crazy. He is old. You will be old someday. Okay? Just give him time."

Two days later, with Lester firmly established in the first floor of the house, a call came for Clark. "Master Jackie, it's Moss. Or do I call you Clark fulltime now?"

"Moss. How are you?"

"The best and doing better. Studio Nine would like to meet with you. Script is getting ready and the director and the lead actors want to have a reading. You up for a little LA LA Land time?"

"I dunno, Moss. My father is not in the best place right now. He's here with Missy and me. I hate to drop everything and come out there. It would mean I'd leave him to her."

"So?"

"That doesn't seem fair. He's my problem. Not hers."

"Dude, the world is waiting for you. Money speaks. And it is speaking loudly. Studio Nine has moved a great deal of cash into your bank account, in case you hadn't noticed. You need to be here. Contractually, you agreed. Remember?"

Clark was silent for a few seconds then said, "All right. Give me a few days. I'll call you."

"That's my Jackie Boy. Get packed. Get a ticket. I'll pick you up at LAX. You are going to be blown away with the set designs and the production they are planning."

"I'll call you with my travel plans, Moss. But tell them, I have to have a quick turnaround. No lingering for parties and all that bullshit. In and out. Script review, a few meetings and then I'm back here. I can't leave her with him for a long time. It wouldn't be right."

"You got it Jackie. You got it. How is Missy?"

"It couldn't be better. Truly good."

"Great give her my love and tell her to get you on a plane fast. And Mr. Cheap Seats, fly first class this time. You deserve it."

It was a Wednesday afternoon, just past the first of November. She drove him to the airport near Longview and he caught a commuter flight to DFW and then on to LAX.

She had not balked in the least about taking care of Lester while he was away.

"It'll be one maybe two days tops." He assured her.

"You go and get your business done. We'll be fine. We'll plot something against you while you're gone." She grinned that devilish smile she was known for. He kissed her and stepped through the metal detector and walked out of the small airport and onto the waiting puddle jumper that would take him to Dallas.

Two days later he called her and said things were about wrapped up and he'd be home by the weekend. She told him not to worry, she and Lester were becoming good friends and he was teaching her the finer points of forty-two.

"Has he tried to wander off?"

"Not even a step."

"He must be settling in."

"Clark, I think we should make his presence here a full-time thing."

"We'll see." Clark said it, but felt a bit of a shiver run up his spine as he considered the possibilities of trying to manage a relationship with Missy and take care of his father all at the same time – all under one roof.

That afternoon, Roberto called Missy and told her he needed to see her immediately. He was in Dallas and wanted to drive over for a meeting. He sounded quite agitated. "I have found something in my audit you need to see."

"Okay. Fine, bring it here. I'm at the house."

She called downstairs to tell Lester she had a business meeting in a few hours and if he needed anything to ask the housekeeper, a lady named Lucy, to get it for him.

Lester yelled back that he was going to nap. "We can play forty-two later." She agreed and got dressed to meet with Roberto. She wondered what he had found that was so important.

When he arrived and she saw what he had, she knew why it couldn't wait.

## Chapter thirteen

Missy had Roberto help her move Lester back to Whispering Pines. She promised the old man it would only be for a few days. She had to go away and do some business. She would leave Clark a note and he would come retrieve his father from the care facility.

The old man put up a squabble, but soon relented, noticing that both Roberto and Missy had very stern faces, saying that something very important had arisen from the auditor's sudden appearance at the house. He got into the passenger front seat of her car and Roberto loaded two suitcases into the trunk and slipped into the backseat. She drove straight to Whispering Pines. Lester thought they were traveling way too fast, but didn't say anything about it. They got him out and the office personnel from the home came and retrieved Lester and his luggage, "Les, we're so delighted to have you back with us," said a lady with a Whispering Pines name tag which read: Edith.

"It's for just a few days, right Missy?" Lester asked, looking for affirmation.

Missy nodded and headed out the door with little or no good-byes. Roberto followed her and Lester watched as they drove away. Again, too fast, thought the old man. He was escorted to his apartment by two friendly orderlies.

Missy left a note on the kitchen bar, a peninsula that jutted out from the east wall into the heart of the giant cooking area. Its marble surface was totally bare except for the note that she had typed out. Clipped to her note were four printed sheets of paper.

Clark tried on three occasions to call her. But there was no answer. He worried something might have happened to Lester. Or to her.

He flew into the small commuter airport just outside of Longview and called again. No answer. He went to a counter and rented a car and drove the eleven miles into Kilgore and up the long driveway to the house. The oak trees were just starting to turn their dull yellow. An early autumn sun draped the house and the estate in a warming glow. There, in the driveway, was her SUV. He approached it, and for some reason felt its hood. Ice cold. It had not been run that day. He opened the side door off the portico and entered the den. He called out for her. "Missy. Missy are you here?"

Nothing.

Next he yelled for Lester. Again no reply.

The note that Rusk held in his hand was from the lawyer investigating the rigs that were in question. There was no denying it. A deviated well was sucking oil out from under his lease. A second note registered it was also happening at two other sites. The lawyer spoke up and said they hypothesized that at least three other Rusk leases were involved.

"Son of a bitch," said Rusk as he stood and began to pace around in his large office.

"We have no way of proving who did it. I mean who gave the order? That's what we will need to get compensation. We will need a finger on the smoking gun's trigger, so to speak."

Rusk walked to the floor-to-ceiling windows and stared out at the downtown below him. It was a series of short commercial buildings towered over by silver painted derricks almost as far as the eye could see. Pump jacks were operating feverishly on some sites, while others sat sill, waiting on their monthly allotment dates to kick them on. The field was regulated in this way to prohibit the pool of oil, which lay beneath East Texas from being depleted too rapidly. At Christmas time, the derricks in the downtown area were strung with colored lights to make the entire area seem as though giant holiday trees surrounded the city center.

"Who?" asked Rusk.

"Who? What do you mean who?" asked the lawyer.

"Who is vulnerable in this? Who could we get to sing?"

"Well there is the driller himself. He got us all this information to begin with. Like he knew exactly where to look."

"E.C. Humphries?"

"No. His boss."

"Harvey?"

"Yes. Lester Harvey. He's the most exposed. Plus he was still under contract with you when he took on Scroggins as a customer."

Rusk thought for a moment and nodded. "Ruth," he shouted. The polished oak office door opened and a woman in her late 50's in a dark business suit stepped in.

"Yes, Mr. Rusk."

"Ruth, see if you can get Lester Harvey on the phone. It's quite important."

"We should do this face-to-face," added the lawyer.

"Ruth. Wait. Ask him if he can come up here and have a conversation with me. New project."

"Yes, Mr. Rusk."

She disappeared back behind the huge doors and in a few minutes returned with word that Lester Harvey would be at Rusk's office at two o'clock."

The lawyer nodded. "Might be wise if you two had this conversation out of hearing distance from legal counsel. If you get my drift."

Rusk agreed and the lawyer departed. The oilman ordered lunch: a tuna sandwich and an iced tea. He spread out the map he had shown Harvey earlier with all of its colored dots. He studied them and knew what was about to transpire. He had felt it coming on for sometime. Now he could prove it. And he wanted Lester Harvey to help him. But he would have to offer his old friend something in return; something to offset Harvey's own involvement. What did his lawyers call it, quid pro quo? Yes. He would have to exchange something of value for Lester's testimony. Something that would be of great value to Lester. But what?

At two o'clock precisely, Lester strode into his old friends office and plopped down in one of the cowhide, leather chairs which sat across from the massive desk. Lester immediately recognized the map spread out over the desk. "That again?" asked Lester.

"Yep. This again. Only this time I need more information."

"Hell, I got you everything I had," said Lester

"Not quite everything, Lester. I need a bit more."

"Like what, Howard. You know the deal. He deviated the stem right under a dozen wells. Yours included."

"And you'll testify to that under oath?"

Lester shook his head. "Might need to talk to E.C. about that. He ran the rigs."

"E.C. Humphries?"

"Yeah. He was my drill foreman on most of those wells." Lester got up and studied the map with all of its dots. There were twelve wells circled in red ink. "As a matter of fact, I think E.C. probably drilled each of those."

"And E.C. is good at what he does?"

"Howard, you know E.C. He's the best in East Texas. Nobody's a better driller than he is."

"But I imagine E.C. doesn't deviate a stem unless he has orders from someone up the chain of command. Am I right about that, Lester?"

Lester nodded. "Sure."

"And who was above E.C. in your chain of command at Lincoln Drilling?"

"You know goddamn good and well it was me."

"And did you give orders for E.C. to turn the pipe and venture under my leases?"

"No. I told him to do what Scroggins said for him to do. Scroggins was the customer. He was paying the bills."

"But you knew what was happening?"

Lester stalled. He was getting close to a line where he might incriminate himself. "What do you want, Howard?"

"A deal."

"What kind of deal?"

"I drill a well and I'll pay you to drill it. Then you drill one for yourself and I'll pay for it, too."

"We've been here before, Howard."

"Right you are, but oil and gas prices were a lot less then. Now, you'd get very, very wealthy. Very wealthy in a deal like this."

"A man can only spend so much money, Howard."

"But you could pass it along to others. You have two sons and a lovely wife. Buy a big lake house out at the country club and retire out there. Six wells. That's all I ask. Six wells. Three for me. Three for you. And testimony against Scroggins."

"Let me think about it, Howard." He stood to leave, Rusk remained seated behind the desk and map.

"Well, don't think too long. My lawyers are quite antsy and they have you in their cross hairs as an accomplice in this crime."

Lester knew that had been coming. He was prepared for it.

"That would be very hard to prove, Howard. Very hard indeed."

"But it would drag you into court for a long, long time, Lester. A long and painful time. And in the end, what would you get out of it, even if you were exonerated? Nothing. My way – you'd make a fortune and have your sins absolved. All in one fell swoop." Rusk lit one of his ubiquitous cigars. "It's a Cuban. You want one?"

"Don't smoke anymore. Doctors say its not good for my heart."

"Neither is keeping dark secrets. It is the same as lying, Lester. The very same."

Three days later Lester Harvey and Howard Rusk were partners once again. It was as if nothing in the world had changed. Almost nothing.

Lester still had another partner. And he had not mentioned that to Rusk.

There are accidents in the world – things that do not go as planned. Events that should have occurred, but for some reason fate intervened and changed the script. In the case of Clark, he didn't walk through the kitchen of the mansion, but instead, wandered through the den and then down the long hall to his father's room, where he saw it empty. The closet cleaned out and the drawers open with socks and underwear gone.

He bolted out the door and back to his rental car and drove toward Whispering Pines. He figured something had happened, he didn't know what, but he was sure she would have returned his father there. It was safe there for him. She cared for him and if she was going somewhere in a hurry, she would have taken him there. For his own good.

## Chapter fourteen

The old man was sleeping in his chair with the TV playing softly: a game show with some presenter offering contestants prizes for guessing the price of merchandise.

A woman appeared in the doorway, "Clark?"

He turned and said, "Edith, did she bring him back here?"

"Missy? Why yes. Yesterday. Left him here in a hurry."

"Was anybody with her?"

"A man. Shorter than you with curly black hair and a thick mustache. Quite handsome."

He led Edith back to the office where he retrieved his checkbook from his coat pocket. He wrote a sizable check and said, "This is for him. Take care of him. See that he gets anything he needs. I'll forward you an address if you need more or if you need to reach me. I've got to go just now. Tell him I came by and I will be back for him. Soon. I promise."

With that Clark drove back to the mansion and pulled in behind her car. He entered the house from the portico and walked into the kitchen. That was the first time he saw her note. He picked it up and began to read. Soon he slumped into a chair that was next to the breakfast nook across from the marble kitchen bar. He was having a hard time focusing.

Everything was a blur. History had stopped. It now was rewinding and trying to repeat itself.

He could feel the pain from the past return. What joy he had shared once with Missy was now gone and in its place was a burning – some of the heat from anger – some from angst – and a lot of the burning sensation from pure loss.

He read the note and then began to study the pages she had attached to it.

The trial was fast. A jury awarded Howard Rusk, et al. a huge sum of money in penalties and lost compensation. But he knew he would never see but a fraction of the reward. Scroggins was gone. Disappeared. On the lam somewhere. Most of his money moved overseas. Deposited into banks that no one in the states could get into.

The jury dug deep and came up with a plan that gave Howard Rusk rights to future earnings from the Scroggins' wells. This was complicated because there were silent partnerships behind the wells themselves. Paper companies that stretched far into the distance. Boards of directors and owners whose names were not familiar with Howard and his legal team.

With one exception.

In one filing with the court, there was a document naming Lester Harvey as a financial partner in S&H Limited. S&H seemed to have some ownership in each of the wells that had been brought under question in the court in Longview. The judge called for a recess to allow a grand jury to be convened to investigate further the financial web that surrounded the civil suit Rusk was bringing against the Scroggins empire. The judge reasoned that criminal acts had been committed.

It was that grand jury that discovered Lester's deepest and darkest secret. He had profited in each and every transaction that Scroggins had done. And profited greatly.

The Gregg County district attorney was a political animal, if not a great lawyer. He decided not to make the grand jury's findings public at first, but rather, he would let Rusk's team know what they were dealing with privately. He knew Rusk was a powerful man and held great resources. Re-election wasn't that far away and he might need a favor later, closer to election day.

Having Lester Harvey as their key witness, in the civil case, was a complication. In fact, the D.A. told Rusk's lead attorney that he found Harvey's presence in the civil trial as a liability. The Rusk team might have to disclose that Harvey was now a partner with Rusk and yet his testimony was a conflict of interest. Self-interest. Harvey stood to make a large sum of money from both sides.

After Scroggins just up and disappeared, the DA knew he could turn the grand jury information over to the Rusk legal team with little to no opposition from the remaining Scroggins defense team.

It happened that the evening of the release of the findings, the Rusk family and the Harvey family were planning early celebratory champagne for having won in court. A matter of days, thought all concerned. The jury had spoken and now the judge had to agree to the settlement terms. It wasn't the huge award that all expected, but it was justice. "And justice is what I was after all along," said Rusk. And he believed this. Until the lawyers showed Howard Rusk the findings of the Grand Jury and the information they had uncovered.

That is when all hell broke loose.

It started on the deck at the marina, when Howard ordered his two daughters off the boat and back home. No questions asked. Lee and Missy were upset. Missy cried and the two girls loaded into a car driven by a Rusk lieutenant, who had been summoned to the lake to retrieve the two girls. Rusk did not want them to see the fracas that was about to erupt on the water's edge.

His voice was loud and accusing. People at the marina and on the docks stopped what they were doing to stare at Lester's boat and the melee that was resounding from it.

"You son of a bitch. You two-timing son of a bitch." Howard was yelling, thrusting a piece of paper into Lester's face. Clark stood to get in-between the two men, but his father pushed him back into the pilot's chair.

"Take us out into the lake so we aren't a public spectacle here," ordered Lester to Clark, who sat next to the boat's controls.

Clark started the two robust black motors on the back of the barge. He eased the throttle forward and the boat began to lurch against the lines holding it steady. "Lee." Clark yelled out. His brother hobbled to the dock side and released the lines securing the boat, as they began to navigate out onto the dark lake, as it was now well past sundown.

During this time, the two men stood eye-to-eye with Howard doing the yelling and Lester continuing to push him away. A crowd had gathered dockside, watching the vulgar disturbance. "You knew all along. You played me. You are a two-timing rat. A fucking rat."

"Howard let's drop it.  Not here. Not in front of our wives. And my sons."

"Screw them, Lester. They should know what their father really is. What a foul human being they have for an old man."

Clark again stood to separate the two men, but Lee caught his arm and pulled him back. Lester flashed him a look that said 'don't get involved in this.' The boat was moving forward, aiming straight toward the cut with its armada of sharp rocks protruding from the dark surface of the water. The wind had kicked up and the waves were rolling quite high.

Now Ruth, Rusk's wife, stood and on shaky legs took a step toward her husband. "Howard, really. Not here. Not now." He pushed her away and she lost her footing and as the pontoon boat rolled across a breaking wave, she fell about the deck. Willie tried to help her to her feet; both women were yelling at their husbands to settle down, but the two men were now into throwing punches. Not just insults.

One of Rusk's punches landed squarely on Lester's right-hand jaw in full force. It spun him down and onto the boat's controls prompting the giant Evinrude engines to roar into life and the bow of the party boat pitched up in the night air as the craft launched itself straight into an oncoming rock. The barge hit the rock on the port side and sent Ruth overboard, hitting her head on the right-hand motor and then in full flight she struck a rock and slid beneath waves of the dark lake water.

Willie yelled and Clark grabbed the throttle and reversed the boat. A huge gash had appeared in the front pontoon on the left side where it had struck the rock. Lee grabbed a flashlight and searched the surface of the water. Nothing. No sight of Ruth.

As he stood close to Rusk, Clark could smell the odor of alcohol. The oilman had been drinking before the incident. Rusk was about to dive in for his wife, but Lee grabbed him and Clark said, "I'll go. You stay. Dad, back the boat up some." With that, Clark dove in and began to fish around with his hands trying to locate Ruth's body. He dove deeper and deeper, swimming next to the slimy rock. The water was dark and murky. He could see nothing. Soon he was winded fighting the current driven by the wind and Lee took over and Clark climbed back into the boat, which was now listing rather precariously on its left side. Willie held the flashlight just at the edge of the water to give her sons some light in their exploring. After several attempts at diving deeper and deeper, Lee, also surfaced and shook his head.

"Get Lee back in here. We need to get this boat back before we all drown." It was Lester, who was now seated in the pilot's chair working the controls of the powerful outboard engines. Rusk fell to his knees in tears.

"Ruth. Ruth. Ruth." he cried over and over. "She can't swim."

Clark eased himself back into the dark water and told his mother to hand him the flashlight. He assisted Lee back into the listing party barge. "I'll stay here at the rock. You guys go to the marina and get help. Get the sheriff. Get an ambulance. Get divers." Clark was yelling instructions as fast as his mind would cooperate with his tongue.

He watched as the barge slipped into the night and tried to speed away in a most clumsy manner with part of its front pontoon torn apart. The boat limped toward the marina, which was a lighted area on the far shore. He slowly got a foothold on the rock and climbed up and turned on the flashlight to lead searchers to his location. He was about to take a seat on the rock, when he saw the body.

She came floating up about ten feet from where he was perched. Her red and white cotton party dress floated out from her thin figure like a parachute. He placed the light down on the rock aiming it at the marina and dove into the lake again. This time, the water felt cold. He had not noticed it before. But now it chilled him as he grabbed Ruth and pulled her to him. She too felt cold. He swam toward the rock on his back carrying her across his chest. Backstroke by backstroke he plowed through the rough water toward the light he had placed on the protruding stone.

Suddenly he could see other lights racing toward him from the area of the marina. One. Two. Three or more boats were on their way. He tried as best he could to hold her head above the splashing waves, but he knew instinctively she was gone. She was dead in his arms. Gone.

Aloud, for no reason at all he whispered, "I am so sorry, Missy, so very sorry."

# Book Three

## Chapter fifteen

Lee called her multiple times on the phone. But she never took his calls. The housekeeper simply said that Miss Missy wasn't available. And she would hang up. She hung up on Lee and she hung up on Clark. And soon he learned that her father had sent her away. He had sent both daughters away. Lee was devastated. Clark was as well, but he kept his loss a very silent secret.

After her mother's funeral, Missy was sent to Europe to do the things a fashion model does. And Clark was preparing – with the lawyers that seemed to circulate around the house at all hours–preparing for his testimony.

The trial was a sensational event. Not like an oil property trial where one or two parties' appeared before a bored jury and arguments were made about money and property – about leases and slant-hole drilling. No, this was big. It was news.

It was murder.

"How long did you search for Mrs. Rusk?" asked the prosecutor.

"Several minutes. Maybe ten. Then Lee took over." Clark squirmed in the witness chair. It felt strangely uncomfortable, as if the entire weight of the world was leaning on him. The fluorescent lights in the ceiling of the courtroom shown a bluish green down onto the proceedings. The wooden walls were old and stained with dark brown age. Photographs of the last three U.S. Presidents were hung in order of their service; below them a picture of the current governor of Texas. The jury box had an oak railing across the front, separating it from the rest of the courtroom; and twelve people sat behind it. Sat there staring at him. He didn't know any of them, although he thought a man on the back row looked somewhat familiar. Judge Reynolds was presiding. Andy's father. At times it was comforting to know he was there, at other times, Clark wished it had been a total stranger.

"Why did you stop?"

"I got winded," explained Clark.

"Winded? I see...Don't you play varsity basketball?"

"Yes but the water was very rough and..."

"And how long did Lee search for Ruth – for Mrs. Rusk?"

"About the same. I'm guessing ten minutes or so. It was very cold – the water. Plus, Lee's leg was injured and he could not stay in the water long."

"And who was at the controls of the boat when the incident occurred?"

"I had been. But I got up to step in between my father and Mr. Rusk."

"They were fighting? Correct?"

"They were having words, yes sir"

"And when you left the controls of the boat, where was it headed?'

"It was in neutral. I left the controls in neutral."

"You are sure?'

"Yes."

"And what happened then?"

"My father pushed me back down and Mr. Rusk continued to yell at my father calling him names."

"Did Lee grab you at some point?"

"Yes. I was about to try and separate them again, before a real fight broke out, but he grabbed my arm and pulled me back. That's when Mrs. Rusk spoke up."

"Where was she standing when this happened?" The attorney took a step toward a diagram of the pontoon boat resting on an easel.

"She had been in the aft seat. Port side. That's the left side. But she stood to try and restrain her husband. He pushed her away and she fell."

"Where did she fall?"

"She fell to the center of the boat. Behind the middle console. My mother tried to help her up."

"Then what happened?"

"Dad and Mr. Rusk got into actually throwing punches."

"Who threw the fist punch?"

"If I remember correctly, it was Mr. Rusk."

"He's lying," shouted Rusk aloud in the courtroom. Andy's father banged his gavel several times and admonished Rusk's lawyer to control his client. He then looked at Clark and said for him to continue.

"Mr. Rusk hit my father on the side of the head and knocked him into me."

"And where were you seated when this occurred?'

"I was in the pilot's chair. Mid-boat on the starboard side."

"That's the right side, correct?"

"Yes sir."

"And what happened then?"

"I must have grabbed the steering wheel and the boat turned and my father's weight came down on the throttle and we shot forward toward the rocks."

The prosecuting lawyer walked to a diagram of the boat and of the rocks at the cut of the harbor, which led out from the marina. "You were here," he said pointing to the pilot's seat, "and your father fell on top of you and his arm or hand hit the throttle and it caused the boat to launch out of the water and hit the rock."

Clark nodded.

"You'll have to speak up so the court reporter can record your answer."

"Yes. The boat struck a rock."

"Lee was where? Here, I believe you said?" The lawyer pointed toward the front of the boat where Lee and Missy had been seated when her father came and forced the two girls away and sent them home.

"He was no longer that far forward more like here." Clark pointed to a bench seat near the pilot's chair.

"I see. So Lee is here. Let the record show that Lee was parallel with his brother in the boat. Your father is on top of you. Mr. Rusk is attacking him and Mrs. Rusk now goes flying off the aft section of the boat. Now how is it that your mother, Mrs. Harvey, didn't see anything like this – or certainly couldn't remember it? Or Lee or your father?"

"Objection. Calls for speculation," said the attorney who was seated at the defense table.

"I'll allow it. The witness was there and had a view of everyone on board," said Judge Reynolds.

"Let me ask it another way. How was it, with your father on top of you and Lee reaching for the two of you and for the controls of the boat, that you could see what was going on in the aft of the boat?"

"I never said I could."

"But you said, Mrs. Rusk hit her head on the boat motor and then on the rock as she went over and into the lake."

"Yes. Well, there was blood on the motor and on the rock and I saw her slide down the side of the rock and into the lake."

"Did you see Mr. Rusk push his wife?"

"Good God, no."

"Did he go after her?"

"No. Lee and I stopped him. He was ...or had been... drinking. He reeked of alcohol. He had no business diving into that lake in the shape he was in."

"That's your medical opinion?"

"No sir. You know I am not a doctor..."

"Then how..."

"Allow me to finish..." Clark was flustered and angry.

"Counselor, let the witness finish." It was Judge Reynolds.

"Mr. Rusk smelled of alcohol. He was tipsy. He was having a drunk fight with my old man. You've seen one you've seen a hundred. The lake was rough that night. A wind was up and the waves were higher than usual. He was wobbly on his feet and was rocking back and forth. He grabbed at my father as much to steady himself as to push my old man around. But when Mrs. Rusk fell in, he slumped to his knees and yelled for her. We restrained him ... Lee did. And I went overboard to search for her."

"And what was happening on board during this time?"

"I have no idea. I was underwater looking for – searching for – Mrs. Rusk."

"And y'all never found her on your first dive nor Lee's dive...is that correct?"

"Yes sir. I saw that the pontoon boat was starting to list rather badly with the hole in its left side and I told Lee to get everybody back to the marina and I'd stay on the rock with a light to guide rescuers to the spot."

"That's a lot of quick thinking, young man."

"It just came to me. My mom handed me the flashlight and I placed it on the rock so that boats coming out of the cut could see where we were."

"We?"

"I was hoping to locate Mrs. Rusk. That's all I was thinking about at that time. To locate her and for this terrible incident to be over."

"And how did you find Mrs. Rusk?"

"She surfaced face down about fifteen yards from the rock."

"Was she dead then?"

"I can't say for sure. But she was very lifeless and very cold."

The prosecutor picked up a set of photographs and brought them to the witness stand for Clark to examine. "With permission, your honor?" The judge nodded. "This picture shows the boat motor that you say Mrs. Rusk hit her head on."

"Yes sir. That red area there is blood."

He placed another photograph in front of Clark. "This is the rock, you say the boat struck..."

"No sir. The boat struck a smaller rock forward of that rock. Mrs. Rusk went over the aft edge of the boat and hit her head on this rock about there." He pointed to a streaked area of the gray stone. "It too had blood on it."

"Did you actually see Mrs. Rusk go under water?"

"Yes. But the boat was hung up on the rock below it and with Lee grabbing at the wheel we were turning and I lost sight of her on our next revolution. That is when Howard...Mr. Rusk...was starting to go into the water and Lee and I stopped him. I went in for her."

"By this time she was gone from sight ...is that correct?"

"Yes sir. She had slipped beneath the water's surface."

"Allow me to read for you from the transcript of this trial... two portions. One is from your mother's testimony and one from Lee's...your brother." The lawyer grabbed a transcript from his table and introduced it as evidence and the judge allowed it, even though Clark's lawyers, as well as Rusk's lawyers were protesting.

"Mrs. Harvey, what happened after Mr. Rusk struck your husband?"

"I do not know."

"You don't know?"

"I do not remember."

The lawyer turned a page over and began to read from another transcript.

"Allow me to move on to Lee's portion. 'Lee, when your father fell onto Clark and the motors raced forward what happened in the rear of the boat?'

'I do not know. I wasn't looking that way, I was trying to separate my father from Mr. Rusk, as well as wrestle the controls to neutral. The boat was out of control.'

'You do not know what was going on aside from the boat's motors racing?'

"That's all I can remember.'"

"And yet, here you are, Clark, telling this court you saw Mrs. Rusk fall overboard and sink into the lake after striking her head on the rock. You are going to stick to that story?"

"Yes sir." Clark said, yet he was most confused as to the motive of the D.A. and didn't understand why he was being drilled so hard. Everyone else had said I don't know or I don't remember, and that was that.

The prosecutor and the defense attorney for Howard Rusk were asked to appear in a side bar and Clark was asked to step down from the witness chair, but admonished not to leave the courtroom. After a few minutes, Judge Reynolds sent both attorneys back to their respective seats and promptly declared the trial over.

A second trial was held two months later and a jury came to the same conclusion. Everything was circumstantial evidence. Not enough to convict.

Only this time, the defendant wasn't Howard Rusk, but rather Lester Harvey. But the outcome was the same. No one was talking. No one was telling what they had seen. No one could remember. No one that is, except Clark.

One month and twenty-two days later, Clark left home for nineteen years.

## Chapter sixteen

Clark took the papers along with her notes from the kitchen bar and moved to the sofa in the living room of the Rusk mansion. Turning a floor lamp on, he began to read her note.

Clark,

'A lot of time has passed us by. And I am afraid, thanks to my sister's inability to tackle all the paperwork associated with this messy estate, I have been the one appointed to make sense of it. To that end, as you know, I enlisted the assistance of Roberto. He has been a godsend. Sifting through the layers upon layers of contracts and tax receipts – files and records. It is a huge undertaking, but he has done it and was almost finished with his job, when he ran across a note left in the next-to-last box. It was addressed to me. In fact, there was one to me and one to Ellie. I have forwarded her note on to her.

'The note was written to me from my father. He wanted me to have it to help guide me in my life. I am going to share it with you, in hopes it helps guide you as well.

'I will miss you. I will miss you so desperately that I can't put in words how much. But what we once had is over. Those days are now past and gone. Sealed and over.

'Please, I beg you, please do not try and find me – do not try and reach out to me.

'Somewhere deep in my heart, I will always love you. Perhaps I always have.

'Love Missy.

The next pages were typed on HAR stationery, complete with a gold and blue seal embossed atop each page.

'Dear Missy,

'I promised your mother, long before her untimely death, that I would always take care of my daughters if something happened to her. I would see to it that you two were safe and well appointed for in their needs. To be sure, I never thought I'd have to end up writing a note such as this. But then again, I never thought I'd be the one to outlive Ruth.

'By the time you are reading this, your sister is busy trying to figure out the ins and outs of the estate. Give her some slack for it will take a while. As I have said over and over: Trust no one. Don't even trust the lawyers and accountants. They all have their hands out and want a piece of what is yours.

'But this note is not about dollars and cents. It is not about things owned and things borrowed or even things we can share with one another – not in the way estates go. It is about you knowing the truth. You deserve that much.

'Allow me to tell you a story, which you may or may not know about. It started way back in the late 1950's and early 60's. My original fortune was already thriving. Your mother and I were comfortable and were building out our mansion to the stately manse it has become. Life was good. Very good.

'Then I met a man. A man named Lester Harvey. Lester was a driller. Even though he was much younger than I was, he knew how to put a hole in the ground and how to put pipe around that hole and how to suck oil up out of the ground. It was as though he had an innate sense about the business. He worked for one of the big companies – if my memory serves me correctly I think it was Humble. But it may have been Shell, I do not remember for sure.

'But I do know that the young man had raw talent: excellent talent and it was being squandered by the brass out of Houston, who ran the majors back then. So I told your mother I wanted to take this man under my wing and tutor him; and in turn, he could tutor me. A partnership of sorts was launched that lasted decades. Profitable decades. Times were good and we prospered – the Rusks and the Harveys.

'The Harveys moved out of the oil field camp – away from the small huts that the majors had built to house their workers, and bought a home of their own on the east side of the town. A small house, but a nice house. And they soon were having children. At the same time your mother and I were having Ellie and you. And while our families didn't really socialize, we kept in close touch. Partners will do that.

'Lester was a bit raw around the edges. It came with his position on the well having to supervise roughnecks and roustabouts and keeping them in line. Having to drag workers on a Monday morning out of the drunk tanks, get them back on the rigs to continue our work. He was a hardscrabble kind of guy. Not easy to get to know, and not one for many words. But I trusted him and depended on him in our company. And for many years, his loyalty paid great dividends.

'His wife, you know her as Willie, was a fine woman and a strong force in the community and the schools. Your mother never cared much for either Lester or Willie. She saw them as below us. To her, we were on par with the wealthiest people in the region. The name Rusk was soon uttered in the same circles as the most prominent names in the state. Governors called on us. United States Senators, as well. Once, Eisenhower called to discuss energy policies.

'But with pride comes the temptation of superiority.

'And yes, we suffered from that, as well. There were several business deals that I allowed your mother to talk me out of sharing with Lester, even though he had helped make this family's wealth greater than it had ever been. I suppose it was his being obstructed from a few of these deals that led him to seek work with Harold Scroggins. For whatever reason, he sided with the devil and that made me trust him less and less.

'And before long I noticed one of Lester's young boys –Lee – coming around. Interested in you. Wanting your attention and affection. Looking back on it, I was perhaps harsh in my actions. Had it been just me, I would have probably looked the other way, but as it bothered your mother, I made alternative plans for you. Boarding school. Then Europe. And there you flourished. I am so proud of you.

'Then there was that fateful night on the lake. And the consequences it led to. I wish it had never happened and I wish it could be taken back. I was a fool for acting the way I did, but so too was Lester and his son Clark. They carry as much blame for your mother's passing as anybody.

'Lester knew of Ruth's disdain for his family. Especially knew of her dislike of Willie. And I am sure he told his boys. But that just seemed to make Lee want you more. And I knew we couldn't have that. And then when your mother passed, I knew you had to go away.

'I didn't want you around for all the fallout of the trials. Both trials were messy. And it seems that only Clark could truly remember what happened. And as much as my lawyers tried to discredit him, he told the truth. To a certain point.

'You see, Lester and I were having a fight over money. Over power. Silly stuff that doesn't mean a thing in the long run. We were drunk, at least I was, and things got out of hand. Clark tried to intervene. When he was pushed away he hit the controls on the boat, causing your mother to fall to her death. Yet, he wanted the blame laid at my feet. Lester, too.

'In the long run, his testimony didn't matter. We both were exonerated and have moved on. But there seems to me that the more one knows the better one can deal with the future.

'I would not be surprised if Lester's boys, some day don't try and make a run for our wealth – your inheritance, claiming a goodly portion of it belonged to Lester for all he did with me, as if we owed them something.

'Just remember this. Lester Harvey and Harold Scroggins tried to ruin me. Tried to steal from me my life's work. And then Lester and his son killed your mother.

'To be sure, I never accused him of this in a court of law, for it would have been almost impossible to prove, according to my lawyers. But I was there. I know what happened.

'The Harveys are not like us.

'They are not to be trusted. No matter how high they try and rise, they will always be oil field trash. Perhaps that is too strong an indictment; maybe just common would be a better word to describe their family. But you, my dear, are anything but common.

'No matter how much money they amass, they will never rise to your equal. They could even become richer-wealthier – but never better.

'And that is why I separated you from Lester's son – why I sent you away. Sent you from our home. To be rid of those who would try and bring you down to their level. Remember that my dear. Stay away from those who have their hands out trying to grab what you have.

'Live in peace and prosperity and know that your mother and I loved you and your sister with all our hearts and souls.

'God Bless,

'Dad.'

Clark took the pages and reread them. Then he walked to the kitchen and lit a fire on the gas range and slowly burned each page. One at a time.

## Chapter seventeen

A week passed. Clark had been summoned to California on business once again. There was much activity going on with the movie and the studio wanted him there for meetings. Moss met him at LAX.

Clark wasn't in a talkative mood as his agent ushered him into his black SUV and began the skillful dance of maneuvering through Los Angeles traffic. They passed Hollywood and the sign on the side of the hill that announced it as such. Into the valley they drove, past studios and past low, flat single family homes until they emerged on the edge of the mountains that rose on the eastern side of the sprawling city. Slowly they climbed the serpentine road that led to Montrose and to Moss's gated community and to his rambling house.

The two unloaded the luggage, which was little more than a roll-on suitcase and a very small bag for a laptop computer. "Get settled in. Bedroom at the top of the stairs.

I've got the kids at Alice's sister's place so we can have some quiet. The Studio Nine people will drop by for cocktails at seven. I hope that's okay?"

Clark nodded.

"Something bothering you?"

Clark shook his head. "Just tired. Very tired."

"Well, grab forty winks and I'll wake you at six so you can splash your face before they arrive."

Clark closed the bedroom door and opened the floor to ceiling windows. The rush of cool mountain air came in and he was suddenly refreshed. It made him think of Oregon and his small place in the mountains. He made a mental note to try and secure a new lease there if it was still available. Next, he pushed a chair to the edge of the window and dialed a number on his cell phone.

It was her number. The phone rang and rang and rang again, but no answer. He had expected as much. He waited several minutes and dialed again. This time a man's voice answered. "Don't call her any more."

"Roberto?"

"Yes."

"I want to speak with her."

"She does not wish to talk to you. You found her note, yes?'

"Yes."

"I think she said all she wanted to say in that note."

"There's a lot of misunderstanding in that note," Clark's voice had an edge of pleading to it.

"Perhaps, but she is settled. In her mind it is settled. It is closed. Do not call again. Ever."

The line went dead and Clark stretched out on the bed. He had a headache and felt lonelier at this moment in his life than he had ever felt before. He closed his eyes and tried to sleep, but all he could see was her smile and her beautiful face. That stupid wisp of hair curling over her eye and her constant flipping it out of her way – that film ran over and over in his head. He wanted more than anything to hear her voice. To speak with her. To tell her what he knew. What he felt – why things had happened they way they did.

In the end, he fell asleep and stayed in that restful pose until Moss awakened him at six thirty.

The Studio Nine people were fabulous and lauded praise on his work over and over again, until it became embarrassing. The executive producer pulled out a timetable and showed Clark a schedule of when he was needed at the casting call and then on the set. Clark agreed, but then reminded those gathered that he only had a few days to spend on the West Coast because he had to get back to Texas to take care of his father. Promises were made to see that his time was used wisely and that he would be back on his way home soon. *The Promised Land* was on schedule and many thought it was going to be a blockbuster. Talk around town – the kind that truly matters– was saying that the novel wrote itself into a mega movie.

"I've got people at the *Reporter* and at the *Times* telling me that this book will make a sensational movie. We believe it," said the executive producer. "We've got an A director, Paul Ridley and a cast that we are assembling that I think will knock your socks off...and if not yours ... then America's." The small bit of humor was a way of announcing to him that he was there as a stamp of approval – a PR function– not as a decision maker. He understood that role quite well. After all, this wasn't his first movie.

The Studio Nine entourage left at ten and Clark went back up to his room to rest without so much as a conversation with Moss. His night was restless. He got up several times and stood in the window facing the mountain. There was a symbolism to it: a huge obstruction to his view – to her– to life itself.

He felt depressed.

Two days later he was back in Texas and immediately checked in on his father. They had lunch at Whispering Pines and Clark found the food bland and not at all what had been promised in the brochure.

"I'll pick you up and take you to a real dinner tonight, Dad."

"You don't have to do that."

"No. I want to."

"Well, if you're going to come get me, let's eat at the club. Maybe some of the old gang is there and I can catch a game of forty-two."

Clark agreed and left, promising his father he'd be back by six. As he drove away from the retirement home, he suddenly realized he had no place to go. No place to call his own, so he decided to stop at the mansion. Perhaps she might have returned and be there. Maybe he could clear the air with her, find out all that was going on in her head.

The giant house looked dark and empty. The front yard had once again appeared as though the gardeners had been dismissed, for there were tree limbs down from a recent thunderstorm and debris was scattered about the property. Patio furniture had blown across the green expanse toward the line of pine trees in the rear of the house. Her SUV was gone from under the portico and the door was locked. He tried his key and surprisingly it worked. He walked into the kitchen and turned on a light. There was no power. She had turned the electricity off. To check his theory, he made his way down a hall with the help of the light on his cell phone into a small utility room and checked the breaker box. It was set in the proper mode for functioning so the power stoppage came from the other side of the meter. He went outside and checked it next. It was not spinning at all.

He turned a faucet on and no water emerged from the pipes. He tried to light the gas stove in the dark kitchen and it too had no fuel to fire its burners. The evidence mounted. She was gone and it looked like she was planning to remain gone.

He went upstairs to their bedroom and found her closet emptied. Dresses, blouses, coats, wraps even her collection of shoes, which at times he had teased her about – all gone. Left was a totally vacant closet.

The remaining clothes on his side were strewn about as if someone had searched them for something. He folded them and went to the dresser drawers inside his closet and got underwear and socks. Downstairs he found a shopping bag and put his clothes into it and started to leave.

He returned to his study upstairs where he had spent time writing, but it was as he had left it. The last vestiges of light were moving away from the windows rapidly and he had to turn his phone off to save the battery. He went back downstairs, carrying a blanket from the upstairs guest bedroom and lay down on the sofa for a short nap. He would sleep there tonight and then decide what he was going to do with his life.

He drove to Whispering Pines and picked his father up and they went and dined at the country club that night. The food was better than the retirement home and two of Lester's friends were there. They all moved into the men's locker room after the meal and played forty-two, Clark joining in, but was very distracted, so much so, that Lester actually scolded him several times for 'lame-brain' moves.

After dominoes, Lester and Clark drove back toward town. "What happened?" asked his father.

"What do you mean?"

The old man turned in his seat to face Clark. "You are here alone. Moody as hell. She leave you?"

"Yeah. Something happened and I don't know what."

"I bet it's that French guy."

"He's Canadian. And I don't know. I don't want to talk about it."

"Okay. Okay. Just asking."

"Well, don't. It's not your concern."

"I liked her. Still do. Hoped you two could work things out."

"You just liked living in that great big house."

The old man laughed. "That was kind of a hoot. Me under Howard Rusk's roof. After all we'd been through. Seemed fitting."

"Fitting?"

"Yeah. Like I got the last say. Like I won."

Clark flashed a glance at his father then returned his attention back to the road, as they drove into Lincoln. "Is it always about winning and losing with you. Always about settling some score?"

"Look, son. Me and Howard Rusk had our moments. Good and bad. The good outweighed the bad, if you count the time I got to stay under his room in that mansion. I could see myself living out my days there with the two of you."

"You could?"

"Sure. Missy was sweet to me. Kind and considerate. And I was taken good care of. Had a maid at my beck and call. Had everything I needed. And life was easy. Great place to hang around until the final bell."

"You thought you'd live there with us. For good?'

"She told me I could."

"Who did?"

"Missy. One day you were upstairs banging away on that typewriter of yours and she came into my room. I was watching TV and to be honest with you, kind of nodding off. She came in, put a pillow behind my back and said, 'Lester, we want you to stay here with us for good. Is that okay by you?' I assured her it was. Being there, with the two of you coming and going and having that Mexican lady as a maid – waiting on me hand and foot – I mean, I had it all. Much better than Whispering Pines ever thought about being."

"Don't get used to that idea. The mansion is all-dark now, the power is out and she's gone. The staff looks like they're gone, too. Everything is shut down."

"But why? Did you two have a fight?"

"To tell you the truth, Dad, I haven't a clue." He did, but he wasn't going to share it with his father. He didn't want to know anything else. There had been a business deal. It went south and then there was a drunken flight and a dead woman in a dark, cold lake and suddenly life was soured all over again.

And now, Missy was gone. Gone from his life. Once again.

## Chapter eighteen

Lester Harvey died on Easter Sunday. Just before noon. The doctor who came to Whispering Pines to check on him, said that it had been sudden – a massive heart attack. A myocardial infarction – that's what the young doctor called it. Clark stood in the doorway as he watched the orderlies lift his limp father's body from the bed onto a stretcher belonging to Wilkes-Chapman Funeral Home. They draped a white cotton sheet over him and began to maneuver out of his apartment. Clark stepped aside to allow them to pass.

"I do not believe he suffered," said the doctor. "I think it was that sudden."

Clark nodded. There was a part of him that wished his father had felt one last moment of pain, but that thought was washed away with a wave of guilt and anxiety. He slowly followed the gurney down the hall and passed the office where the woman named Edith stood.

"Clark, I'll have a refund ready for you tomorrow." He nodded. A refund. It sounded so commercial. *Here's some money returned for your dead father's life. Spend it wisely. It is probably tainted.*

The bright light of midday blinded him momentarily as he slipped on a pair of sunglasses. The black hearse slowly pulled out and headed back down the road. It would make a right hand turn, right in front of the Rusk mansion, just before the college campus and head toward Lincoln, where the old man would be prepared and then buried. His grave would lie right next to Willie's. They were back together again, thought Clark. How fitting. Willie and Lester at peace. Finally.

That week was something of a blur. People came and went – in and out of his vision. He really didn't know where he was or what he was doing. Andy had stepped in and given Clark his lake house to reside in while he got his "feet back on the ground–" a phrase that Andy said over and over that week, as if Clark was just floating, which was how he felt. Nothing to tie him down. Nothing to give him any direction for the present, let alone for the future.

A big funeral was held at First Baptist in Lincoln. Clark had thought the family had become Presbyterians, but then again, the Baptist church was much larger and could handle the crowds. The church was packed. Half of the faces in attendance, Clark did not know. The other half he had grown up knowing. A graveside service was conducted by a minister that Clark had never met. And then there was the luncheon; with people from Kilgore, Lincoln, Tyler, Gladewater and Longview all descending on the church's fellowship hall, to feast on fried chicken, mashed potatoes and green beans. It was all washed down with very weak iced tea. It seemed to be a common ritual – a type of Eucharist for the dead and departed.

A man approached Clark at one point and put his arms around his shoulders and said how sorry he was that Clark had lost his parents. Turned out the man was Jess O'Brien, the English teacher's husband. Clark did not know it, but Old Ironsides had died the week before. That's how life in a small town was. A few births and many, many more deaths to offset the rise of newcomers.

Two days after the official funeral, Lester's buddies at the country club held a special service complete with bourbon and soda, beer and pretzels along with several games of forty-two – all in Lester's memory and with Clark present, hearing all the old war tales and stories of his father's escapades.

By the end of the week, Moss, who had flown in to be with Clark, put him in a car and they drove across the southwest, back to Los Angeles. Moss promising the drive and the alone time would be very therapeutic. It was a two-day trip and Moss did most of the driving and a lot of the talking, but Clark was too numb to really remember much of the conversations.

For the most part, he slept during the journey. Sleep felt good to him. It was an escape.

"You started a new book, yet?" asked Moss hopefully, one afternoon, as they dissected New Mexico.

Clark shook his head. "Not yet. Have some ideas ruminating. But nothing solid yet."

"Don't let that well run dry, old buddy. The kids need braces." He laughed at his own joke.

Clark smiled.

"How about taking that pastor's fire and brimstone we're-all-going-to-die-and-go-to-hell-unless-we-change-our-ways sermon he preached over Lester's body – how about turning that into the basis for a novel?"

Clark squinted out the window as miles and miles of New Mexico rolled past. It was arid land with sparse grass and shimmering heat ascending from the surface of the plains – rising to mountains in the far distance. The blue sky was huge and expansive, broken up every now and then with white billowy clouds migrating eastward. "The sermon was one I've heard a million times before. 'Sin leads to sinners and sinners are led to death and destruction by their own free will. Repent or burn in hell for eternity.' I think God is responsible for all this to begin with. He made man with a free will and knew he was going to sin. Knew it from the beginning. Then he plans this elaborate ruse to get man to worship him for redemption, when it was God's folly all along. Maybe in the end God should die."

"Sounds like a great movie to me," joked Moss.

"I've had enough death and loss for a while, Moss. I just want peace and quiet."

"You going back to the cabin?"

"Yes. A different one. I called the agent and she has one still available between Cottage Grove and Eugene." He reached into his coat pocket and brought out a printout of her listing. He handed it to Moss who took it in one hand and steered with the other. "Needs a fresh coat of paint inside. But that will give me something to do before winter sets in. That and collect firewood."

"You make it sound like the wilderness. It's just on the outskirts of Eugene, complete with running water, electricity and a daily newspaper. I don't think you're going to be roughing it any. And you can buy firewood from a dozen convenience stores and gas stations near by."

"Hey let me have my fantasies, if you will. It's my cabin in the wilderness. The cabin is remote enough for me to hide out. It's bigger and nicer than the one in Bend. And you're right, it does come with many requisites that I like."

"Wifi?"

"Yes. I'll be connected."

"Other amenities?"

"A good size college town attached to it. And all the amenities that come with that. But still a nice lonely cabin," said Clark.

"Good for hiding out and writing?"

"Yes," Clark agreed. "Hide out and attempt to type something that resembles a novel."

"You sound very pessimistic. But then again, you always do just before you start a book."

"Thanks for the encouragement."

"I'm just saying..."

Their off and on conversation about what he was going to tackle next – in the next book – continued well into Arizona, when Clark placed his head against the car's window and went soundly to sleep. As he did, Moss turned on the radio and scored an hour-long, uninterrupted program of Beatles music, starting with 'Paperback Writer'. As he drifted to sleep, Clark grinned. 'How appropriate.'

It was dark when Clark awoke. Moss had pulled into one of those bright, twenty-four hour roadside service stations, mostly designed for diesel-thirsty, cross-country truckers.

"Want me to take a turn behind the wheel? Give you a chance for some shuteye?" asked Clark.

Moss agreed and after filling the SUV, they switched seats and Clark set out for Los Angeles. "Stop us before you get to the Pacific," joked Moss. "I'm not a great swimmer."

As he drove west, he found a radio station playing oldies and turned it low so as not to disturb Moss, who was already snoring. Clark could feel himself relax. There had been so much pressure back in Texas. First his mother. Then Missy. Then his father. It was as if crossing the mountains and getting on the other side of the continent, was enough distance that he could start breathing again. He felt his shoulders relax and his neck muscles loosen.

And he began to think about the next book. Not in terms of a story – but rather the idea behind a story: the first part of the foundation of a book. What writing instructors called 'the conceit'. He didn't have any characters in mind, just the idea that death is a constant for everyone and everything. That life springs from death in many ways, and vice versa. It was the cycle that intrigued him.

He drove through the desert and into Palm Springs, then into the Banning Pass and down into Southern California, its morning lights twinkling back at him as Clark and Moss descended into the giant valley. The city was awakening before them and that seemed to energize him and the ideas of life and death once again danced on the neurons of his brain.

They drove along the base of the San Gabriels until they reached Montrose and then up the winding road to Moss' house, stopping along the way for breakfast. Moss's idea. "Let's eat together before all the chaos of the house. No telling what the kids are up to. I'd like one more meal in peace."

Clark agreed. They found a diner and ordered pancakes and coffee. It was still early and the place had yet to become the noisy, crowded eatery that Clark knew it would become. He sipped his coffee. "I'll grab a cab at your place and go to Burbank. I can catch a plane there to Eugene. You don't have to drive me anymore."

"Clark. It is what I do. I am here for you. If you need to go to Burbank, I'll get you there."

"No. Let me go on my own. I need the space."

"You got it. But keep your cell charged. I'm going to be checking on you. Got to have you at that computer writing," said Moss with a grin on is face.

Later that afternoon a taxi stopped in front of the cabin and deposited Clark at his new home, fresh with a set of keys from his real estate agent.

He called the self-storage company to see if they would be open later – he wanted to retrieve his car; but a message told him that the office was closed until Monday. That's when, for the first time, Clark realized it was Sunday. His whole sense of time and dates was awash in the haze of the cross-country trip and all that had come before that.

He wandered out to the back deck that was surprisingly well cared for, considering the mess he had found inside the cabin. He sat in a deck chair and pulled a wrought-iron table up to him. He jotted a few things down he would need from the hardware store. Paint. That was the main thing. Brushes and painter's tape. A broom and a mop. And some throw rugs to cover stains on the hardwood floors left by the previous tenants. He couldn't tell exactly what the stains were, but they were dark and rather large. He figured a food fight – perhaps wine. He wasn't sure, but a nice throw rug would hide the evidence. In his deeply drunken days he had ruined quite a few floors, so he knew how to hide the crime.

The afternoon turned cool and he ventured back into the cabin, boiled some water and made a cup of tea. He wasn't particularly hungry, so he did not bother with a meal. A slice of cheese and some bread he had purchased on his way to the house did the trick. He sat at the cabin's small kitchen table and turned on his computer. He stared at it for some time. It stared back. He then turned it off having done nothing but look at its glow.

"I'll get back to you later," he said addressing the P.C.

He could feel the drifting again. The silent moving of his consciousness to that place from where he knew it would be very difficult to escape. But at that moment he had no strength to fight it off. He went with the flow and slowly immersed himself, with a stiff drink, into a deep depression. It felt warm and inviting. It was as if he had found an old friend.

Two months past.

He was finished with the painting, and the cabin's refurbishing. But still, he wasn't writing. It didn't bother him. What did bother him was that he was drinking a bit more than he used to. The bottle had become a close companion once again and he couldn't quite seem to walk away from it. Then one morning, he got a call from Moss. "You up for a little travel?"

"Where to?"

"New York."

"New York?" Why?"

"They've got a prize there for you."

"Who?'

"Columbia University."

"What prize?"

"A Pulitzer Prize. For fiction. For Jack Lawrence and *The Promised Land*."

"No shit?'

"I shit you not. You are this year's winner. And the New York PBS station is going to do a roundtable with the winners. A couple of journalists, an essayist and a photographer. And you. All on live TV – to talk about your work."

"They can't do it by phone?" asked Clark.

"You can't phone it in."

"They can pick up my feed on the Internet and use it..."

"No. They want Jack Lawrence in person. His flesh and bones. It will do you good. I'll be there with you."

"That will do you good. Get you out of that noisy house and improve my book sales."

"True. True indeed. Speaking of which, while we are in New York the publishers want to have a word or two with you."

"Good word or two?"

"Very lucrative word or two."

"My favorite kind of conversation. Lucrative words or two."

"You heard from Missy, yet?"

"No. Don't expect to. I think that part of my life is past. Maybe even locked away."

"You gonna write about it? About her?"

"Someday. When I get a new agent."

"Fuck you. I'll meet you at Kennedy. I'm on United."

"What am I on?"

"You are on your own. Get a ticket. Catch a plane. And get to New York. And Jackie, my boy..."

"I know...fly first class."

"See you in the Big Apple."

They checked into The Plaza, it wasn't particularly Clark's favorite New York hangout, but Moss loved it. Famous people tended to float in and out of the grand dame of New York Hotels as if they were trafficked there by the gods of public relations. And Moss liked to rub elbows with them. He was always looking for the next meal ticket. Not that he was obvious about it, but Clark knew him well. This was a *see and be seen* trip.

Snow was falling and Manhattan had her winter finery on display. There were several new shows opening on Broadway and a huge boxing match at the Garden. Two fighters, both with Hispanic names, neither of which Clark knew; yet, Moss insisted that he would try and get tickets to the bout.

They were about to check into their rooms when Moss grabbed Clark's elbow and pulled him close. He whispered, "Are you drinking again?"

Clark did not answer.

"Be careful. You know where that can lead."

"I'm okay."

"Be careful just the same."

The next morning after a room service breakfast and a couple of vodkas from the mini bar, Clark walked two blocks to the studio where the taping was supposed to occur. His head felt good that day. He had wrestled with the demons and lost, but the struggle didn't seem to have done him any damage. It felt like a small victory. He was encouraged. Maybe he could control his desires. Have a drink in moderation and still maintain.

He met with a production assistant who told him that plans had changed and she had a car waiting for him in the underground garage. They were going to the Lincoln Center for the Performing Arts, to a larger venue, so there

209

could be a live audience to watch the proceedings. He didn't know why, but it made him feel slightly uncomfortable. The P.A. noticed and assured him it was one of the smaller stages at the center. "Not to worry, if you don't like big crowds," she said.

"I don't like any crowds, to tell you the truth," he confessed. He then wished he had slipped one or two of the mini bar bottles into his coat: liquid courage, as his fellow drunks called it.

The stage was set up with a semi-circle table. Six microphones sat in front of six tall-back chairs. A moderator's station was at the far end and had a laptop computer and a set of controls. For what, he did not know.

The first five chairs: Two journalists, an essayist, a photographer and Clark. He paced the table. A man entered the stage and introduced himself. He was the director of corporate giving for the Public Broadcasting station. They shook hands. "Where would you like to be seated?" he asked Clark.

"Closest to the door, in case the questions get too personal," joked Clark.

The man grinned. "Relax. This is to raise money. Not to discover your deepest, darkest secrets."

"My deepest, darkest secrets just might help your viewers increase their giving," said Clark, raising his own eyebrows for punctuation.

The man smiled and asked if Clark wanted any refreshments. Clark said whiskey and ice water would be fine. The man called out and a production assistant hurried out and to his side. "See to it that Mr. Lawrence, here has plenty of ice water." The assistant nodded and hurried away. Moss must have warned them earlier.

"So, tell me about the other members of tonight's panel," said Clark.

"Well, there's you. And next to you..." as he spoke the man moved down the row of chairs as if a person was sitting there and he was giving a brief biography to an unseen audience. "...Nathan Ales, New York Times. Traveled with refuges from Guatemala to the U.S. border. Excellent coverage of their plight."

"I guess that rules that subject out for my next novel."

The man continued as if Clark had not spoken. "Here, Alice French. Boston Globe. A striking series of articles about the worldwide revolutions and wars that are pushing the immigrant movement onto western civilizations. Quite striking."

Clark had read a few of the articles. They were terse and very candid when it came to western countries' treatment of certain ethnic groups caught up in escaping the killings in their home countries. People of color being disadvantaged by conflict in their homelands and oppression in their newly adopted lands. The stories were most graphic. He remembered wishing he could use his vocabulary as pungently as Alice had.

"Peter Genolosski. United News. Photographer. Captured a plane crash in Denver as it was happening. He also documented the rescue efforts, which followed. Marvelous photojournalism.

"And last, but certainly not least, Mary Louise Rymann. Brilliant non-fiction writer and biographer. Her study of the men and women in the CDC labs during the Ebola outbreak was riveting. It was less news and more..."

"...Much more a personal saga." The words of his sentence had been finished by a tall, blonde woman in a very professional grey pant suit – a Hillary suit – Clark thought. She walked toward the two men and extended her long arm and hand, "Mary Louise Rymann." He shook her hand and noticed the strong grasp she had and the length of her thin fingers.

"Jack Lawrence. Lowly novelist."

"Don't be silly. We all wish we had the creative drive to conjure stories in our brains instead of traipsing around the world digging into other people's lives and business. We could stay at home, smoke our dope, drink our whiskey, and play our guitars." She had heard an earlier interview with him – it was obvious, since those had been his exact words.

"Well, the dope days are over and my guitar playing scares the neighbors' children. So it's the typewriter and whiskey for me," said Clark, wishing at that moment that he had a stiff drink.

"*The Promised Land* was marvelous, Jack. I read it on the way back from Poland. Riveting."

"Thank you so much."

"I am told they are making a movie out of it now."

"Yes. Studio Nine in California."

"I see. I don't do movies. Don't ask me why. But my neighbor told me all about the movie being in the works. She dated directors from what I hear. And she knows you. Going by another name now do we?"

"I beg your pardon," said Jack, somewhat confused.

"My neighbor calls you Clark. Clark Harvey. Jack Lawrence is your nom de plume. Am I correct on this or has she led me astray and I have stepped into some awkwardness to which I will apologize immediately?"

"No. You are right. Jack Lawrence is my pen name. Clark Harvey is the real skin and bones me."

"Well, I like Jack Lawrence better. Strong, square-jaw type name, if you ask me. Texas. That's home originally? Kilgore? Home of Van Cliburn. What a pianist he was."

212

"Actually, I'm from a small suburb called Lincoln."

"Of course you are. And that is what she said, as well."

The photojournalist showed up at just that moment and took three quick shots with his Leica digital camera and then apologized, just in case no one wanted their picture made. No one seemed to mind. He and Mary Louise hugged as if they were old friends. He was followed by the two journalists and then the evening's moderator was on the stage and the director came in and gave some final instructions. Everyone had a microphone in front of their seat, as well as a lavalier attached to their clothing. "We want you to speak up. The world wants to know what you have to say," said the director, a short balding man with a deep New England accent and tight-fitting khakis and a loose sweater over a cotton shirt. He had a headset with a microphone off to one side. After addressing the guests of the evening he turned his attention to several cameramen and to the floor director.

The night's master of ceremonies was a professor from Columbia University who had a show on the local PBS station. He was a tall, handsome man in his late sixties with an impeccable grey suit matching a head of gray hair. He was an excellent interviewer. He could put anyone at ease and his questions were well rehearsed and pointed at the work, which had won the awards and not some dig in to the recipients' lives. Clark was grateful for that. But he had a curious notion running through his head the entire evening as to who the neighbor of Mary Louise Rymann might be. Who knew his details that well? Who knew his real name? Who knew his hometown? Another secret he had kept guarded from prying literary circles. Even in his books, there was a photo on the jacket with a credit, which merely read: Author Jack Lawrence at home on the West

Coast. It was a photograph of him seated on the sun deck of his cabin outside Bend, where he lived before venturing to Eugene.

"Be a mystery," Moss had taught him. "Make them want to know more about you. Be an enigma. It worked for Dylan."

The participants took their seats, assistants secured their clip-on mics and a sound check readied the room. The stage darkened except for the lighted logo on the curtains behind them. The show's theme song played and pre-recorded voice over said, "Ladies and gentleman welcome to the Creative Roundtable. Brought to you by your local PBS station and by viewers like you. Now, without further to do, Professor Gene Carlisle."

Applause arose from the audience, who was hidden behind a blanket of white stage lights.

"Tonight's guests are..." as the professor introduced the panel, Clark's brain twisted around the minutia of information that Mary Louise had handed him – who had the inside information on him? He tried, as he might, think of a high school friend who might be living in New York who would have known him and connected the dots. Then Clark realized that everyone was looking at him. The professor had asked him a question.

"I'm terribly sorry, can you repeat the questions?" He blushed.

"What does it mean to you to have been awarded a Pulitzer Prize?" asked the Professor.

Simple enough. He rambled on about three minutes hoping to make sense. But so, too did the others. Phrases such as a *true honor*, *undeserved*, *so grateful*, *never dreamed I would be here*, were brought up by several of the panel. Next the professor asked what each person on the stage thought was the key to their success in the field in which they had received the award. The photographer said, "Pure luck on my part. No planning really. I was taking pictures of jets coming and going with a beautiful snowy backdrop there in Denver, when suddenly all hell breaks loose. I just started pushing the shutter button as fast as I could. I was capturing history – nothing I had planned to do. It just rolled out before me."

The audience loved his honesty. This wasn't a man who had staged anything. He just focused his camera as the world – and a jet – exploded in front of him. As he spoke, images of his photography appeared on a screen behind the panel. The audience responded with much volume to the dramatic shots.

The professor turned to Clark next. "Mr. Lawrence, your book *The Promised Land*, certainly was no accident waiting to happen." The audience laughed. It had been six years between his books. A lifetime in the publishing game. "I hear writing comes easy for you. Are you always creating?"

"Thank you. But I'm not too sure that *easy* is a word I would attach to my creative process. There are days I sit at the typewriter and nothing is there. Nothing. A blank canvas and suddenly the muse is awakened and four or five pages come pouring out. From where, I do not know. How, again no clue." Applause. He was handed a book with a page marked.

"Would you mind reading us the highlighted section, Jack?"

Clark picked the book up from the table and studied the front cover. He had never liked the artwork. It felt too ordinary to him. Too direct – not enough mystery in its form. Opening the book to the paper-clipped page, he began to read:

"It was that time when Winter finishes its duties and Spring takes over – takes over reluctantly to be sure, for there are days the two spar for one last moment of power. Winter's last fit and start, but usually to no avail. Spring is younger, fresher, more lively. Spring counterpunches and weaves and dodges on fresh legs and with youthful zeal. Winter jabs – punches blindly but is winded and can't last long. The bouts are short. They grow shorter as the days grow longer. And soon, like every other year since the beginning of time, Winter goes back to its corner and rests, and then, as a lost champion, is escorted from the grand arena. Defeated.

"It is how the young man felt as he watched her. She was his love. Had been for eighteen years, but now the fight had left her. Now she was being lowered into the warming ground for her final rest – perhaps accompanied by the last of a thawing Winter. He then thought of his own mother, who had passed away on the plains of Kansas during Winter's heyday. The ground so frozen you could not dig a grave until well into the rein of Spring – even perhaps to the days when Summer itself was peeking over the horizon. She had been wrapped and boxed and stored in the barn on the farm, until the land was thawed enough to accept her.

"He watched as his father came near her coffin in the drafty barn. He truly missed his wife. She was everything to him. Daily, the old man would go to the barn and crouch next to her on his tired, achy knees – his droopy overalls dragging into the loose straw. "I hope you are happy now, my love. I hope where you have gone it is warm and you can cozy up with a good book, or sing a hymn with friends. I hope there is a seat close to your table I can fill soon. So we can be together again. I hope that more and more each day. I hope, as you have done, I hope, I too, can see the promised land. His father would say this everyday and then go out and till the soil and plant the seeds and harvest the crops. Season after season – for ten long and lonely years.

"It was on the edge of battle between Winter and Spring two years before the young man's wife died, that his father passed away. The farming came to a halt. The tilling, the plowing, the planting – the work stopped for a day. He was placed into the ground next to his wife and the doors to the promised land opened and swallowed him up.

"And now, the young man's wife was going there, too. Some disease the doctors couldn't catch up with – was taking her from him. And, like his father and mother before him, he hoped he had what it took to enter the promised land and see her once again. To be with her. Until then, Spring reminded him the farm and its chores awaited. It was time to get back to work. Time to plow. Time to prepare the spoil. Time to sew. It was time to move on. Spring, as warm and as soft as she appeared, was a demanding tyrant."

He looked up and the applause was deafening. People loved the reading. It had taken him six weeks to write that. Well, to finish it. He had written at least thirty different versions of the passage, but was never satisfied with it. Then one day he sat at the computer and closed his eyes and visualized the service. The casket being lowered into hallowed ground. And he typed. For one entire afternoon he typed. And it was done. *The Promised Land* was finished. As he sat there, one of the journalists leaned over and whispered, "I wish I had written that."

To him that was an honor greater than anything anybody could bestow on him with a medal or a certificate.

Moss hugged him during a break. Back on stage the PBS people were asking for donations to support programming like this; reminding viewers it took funds to continue to provide New York with quality broadcasting. He went to the bathroom and came out and Mary Louise was sipping from a water fountain, a paper collar wrapped around her neck to keep any wayward droplets from staining her dress. The P.A. removed the paper as Clark approached, "Say Mary Louise, who is your neighbor that knows me?"

"Oh, her name ... it is Missy Rusk."

Clark didn't remember much of the rest of the evening. Moss assured him he was fine. Joking and compelling and he even read two other selections from his books; one from *The Promised Land* about the building of a new barn, symbolic of life and the on-going spirit of the emerging American dream: a dream of hope and of the future. A dream when the young man in the book still had the love of his life by his side.

More applause and adulation. More questions around the table; Mary Louise got long-winded in a response about how she moved so effortlessly through impoverished people in Chad and Kenya where the CDC had conducted trials of a vaccine. Her story was at once heroic and a bit flamboyant. But the audience loved it. Then back to him again.

He was asked to read another passage, this one, from his award-winning, best-seller *Angels and Whiskey*. The action occurs after the time a young man's wife has passed away from a gruesome accident. It was a recurring theme in Jack Lawrence's work – lost love. For the young man, it was a dark time – a time of trials and tribulation. Clark cleared his throat and adjusted his reading glasses.

He could identify with the young man about whom he was to read.

"The house was cold. It creaked in the darkness of night from the wind that howled outside, trying its best to break inside. It was a damp cold – a wet cold – with a storm fresh off the sea slamming the docks of the small fishing village where he called home since moving from the city. It had seemed so peaceful there when they moved. Both wanting to escape the chaos of urban life and return to the peace and quiet along the coast – where they could settle in and he could write and she could paint and collect her cats and dogs.

"The assault outside was in full attack mode. Nothing stood in its way. He slumped into the chair, drained from the long walk up the hill; wet and tired, but glad to be within the walls of the drafty house, with its fire all but embers in the rock fireplace. Both the dog and the cat lay on the hearth as close to the grate as they dared, just for the warmth the faint orange glow promised them. They had both been adopted off the streets in the city. By her. She had found them and brought them into the family. No questions asked. One day, they were simply two new members of the household. He had no idea from where they came or to whom they belonged. Now they were his concern. For she was gone. No longer there to take care of them – or him.

"The house was dark and lonely. He stood and walked to the cabinet above the wooden bar. He opened it and looked inside. It had not been touched for years. Dust covered the bottles. He reached for a bottle of whiskey. He shuddered, remembering the danger it posed to him; recalling the battles he fought to get out from under the control of the alcohol. He remembered the long nights he floundered lost on the streets of the city, not sure where he was; or the times he would awaken in a strange bedroom with a strange woman and still not know where he was – or who he was for that matter, because he had morphed into a something of a shadow of his former self. He no longer wrote. He no longer created. He was simply an empty shell – waiting for more whiskey. He opened the bottle and smelled the vapors: Intoxicatingly sweet and urging him to take a sip. One simple sip. What could it hurt? And yet she had always been there to retrieve him from his destruction and nurse him back to health.

"He placed the vessel's mouth to his own. He tilted it upward until the rush of sweet, burning bourbon came across his parched tongue and ran down his dry throat. He guzzled the amber liquid and slowly closed his eyes. He had no idea where he would awaken or with whom. But at that moment, the pain was being washed away. And he was most grateful for that. Tomorrow – well, tomorrow would just have to wait.

"She had been his salvation. His angel. She had rescued him from the rivers and rivers of drink that he swilled in – she had given herself to him to bring him up from the darkness. She was his light.

"And now she was gone.

"He drank another sip. Slower this time. Enjoying the burn. Waiting for the dullness to ease over him, to take away the remaining pain. He realized this was why he had kept the liquor there – close by. Because he knew he would not be strong enough to face life alone– he would need help. And there in that bar's cabinet he found the help he sought. Even if it was destroying him at the same time.

"He took another drink...

"... and another.

"And then there was darkness."

There was a round of applause and the professor looked at Clark and asked, "It is said that *Angels and Whiskey* is autobiographical. Is that right?"

"I don't remember," joked Clark. "I might have been under the influence myself when I wrote that."

Laughter filled the hall, although it was a slightly polite and nervous laughter.

"I would say that the theme of lost love is something that plays a big role in your novels. Why is that?" the question had come from Mary Louise.

Clark thought about that for a moment – perhaps a bit too long, for the professor was about to ask another question to break the dead air silence, when Clark spoke, "In my life I have loved one woman. With all my heart and soul. And she was taken from me. And when I write of lost loves, I am reliving that moment I had with her and then her exit. It is painful. Very painful. Crippling really. So in my work, I try and show people there is a path away from that pain."

"And it doesn't have to be the bottle or the needle," said one of the journalists sitting next to Clark.

"Correct, it does not. And should not. In *Angels and Whiskey* he finds his purpose again and emerges stronger from his battle with the bottle. It is something I had to do myself. I had to find a way out from under the drowning of alcohol."

"That's an interesting phrase, Clark. Drowning of alcohol..." the professor was probing. It felt personal and not literary, but it had been asked, so Clark went there.

"If you are an alcoholic or a recovering alcoholic, you know the feeling. It is drowning. It is not being able to get your footing and you continually fall back into the darkness that alcohol or drugs present.

"To be sure, it never appears as darkness in the beginning. Like the young man in the novel, it was a warm, peaceful escape from the pain and suffering he was feeling. I can relate to that. So I wrote about that.

"Perhaps that is why some critics have said *Angels and Whiskey* is autobiographical. But really, I think it is just a damn good story about a very brave young artist."

Again there was applause. Moss, off stage, was loving this. The time on camera with this kind of dialog would translate into book sales. And that meant money. Lots of money.

## Chapter nineteen

Two days passed and Moss and Clark ventured over to the offices of Simpson House Publishing, one of the largest independent publishers left in New York. Moss had persuaded Clark to choose them a dozen years ago because they were far less corporate than others, who were owned by media moguls or hedge fund managers. Simpson House was not a product of mergers and acquisitions, but rather the long-suffering brainchild of two book lovers, Mike Simpson and Teddy Griffin.

The offices at Simpson House were a true depiction of bipolar architecture. The front half of the company's headquarters was bathed in chrome and glass with heavy doses of teak and walnut features. Large, filled-to-overflowing book shelves punctuated every conference room and on every conference room door was the Simpson House logo etched into thick beveled glass.

Offices along the wood paneled hallways were immense and very well appointed with mid-century modern furniture and modern surrealistic art adorning their walls. But at the end of the hall was a walnut door, which led to the war room: a single open concept room painted in bright white with a labyrinth of dozens of metal desks separated from each other by wainscot-height metal and plastic partitions. The entire arena had a daily newsroom feel, but more refined in some way. And much quieter. Men and women were engrossed in reading manuscripts and book query letters. They were surrounded by artwork on the walls – poster-size reproductions of the best-selling books the firm had published as if to remind the readers and editors of the standard for which Simpson House was searching.

Each editor had two readers and they were assigned, in order of seniority, the tasks of approving incoming manuscripts. First, the youngest reader would read the incoming work and make notes as to its potential. The work would then be passed to the more senior reader, who would give the first go–no-go vote. As a final check, the manuscript might pass to the editor who would study the work with his or her underlings' comments in mind. If the editor voted to continue, the work was proofed and comments added to the margins of the manuscript and it was then passed back to the walnut and teak hallways to the marketing committee.

The marketing committee was a body of senior editors, marketing executives, an accountant/cost-controller, the head of sales and distribution, a lawyer and either Mike Simpson or Teddy Griffin. They met once a week–almost always on Wednesdays. It was the most important gathering on the schedule at the publishing house for any week.

Simpson tended to deal mostly with fiction and art books, while Griffin specialized in non-fiction and political biographies. It was in the marketing committee meeting that a decision would be made on the worth of the work and a contract would be prepared based on that estimated value. However, if the committee voted the work down, a rejection letter would be computer generated by a secretary and mailed back to the agent who represented the author to Simpson House. On rare occasions either Simpson or Griffin might scribble a personal note to the would-be author on the rejection form for encouragement. But for the most part, the notes read, 'Your work is not quite right for us at this time. Thank you for considering Simpson House as a potential publisher. And best wishes in the future.'

Clark had dozen of these rejection letters, from publishers up and down the canyons of Manhattan, as well as along the West Coast. But he also owned a note that Mike Simpson had sent him over twelve years ago which read, "Great, great work. We would love to be your publisher on this outstanding project.' Clark kept that note penned to a cork bulletin board above his workspace in the cabin.

Clark had been in the Simpson House offices once before. They always felt cold and aloof to him, like ogres watching over a child trying to decide if they should kill it, take its head off or leave it the hell alone and see if it can survive on its own.

There was a great deal of power vested in these offices and he could feel it. It oozed along the hallways and out from the offices. The people there held the livelihood of hundreds of writers from around the world in their hands and they tended to know it and even acted like they knew it. There was a subtle, but still obvious superiority to the publishers' mannerisms, like a crowned member of some royal family left to see after the serfs of the realm.

Simpson came out of his huge office and shook Clark's hand. "Fucking Pulitzer Prize winner. I can't believe it. I can't. Way to go!" He slapped Clark on the back as if they were footballers on the same team.

"Thanks," was all that would come out of Clark's mouth, for at that instant he saw down the hall, emerging from another office, Mary Louise Rymann. And Clark knew he had to talk with her.

His stare caught the attention of Simpson. "Oh you and Mary Louise were marvelous on the program the other night. Mary...Mary Louise... come. Come join us. Two Pulitzers in one hallway. Marvelous!"

The journalist immediately saw Clark next to Simpson and stopped her conversation with whoever was behind the partially opened door. She smiled and nodded and then excused herself from the unseen party.

"Jack Lawrence. Or is it Clark here?" she said as she approached Clark, Simpson and now Moss, who was joining the gathering.

"We go by Jack here, Mary Louse. It's tradecraft. Keeping the nom de plume intact," laughed Simpson, who probably had to juggle dozens of names of authors and their publishing aliases.

"Mary Louise, good to see you again. I didn't know you were published by Simpson House," said Clark.

"Oh sure. Mike Griffin and I go back to college days at Yale. By the way, I didn't have a chance to tell you the other night, what with the crowds of well-wishers joining us on stage after the show...but your reading – your work – it was suburb. Simply brilliant."

"Our Jack can write a good English sentence or two," crowed Simpson, placing his arm around Clark. We just hope he has a few more sentences stored away in that brain of his."

"I can assure you he does," piped in Moss.

"And Mary Louise what is your next venture?" asked Clark, trying to turn the embarrassing conversation that was focused on him toward her.

"I'm just sending to press one about firemen in New York City. Next will be an expose' on the loss of life, homes and livelihoods of people caught in the melee of volcano eruptions transpiring now." Her voice lowered as if she were telling them a little-known secret, "You know there are more active volcanoes at this time than at any other period dating back to the dinosaurs."

"I did not know that," said Clark.

"And the men and women who live under the shadow of these mountains – these enormous killers – are constantly living in fear of an eruption. And when it comes, my story documents their flight to safety and a new life."

"My God that seems so dangerous."

"It is. I have lost two research assistants in three years."

"Quit?"

"Killed." She said, with almost a hint of smile on the corners of her ruby red lips. A devilish smile – but just. "Someone has to do the initial ground work."

"And it's not you?"

"Mercy no. Not anymore. Now, I write the stories, but others dig the facts for me. It is like having a field producer on a TV news crew. That's where I got the idea for my structure. Think *CBS 60 Minutes*. A producer – in my case a researcher – goes out, finds the story, digs up the facts and then brings it back to me and I put out a book."

"It's like a cash cow," said Simpson, adding the publisher's monetary touch to the conversation. "And speaking of cash cows, I'm afraid, Mary Louise, we have to steal Jack and Moss away and do some business."

"Jack, let's do lunch while you are in town," she said.

"Yes. I'd like that. Today perhaps?"

"Can't today. Have a noon interview at ABC with the *Good Morning America* folks. Maybe drinks at the Haps."

"The Haps – say around six?" he offered.

"Six at the Haps Bar. Look forward to it. And don't bring these stuffed suits with you." She smiled. "We've got to let our hair down and get to know each other. You and me."

"It's a date. See you at six."

The meeting with Simpson House was most successful. Besides the organization of a new national book tour to promote Clark's award-winning novel, a big advance contract was agreed upon for a new, yet-to-be-written book, as well as the paperback rights to *The Promise Land*. Moss held off the international rights for further discussion, although Simpson House was pushing for their subsidiary in The Netherlands to get the European rights "ASAP, my friend. ASAP" said Simpson. Moss believed that the publisher, if they felt threatened on losing the international rights, might sweeten the deal even more. As it was, Moss took a check for more than three million dollars and placed it carefully into his briefcase. He tapped the case on the elevator going down after the meetings, "Down payment, my dear Jackie boy, down payment."

## Chapter twenty

She wore very tight pleated jeans and an embroidered western shirt. Not at all what he expected, from this uptown New York fashionista; although the western motif was finished off with exquisite turquoise jewelry, including a rather large broach from a posh Santa Fe jeweler, known for encrusting diamonds with the turquoise. Even the faux rattlesnake boots were a bit too stylish for pure western. Clark assumed they were Italian. He had never owned a pair of boots. Well at the age of four maybe, but not since then. He was more a boat shoe or moccasin kind of guy. His taste in western wear ended at the Mississippi River and didn't pick up again until it was deep in L.A. – somewhere near the Santa Monica pier.

"Clark, or should I call you Jack? I am confused."

"What would you call Samuel Clemens?"

"I'd call him dead and gone."

"No really."

I wouldn't call him Mark if I knew him well, but then again, I don't know you well, *yet*."

She let the word 'yet' linger just a tad, too long. It made him feel slightly uncomfortable. She was his senior by a good five – maybe ten years. But one could tell she still liked to prowl the streets: a cougar hunting for her next victim. And he didn't feel like becoming prey.

He thought about her usage of the word "yet". He thought how in the language in which he worked, a word's definition often has less to do with its meaning and its consequences than the manner in which it is written, or more often, spoken. He let his mind conjure that notion. A pause, a silence, a moment passing said right before a word or immediately after, can change the momentum of the thought behind the word; behind the sentence itself. It can redirect the thought behind the definition of the word. The utterance of the word can steer a sentence in a new direction, a new aim; as if pulled slightly off course by some unseen magnetic force, and redirected to other implications. Yet. Yet. What did she mean by *yet*?

Was it simply time she was referring to, or was it a door opening, an unspoken invitation, a subtle hint as to what was to come?

She was a writer. An award-winning writer. Her vocabulary was rich – she knew her words and she used them carefully. And that made the slight pause lingering before the word *yet* even more dangerous, at least in his mind.

He let the notion pass. But he was often finding himself second-guessing people's intent by the words they said and in the order and the meter in which they used them. However, her *yet* nagged at him.

Haps was busy. A crowd was watching a sporting event on a big screen TV in the back and was yelling at something every so often. The waitress brought them the wrong drinks the first time and then returned with apologies and free liquor for the next round, all the while smacking her gum rather crudely. Clark was drinking club soda, straight with a twist of lime. Mary Louise was having a gin and tonic.

"You know, I am a good reader of people," she said.

"You are?"

"Yes," she said. "It's how I make my living."

"I could have sworn you were a journalist."

"Listen to me. If this weren't in a bar and we were in my office and I had a shingle to hang out, instead of a typewriter, this would be costing you $150 a hour."

"I'm all ears."

She leaned in. "There's a look. You know it when you see it. A look in someone's face – really in his or her eyes. Bored – they glass over. Interested– they brighten up."

"I hope this isn't costing me $150."

"Shut up and hear me out." She scooted closer to him, her knees touching his. Her long ruby red finger nails slowly stirring the tops of the ice cubes floating in her drink. "You and Missy Rusk were an item at one time."

"And she told you that?"

"No. At least not in words."

"What? She sent you a signal?"

"In a manner of speaking, yes. Yes she did." She took a long sip of her cocktail and then set it back down on the napkin. She tapped his glass. "Drink up. This could take a while."

"Good therapy. Get the patent drunk and then tell him he needs more treatment." He really didn't mind. The thought of alcohol felt good running through his system, even if all he was having was fizzy water and lime. The memory of the warm, peaceful slide into a dark place generated by a stiff drink (or twelve) was most inviting at that moment.

"Shut up. So I'm getting the keys out of my purse the other afternoon and Missy opens her door and sees me. 'Saw you on TV last night,' she says to me. 'You and Clark.' Well, I go through the rundown of the people on the show – on the stage that night – and I don't come up with a Clark. Then I remember she calls you Clark. 'Where's this Clark coming from?' I ask her and she says, 'Back in our hometown in Texas. He changed his name when he wrote his first book. Changed it to Jack Lawrence. But to me, he is Clark Harvey.' And as soon as she said your name I saw it."

"You saw what?"

"That thing I was telling you about. That $150 an hour thing."

Clark frowned not following the conversation. "Her eyes. Her face. There was a spark behind those dark, depressed eyes. A simple glimmer of a small spark trying to light a fire."

"Were you drinking before we met tonight?"

"Shut the hell up and listen to me. There's more," she said.

"Okay."

She took another long drink and motioned to the waitress for another round. "When you see it, you know it. Like my first husband."

"I didn't know you were married."

"Twice. The second one was a shmuck. Lost everything to Bernie Madoff. Well, not everything, but enough that he... well let's just say he went away."

Clark nodded. There was no sense in asking for details if she didn't want to dish them out. He would circle back around for more of the story later. For now he wanted to know about her across-the-hall neighbor.

"Now my first husband, James. He had it. That spark. He could come into a room and light it up. He was like the beacon in a lighthouse. Even if he were down and angry, there was still a bit of James tucked away inside that you could see and count on."

"I take it he didn't invest with Madoff?"

"Never got the chance to. I got an assignment with National Geographic. The lives of natives on newly ceded national park lands in Africa. The magazine wanted to chronicle their successes and failures now that the land around them wasn't wild, but was rather protected by the government. They wanted to know what the natives' culture was like – how it had changed. James wanted to go to Africa with me. He had the time available, at least for a few weeks and I could use a handsome baggage boy." She grinned, fondly remembering her husband. Then the smile faded. "So together we went Kenya, South Africa, Zimbabwe. It was there it happened."

"What?" Clark asked.

"James was in front of a charging rhino. He was trampled to death." She paused for a long time.

"Jesus."

"Yeah. The flame went out rather quickly."

"That was horrible. And you witnessed it?"

"Ten feet away," she said as new drinks arrived at the table.

"I mean, what did you do?"

"I cried. I was young then. Impressionable. Blamed myself for allowing him on the trip. National Geo got real angry with me for having him on the mission. They blamed me, as well. It was stupid, really."

"And then number two shows up?"

"Not for some time, but he's not the reason for the story. The reason I'm telling you about James, is that I could always see his spark. Always see the light inside of him. And she's got that same spark."

"Missy?"

"Yes. Missy. Your Missy."

"My Missy?"

"Look, when I used your name. When we talked about your book. When I mentioned the TV taping, her light came on and the darkness of whatever is inside of her – went away. If just for a brief instant. I could see it."

"And..."

"And don't you get it?'" Mary Louise shook her head. "She still cares for you?"

"Isn't she married to that Canadian by now?" asked Clark.

"I haven't met any Canadian. In fact, she rarely has guests over at all. Except for her sister – what's her name? Ellie? Except for her, Missy is pretty much a hermit. A loner."

"That doesn't sound like Missy. She was always the center of attention. The light of the party – like you were talking about. That was Missy."

"And I'm giving you a piece of intelligence – from behind enemy lines. The lady is in love with you. Oh, she may hate your guts on some level, that's between the two of you. She may even choose not to see you, but I can tell you that Missy Rusk is in love with Jack Lawrence or Clark Harvey or whoever you are."

"She left me a note which said never try and speak with her again. She even had the Canadian guy answer her phone and say..."

"Forget Canada. Forget him. I'm talking about ... I can tell these things. They are spiritual. Like when I saw pilgrims seeing the Blessed Virgin the first time in Loreto. Their eyes glisten. And I'm not talking about the tears. I'm talking about something spiritual deep inside of them welling up and was trying to escape. That's her look. Your name – pow – the glow – the spark. It is real."

He sat back and took a long sip from his drink, wishing at that instant it was laced with something that was stronger than simply lime juice.

"You don't get many chances in this life to have that look showered on you. Don't waste it sitting in dark bars with crazy, horny journalists and oppressive agents. Go see her. Go to her."

And so he did.

## Chapter twenty-one

Mary Louise knocked on the door across the hall from her condo. A voice from within yelled, "Whose there?"

"It's me. Mary Louise."

"Coming."

First the sound of footsteps on the polished hardwood floors – heels reasoned Clark. She loved to wear heels, they made her feel taller and sexier. But who was she being sexy for? His mind began to race. Then the hardware on the door began to move, as she unlocked the myriad of devices keeping the world at bay. Clark kept to the far side, so he wouldn't be seen in the peephole if she looked, and as many locks as she just attended to, he knew she would have looked. The door opened and Mary Louise stepped back and Clark stepped to the forefront.

Missy stood there for the longest time looking first at Clark and then to Mary Louise and then back to Clark. Finally she did something that neither Mary Louise nor Clark had expected. She crumpled onto the threshold in a pile of sobbing tears.

They moved her to a sofa and Mary fetched a glass of water. "Should I put a splash of scotch in it?" She asked and Clark nodded to the affirmative.

"But not much. Just enough to lessen the shock."

"Shock? I thought you two knew each other and were close," said Mary Louise.

"She thinks I tried to kill her mother."

"My God, Clark, why didn't you tell me that? I would have never gotten us intertwined in such a mess." Mary Louise brought the drink over, its amber liquid slowly dissolving the ice.

"Here drink this," said Clark.

Missy sat up a bit and grabbed the tumbler and sipped rather strongly then coughed. "Why are you here?' She asked looking directly at Clark.

"I heard you were being a loner."

"Can we go back to the part about you killing her mother?" Asked Mary Louise.

"Not now," said Clark.

"Do the authorities know?" Again Mary Louise was pushing.

"Yes. There was a trial."

"Good God, Almighty."

"Not about me. First her father, then my father."

"Two trials?"

"Yes."

"And?"

"Acquitted both times. It was an accident," explained Clark.

"And I accused Clark of doing it." For the first time Missy entered the conversation.

"Why Clark?" Asked Mary Louise, trying to play catch-up on the past.

"There was an accident. On a boat one night – a party – lots of booze. Words were had. Things got heated. Punches thrown and her mother, trying to break up the melee slipped and went overboard," said Clark.

"You left out the part about you revving the engines and making her go overboard," said Missy now sitting up and becoming more alert.

"Clark?" exclaimed Mary Louise.

"Missy, I didn't do that. Your father hit Lester and knocked him into the controls and Lee and I both reached for them trying to stabilize the boat. It was only after we got it stopped that we realized your mother had fallen into the lake."

"Why couldn't she swim back to the boat?" asked Mary Louise.

""She had struck her head. Twice. Once on the boat's outboard motor and then again on a rock protruding from the lake. I went into the water after her but she had sunk below the surface. Then Lee went in after her."

"Who is Lee?" Asked Mary Louise.

"My twin brother."

"My Lover. Back then. A high school fling," added Missy.

"Neither of us could find her. They returned the boat to the marina. I stayed on the rock trying to look for her..."

"Enough. Enough. Get out. Both of you. Get out. I don't wish to relive this again. It is over." Missy spoke as she covered her ears.

Mary Louise stood. "Doesn't sound as if it is over. I think the two of you have a lot of discussion that needs to occur. And I am going to bow out and let that conversation begin. If you two need anything, I'm across the hall. And no guns and knives." As she said it, both Missy and Clark laughed. It helped break the ice.

Mary Louise's departure left Missy and Clark on the sofa together. It was deadly quiet in her condo. Even the city's constant den couldn't find a way to squeeze into the stuffy room. Finally Clark spoke, "I'm sorry. I shouldn't have come. I didn't mean to upset you..."

"No. I'm glad you did. I'm glad you came."

"Maybe I should go now. Leave you alone," he said as he slowly stood.

"Yes. Yes, I think so." She said.

He stood and took a step towards the door.

She reached for him and took his hand into hers. "No, sit back down. It's been too long. But don't talk. Just let me look at you."

"But..."

She shushed him. "No talking, Clark. Give me a chance to fall in love with you again."

His first stop on the tour was Cincinnati. A book signing at a big chain book store after a speech at the university, then an interview on a radio station and a taping for a segment on a local morning TV talk show.

Moss called him to check on things; promising to join him in Chicago. There was a two-day stop planned for the Windy City. "Simpson is going to join us. I hear he has a big check for international rights."

"That's nice."

"How is Missy?" Moss asked Clark.

"A bit standoffish, but thawing."

"I can't believe she asked to accompany you on the tour."

"She said she didn't want me out of sight ever again."

"I'd say that was a thawing."

"Maybe, but we still have a ways to go," said Clark.

"Separate bedrooms?"

"You are my agent. Not my mother. See you in Chi-town." He hung up the phone.

"Who was that?" she asked rolling over in the giant bed, the sheets drifting down between her long legs.

"Moss. He and Simpson will be in Chicago with us."

"A bit standoffish and thawing...were you talking about me?"

He nodded. "Yes. Moss was curious as to how we were doing."

"You just made love to me for the third time today. I'd say the thaw has melted."

"Maybe."

"Maybe? What do I have to do to prove to you I am once again smitten by you?"

"You could remove that sheet, spread those beautiful long legs of yours and invite me back to bed to ravish you yet again."

"No way. You've got to go sign books. Besides, I only screw men I truly love four times day. We still have things to work out."

He laughed, bent down and kissed her. She placed her hands into his hair and then down to his neck and pulled at him. He succumbed and dropped into the bed in between her legs. Suddenly she pushed him back. "Go sign your books. I'll meet you for lunch. I'll text you where."

"I should be through by one."

"Fair enough."

He finished dressing and she sat up to look him over. "Lose the tie. Just an open collar shirt works well with that coat for you. Clark would wear a tie, but Jack Lawrence doesn't need one."

He grinned and removed the tie, opened his collar and headed for the door.

"Clark," she said. He stopped and turned. "I am falling in love with you. You know that don't you?"

"Are you falling in love with Jack or Clark?"

"Both I think." She grinned.

He shrugged. "We still have some things to work on."

She threw a pillow at him. "See you at lunch."


The tour was a hit. The book was skyrocketing and his notoriety was as bright as ever. His star was shining...that's what Simpson said and Moss agreed. Even Missy was positive that the book was going to be huge. Over drinks in Oklahoma City, the four of them sat at a table and toasted the whirl-wind success of the novel.

"Funny, the movie has given it a second life – even bigger than before." Said Moss.

"Yes, and the movie is still in production. Just wait until it's really on the big silver screen," said Simpson. "We're talking about releasing the paperback in conjunction with the movie's premiere."

Clark nodded at all of this. He was feeling tired. "I think I'm going back to the hotel and nap before tonight's radio show." In reality, the constant flow of liquor was concerning him. He was fighting an urge to join in on the toasts with something stronger than a cola and lime.

Everyone was suddenly anxious with him. "Just tired, folks. That's all."

"I'll come with you," she said, and rose to join him as they left the table.

On the walk back to the hotel she asked how he was really feeling and he said, "I'd like to be a hermit. To get away from all these people and hands reaching for me. I am tired as hell of signing my name over and over. Good Luck Billie Jo...signed Jack Lawrence. Over and over and over."

"They pay you a lot of money to do that," said Missy.

"No. I get paid to write novels. This other stuff is the marketing department's idea of hype."

"It is good hype."

"I guess." They entered the hotel and rode up the elevator. She was holding his hand.

"And what about you? What are you going to do?"

"Hey I'm on tour with my boy friend."

"Oh, I'm now your boy friend am I?"

"Yes. For the rest of the day, you, Clark Harvey are my boy friend. But I have a secret lover. His name is Jack Lawrence. I just hope they never meet and find out." She laughed and thought it would bring a smile to his very somber face.

"No, I'm serious here. We've got Dallas tomorrow, then Houston, San Antonio, Austin, El Paso, Tucson, Phoenix, then to California. And there it's San Diego, and L.A. for three days and a day off for meetings with Studio Nine then up to the Bay area, then Eugene, Portland and finally Seattle. The marketing department wants to add dates – for us to swing back through Denver, Salt Lake City and Minneapolis before we're through. It's a long slog."

"It's a long slow journey to freedom."

"Freedom?"

"Yeah, once you've paid your penitence you are free to become a hermit again."

"Okay. Let's start there. Are you going to be a hermit with me?"

"I'm not sure I am even going on the rest of the tour with you." It was the first he was hearing of this. "I may peel off when we are in Dallas and go home for a few days. My real estate lady – you remember Jenny Orr – she has a man interested in the old house."

"You're going to sell the mansion– your parents mansion?"

"Maybe. If the price is right."

"I was...it's just that...well, I was hoping we could settle there. You know for a place to have when I'm not up in the mountains typing away. A place for the two of us to call home."

"Clark, it's old and needs a lot of work. Constant maintenance."

"It sounds like me."

She laughed. "It doesn't need that much attention. Or that often." She kissed him on the cheek.

"But seriously. I love that house."

"You love the memories of that house. Let's build a new place. Modern and with fresh fixtures that don't drip and leak."

"I like old places. They have charm and character. That house has tons of character."

"You are a character."

"But think about it, Missy. It is a grand palace of the old oil days. The days of tycoons and ultra wealthy families. Somebody is apt to buy it and bulldoze it down and build apartments on the land."

"Oh, I hadn't thought about that," she said.

"Condominiums at Rusk Place."

"Nice ring to it."

"Tell me you wouldn't cringe every time you drove by a row of three-story brick condos there."

"I'd throw up."

"See? You see?"

"But this guy is offering a lot of money," she said.

"You don't need money. You got your father's inheritance. You and Ellie."

"She wants to sell it."

"I'll buy her half."

"Clark?"

"No, really. I've got tons of money. Investing in that house would be a great idea."

"It's a money pit."

"So? You got to spend it somewhere on something. Might as well be on a grand old mansion once owned by your parents."

"We'll see. I'm still going to peel off in Dallas and go back to East Texas. Will you come there and join me after the tour?"

"If I'm still alive." He said jokingly then he stretched out on the bed and took a long nap with Missy in his arms.

## Chapter twenty-two

The tour was in Salt Lake City when Mary Louise Rymann joined them. Her new book, *Hooks and Ladders*, followed the lives of ten firemen on a week's worth of calls in New York City. Besides her sharp eye and even sharper pen, the book was laced with gripping photographs made by the Pulitzer winner from the night Clark had received his award – Peter Genolosski. Mary Louise and Peter had been working on it for over a year when they were both notified of their win and they both realized it would make their next co-publication a smashing success.

Almost immediately Simpson House made arrangements for a book tour for Mary Louise and it just so happened that Clark's tour and her tour crossed paths in Utah. Not Mary Louise's favorite place on the world's stage. The native New Yorker and globetrotter was not impressed with the limited bars and the curfewed hours of those said establishments. But hate it as she did, Mary

Louise knew how to throw a party. She invited Clark back to her hotel suite, along with a small entourage of hangers-on who had followed her out from Chicago, where her last signing had gone on for two days.

As Clark was about to knock on Mary's door when a very friendly face opened it, and surprised by what he saw, said, "Clark? Clark Harvey." It was Andy Reynolds from Lincoln, Texas.

"Andy, what the hell are you doing here?"

"Business. And then I met this wonderful lady. Seems that you know her, as well."

"You met Mary Louise Rymann?"

"One and the same. Going to get some ice. Be back in a sec." And with that, his old high school buddy traipsed down the hall toward the hotel's ice machine.

"Clark, get in here," it was Mary Louise yelling across a room full of beautiful women and handsome men and one rather large body guard-looking fellow who was wearing the tightest black t-shirt that Clark had ever seen. The man's muscles seemed to ripple out of his very short sleeves. "Get yourself a cocktail. The Mormons closed us down in the lobby bar but we are still in the party mood."

"I had no idea you knew Andy." He said.

"Who?" she yelled back over the music and the loud den of voices carrying on dozens of conversations. There was even a guy in the corner with an acoustic guitar playing Neal Young songs, but it was doubtful that anyone, other than those closest to him heard any of what he strummed.

Clark waved to her and she moved over some bodies lounging on the floor as the smell of weed wafted in the air. She approached him. "Andy," he said, almost shouting. "I didn't know that you knew Andy."

"I just met him this afternoon. He was at my book signing. And looked like a very handsome – and willing chap, if you know what I mean?" He nodded. "How's our Missy doing?"

Clark smiled. "She's good. Very good. Back home putting the touch-up to her parent's home for a potential buyer...or back home putting the touch-up to her parent's home for us. I won't know which until I get back." They both laughed.

"When is your tour over?" She asked.

"I've got a few dates left. Maybe at the end of this week."

"Lucky you. I'm on the road for another two months," she said frowning.

"Wow, that's a long time," he said.

"You're telling me."

"I saw your new book. Looks great. And Peter... looks like he did a brilliant job with the photography."

"He's such a dear."

"Who's such a dear?" asked Andy as he came barging through the door with a bucket of ice overflowing, cubes spilling about onto the brown carpet. "Drink up folks, before the Latter Day Saints come and shut down the ice machine, too."

Everyone laughed and before Clark knew it, the party had surrounded him, because he was the closest one to the ice and the make-shift bar. He left at two that morning. Andy and Mary Louise seemed to be deep into some very heavy and very close conversation on the sofa when he exited the suite.

The next morning, Clark was staggering out of his own room, trying to fight off a lack of sleep rather than a hangover, when he spied Andy slipping on a shoe and buttoning his final button on a shirt that was yet to be tucked into his trousers. He didn't see Clark, instead he went the other way.

That afternoon, when Clark returned from his appearance at a university and at their radio station, he ran into Andy in the hotel's coffee shop.

"My God she is a beast in bed," said Andy "A true beast."

"Who is?" asked Clark.

"Mary Louise. That's who. And my good friend did you know she had the crosshairs on you in New York... the night you guys were on TV. She wanted to make you. Then she discovers you are in love with her next-door neighbor. Go figure."

"You win some. You lose some."

"You ever make it with her neighbor?" Asked Andy.

Clark realized that Mary Louise, through oversight or through the better part of discretion and privacy, had not told Andy the entire story and there was no need to feed him with fodder for gossip back in East Texas. "Nope. We were ships passing in the night."

Too bad man. I gotta tell ya, man, Mary Louise is an animal. I've got the scratch marks to prove it. Too bad you missed out on that one."


The tour concluded in Kansas City. Minneapolis, Denver and Salt Lake City had been added following Seattle and that took eleven more days than he had planned for. He flew back to Oregon to grab fresh clothes and his laptop computer, which he had not had with him on the cross-country sojourn. He had felt rather naked without it. Constantly borrowing Moss's to email himself notes about ideas for future work. He even found himself working out of a hotel business center in Kansas City, while a salesman of women's underwear was next to him on the phone trying to make a deal with Target Stores.

He flew into Dallas and then rented a car and drove the two hours east to Kilgore. Pulling up at the entrance of the mansion, he was surprised at its appearance. The grounds were manicured once again, the paint of the house looked fresh and a roofing crew was busy at work trying to finish before the spring rains chased them down.

As he parked under the portico behind her flashy red sports car, he made a mental note to buy a new car, one that would carry more than two people and a small dog, which she had also purchased while apart from him; and it came yelping out to greet him.

She appeared at the den door facing the portico as he unloaded his two suitcases and his computer.

"Looks like you're planning on moving in."

"I heard the old place was for sale."

"No, a beautiful woman and her handsome boy friend purchased it. It's all theirs. Well, when they sign the papers for it and he forks over some cash."

"Oh yes. I read about that, but I hear he invested all of his cash into strip clubs in Southern California."

"Well," she said, taking off her blouse and waving it over her head, "Looks as if the woman will have to start dancing at his clubs." He opened the screened door and she fell into his arms. They barely made it to the sofa before they consumed each other in heated passion; the small dog racing about barking through the entire ordeal.

After they dressed and had refreshments, he asked, "What's the dog's name?"

"Oscar."

"Oscar?"

"Yeah. Like the one you're going to win for having a screenplay adapted from your wonderful book."

"Oscar the dog. I like it. Oscar the gold statue I wouldn't hold my breath. I've seen some of the dailies. I'm not sure how well *The Promised Land* is translating to the movie screen."

"Don't be so pessimistic. Moss says it is looking good."

"So, you've spoken to Moss have you?"

"Not more than twice a day. He uses me to check your vital signs from a distance."

"Well, my most vital sign says I am glad to be here and here feels suddenly like home."

Missy kissed him and said, "I've got a surprise for you."

"What?"

"Put your bags down upstairs and come back and I'll show you?"

"After unpacking, he ventured back downstairs and into the large kitchen. Missy had been cooking: an art form of which he felt she knew little about. But it smelled delicious. And he said so.

"It's for dinner. So back away a bit and follow me."

They wandered out the den door and under the portico, the row of pine trees lining the east side of the property were just beginning to release their stringent pollen and the wind blew it about like yellow snow. She took his hand and led him onto the rock patio facing the long flowing hill. In front of him was a garden, surrounded by a white picket fence and a rainbow of colors from wild flowers at the base and perimeter of the fence. "The flowers keep the bugs out."

"Out of what?" He asked.

"Out of our garden. I've got root vegetables, cauliflower, melons, corn and beans."

"Wait. You're growing a garden?"

250

"Yep. All by my lonesome self. Planted every seed and thing-a-ma-jigs."

"Nice technical term."

She laughed. "To be totally transparent I did have a few helpers. Raul and his sons."

"Who is Raul?"

"Lucy's husband. The housekeeper you know? We have a housekeeper and a yardman. He's Raul. But I picked everything out myself."

"Did you even get your fingers dirty? I mean under those long fingernails?" He asked with a grin on his face.

"I'll have you know, they were covered in dirt and mulch everyday. Open the gate and go in." He did and what he found was a meticulous garden hoed and weeded and growing green and verdant. There were irrigation hoses running down the small mounds where stalks of various varieties of foods were emerging and in the corners, sprinklers sprayed a mist out over what would become corn plants, and bean vines.

"I never knew you had a green thumb."

"Neither did I."

"I mean who would have thought it. Super model Missy Rusk as a gardener."

"I don't know about the super part of that description, more like former model...But I'm growing something else."

"Yeah? We have hidden pot somewhere?" he asked smiling.

She took his hand and placed it on the stomach. "I'm growing a baby."

## Chapter twenty-three

*The Promised Land* won three awards. Best director. Best screenplay adapted from a novel. And best Picture. A rather grand night in anybody's book. He was photographed and interviewed and then shuffled to the side so that the actors and actresses and the director and producers could bask in the glory of the evening. Moss called him on his cell phone and said he had looked simply marvelous on the red carpet as he was interviewed on network TV. "That tux made you look rather handsome. I hope Missy got to see it. So, Jack my boy, got another one in you?" Asked Moss, ever pushing his client for more things to sell.

"Yes, as a matter of fact I do. It's almost finished."

"Well done, lad. How's mother?" Moss's affectionate word now for the very pregnant Missy.

"Big as Connecticut. I swear there are twins inside of her...or an LA Laker."

"When are you headed home?"

"Tomorrow."

"Got time for a quick breakfast?"

"Not this trip. I need to get home and see after Missy."

"Send her my love. And send me that new manuscript."

He arrived back at the house in Texas at two the next afternoon. He was worn out but happy. She met him at the door and hugged him. "You looked so adorable on TV, Mr. Jack Lawrence." He held her. It felt good to have her in his tight hug. The smell of her hair was a musk that made him feel safe and loved. She nestled in his arms. This was how home was supposed to feel. Her bump, having grown into a full-scale mountain as he called it, pushed against the two of them as they hugged. The baby kicked and she winched. "He's going to play soccer, I think," she said.

"Moss said my tux made me look cute," said Clark.

"Did he use the word *cute*?" She pushed away and looked at him.

"No I did."

"You looked handsome. Never cute. Lets go to the patio. Cute? No one ever says cute. It's warm out there and we can rest. All three of us. He opened the door and she waddled out. He placed his suitcase down in the hallway and left a box next to his PC on the kitchen island. He ventured out to the patio and she was slowly depositing herself into an Adirondack chair.

"These new?" He asked.

"You like them?"

"They look good with your garden."

She smiled. "A lot of blooms and a lot of fruit. I'd say it is going to be a bumper year.

He rubbed her belly. "I'd say so."

They sat in the peaceful sun, as it glowed on the garden, sending a warm orange cast across her vegetables and root plants, across her rows of melons and squash, which were ripe and ready to pick. The bees buzzed about looking for more blooms from which to harvest nectar. He closed his eyes and dozed off. After a while, the housekeeper, Lucy, came out and Missy asked for a water. "And bring one for Clark. He'll be thirsty when he wakes up." Oscar yelped twice and followed Lucy back inside. Missy closed her eyes, too and let sleep flow over her.

It was peaceful in the garden. She loved it.

They dined on home-grown fruits and veggies that night, and a pie that Missy had made herself. It was a blueberry pie and she had bought the blueberries from a roadside vendor. "They're East Texas blueberries. From near Tyler," she said as he helped himself to a second piece. "It's the only thing that didn't come from our backyard. I'm thinking about planting blueberry bushes next year. Along the back fence. By the fig trees. What do you think?"

With a mouthful of pie, he nodded his approval.

The sun was beginning to set and paint the back of the house with that special afternoon-turning-to-evening golden glow. "Let's go watch the sun set on the patio." He said.

She nodded and said, "You go on, I need to take care of a couple of things. I'll join you out there."

He left and she could see him through the den windows settle into one of the new white chairs on the stone patio after having dusted the yellow pollen off of it. He dusted her chair next to his, as well. She picked up the dishes from the counter and placed them into the sink. Then she noticed the box next to the computer. It was the size that held a ream of paper. She opened it and realized it was a printout of his new book.

She looked to the patio again and he was gazing out beyond the garden into the valley. There were a few straggling golfers on the course below trying to finish a round before nightfall.

She lifted the text and turned to the last page: the ending of the book and began to read.


*People die. All people die. Doctors, lawyers, priests, ditch diggers, farmers, teachers, cooks, crooks, policemen, road workers, evangelists, housewives...even kings and queens...every one eventually dies. It is the rule of the game all humans play.*

*No one beats the rule.*

*Money can't beat the rule. Bend it for a time, for sure, but it can't win in the end.*

*Science can't beat the rule.*

*People die.*

*That's just how it is and how it is going to be. Until we are all gone.*

*He knew one thing. As long as he could see her −as long as he could touch her and smell her next to him− that part of him would never die. That part of him would love her forever.*


She closed the book and smiled. She thought about how content she was now. How grounded this crazy writer made her feel. Finally her life seemed settled. She was at peace.

Then she thought of all that had gone on before them − before now. Her parents. His family. That night. Their secret love affair. Their time apart. It was from a past era. Almost like it never existed. It felt like a dream− a fantasy.

Even the money by which they lived was from that era – from before. It came from the past. But it was still there. It was still coming to the surface and feeding them. Caring for them. Looking after them. It may have been tainted at one time or another, but it was now theirs. Wherever it came from, it was theirs. Together.

She went out to the terrace and carefully eased into the chair next to him. He took her hand and held it tightly. The last glow of afternoon light had finally succumbed to the darkness of evening. The stars were struggling, trying to unmask from the dark night sky to watch down on them. "Ellie wants to have a party for us."

"For the baby? A shower?"

"For our wedding," she said looking straight ahead, knowing this was the first they had talked about it – at least in a long, long, time. She looked straight ahead knowing he was staring at her.

He simply nodded. After a few seconds he finally spoke, "Okay by me. But I have one question."

"What's that?"

"Are you going to be Mrs. Harvey or Mrs. Lawrence?"

"Let me think on that. Right now, I think I'm just going to be happy."

## Chapter twenty-four

The paint in the baby's room was drying. It was the third round of application the small nursery, just off the master bedroom, had endured. The first two coats were discovered to have contained lead and the room had to be stripped, sanded, primed and painted all over again. Twice. It was a pale blue, with darker blue trim around the windows and door.

Missy had picked it out when she found out that the baby was going to be a boy.

Ellie had supervised the paint contractor, as well as watched over H.J. while Clark was busy either locked away writing or visiting Moss, who was still in the hospital. The agent having graduated from the ICU wing and was out of the critical care unit, was now in a rehab ward that can only be described as high-tech. There were electronic, computer-controlled apparatuses for breathing assistance, walking assistance, climbing assistance, even a small electric crane that could reach down into his bed and lift him up, so orderlies could change his bedding and his underclothes.

Clark visited him every day. And while Moss could not yet talk, he could wink and smile and that let Clark know that his dear friend was aware that he was near and cared about him.

The doctors said the recovery was going to be long. That meant painfully expensive, as well, but Clark told the hospital that if insurance wavered in the slightest, he would foot the bill. Nothing was too good or too expensive for Harold Moss.

H.J. had just turned two. He was walking and beginning to turn single words into short sentences. And he was fighting his daily naps, although when he missed one, he was usually asleep before dinnertime.

H.J. loved it at night when Clark would pick him up, put him in his lap and read a book to him. He did this every night no matter what.

Ellie had her own room downstairs, the one Lester had used for a short time. And if H.J. made a sound in the evening, she was usually there to take him so that Clark could rest through the night.

Missy and Clark had named the baby Harold Leslie. Harold after her father and Leslie as a combined tribute to both Lester and Lee. But Clark had a hard time with calling the child either name, so they settled on H.J. It was a source of laughter to them. At first this tiny ball of protoplasm in diapers and a tee-shirt rolling around on a soft blanket being called H.J.

To Clark, H.J. was something you would call your accountant or lawyer – maybe even your editor or the guy at the service station who checked your tires and cleaned the bugs off your windshield. H.J. was such a grown-up sounding moniker for a baby. Like an adult man's name attached to an infant. Missy told him not to worry, H.J. would grow into his name. He would grow into his initials.

And so they had an H.J.: The perfect baby. Healthy in every way. He ate like a horse and he was as strong as a mule. And smart, oh my god Clark thought *he just might have the smartest baby on the planet.*

Ellie came into the den and picked H.J. up from the blanket where he slept. He was getting almost too big for her. "I'll put him down upstairs. Maybe he'll sleep a bit this afternoon."

Clark nodded. He watched as his sister-in-law exited the room with his son draped over her shoulder. He scanned the room. In the corner was a stack of magazines he had collected with Missy's pictures either on the cover or on a spread inside. He planned to wrap each in plastic freezer bag, the kind with the zip lock to preserve them. Then he would place them in a secure plastic tub, which he would put in the attic. Some day H.J. could visit them, turning the pages and seeing the beautiful mother he had.

It made him sad as he remembered.

The delivery had been uneventful. A quick drive the eleven miles to Longview, have a baby and then come home two days later. No complications. No post-partum blues. Nothing out of the ordinary.

And that was fine with him. They were happy. Their child held in their laps between them and their love growing. Life in the mansion was just what he wanted it to be. Wonderful.

Ellie had even come down from New York City to help plan a small and very private wedding. *No more than twenty people,* he had said and the list had grown to fifty-three within the first ten minutes. Missy had promised to edit it, but she had not gotten around to it for the first month.

Ellie was due to leave the next day. Moss, who was passing through on his way to a writer's conference in Georgia, was under the roof for a few days helping out where he could and encouraging Clark to write. Clark needed a proper finishing to his new book, *The Circle of Lives.* Simpson House was excited about it, having read an early manuscript, but Clark was not settled with the ending. Simpson and Griffin had both expressed that they liked the ending, but if he wanted to add a bit more, they would consider it. But Simpson cautioned, "Don't guild the lily, Jack."

"It needs something else. It's too quiet," he told Missy one night as they lay in bed talking about the things in their lives. "It just sits there like a lump on the log."

"I want H.J. to go to Yale," she said, not responding to his comments about the ending of his new novel, which she had read and marked-up for him in an early draft– a draft he called his pencil version, although it was typed on a P.C.; the title told him that it was far from complete – just a refined sketch of what was to come.

"Is Yale before or after pre-school," he joked.

She playfully punched him. "I'm just planning. You've got to have a vision for your children. What's wrong with Yale?"

"What if he gets accepted to Berkley or MIT?"

"Fine. But only those." She hugged him and then kissed him. "Your ending is fine."

"I suppose."

"Ellie is leaving tomorrow," Missy said.

"Think Lucy can handle the load?"

"She has had five children of her own and two grand children. She is qualified, I do believe. Say, I was thinking of getting out and taking a drive tomorrow. I need a bit of space and fresh air. Maybe go walking over at the park by the lake."

"I've got a call in the morning. Some college in Kentucky wants to interview me."

"I can drive myself."

He looked at her and shook his head. "No. The doctor said he didn't want you to drive just yet."

"I'm fine."

"You've blacked out twice. Let's take it easy."

"I didn't black out. I just felt faint. Besides, he said I could walk. It would do me good."

"Okay. But..."

"...I could have Moss drive me."

"That would be better. By the time you guys get back we can have lunch on the patio. Before Ellie leaves."

"Will you cook burgers out?"

"Chef Harvey at your service, ma'am."

They never ate the burgers.

The call came in at around 11:40 am. A woman at the hospital in Longview asked if he was Missy's husband.

He said he was, although it was premature because it wasn't official yet. She said there had been an accident and he was needed at the hospital immediately.

He raced into the nursery and told Ellie something had happened and for her not to leave yet, but to wait by the phone. He got into Missy's sports car because it was parked behind his SUV. Onto the Henderson Highway he turned north and drove the ten miles to the Longview hospital.

Ellie had stayed on. Instead of planning a wedding, she now coordinated a funeral and a wake.

The house was quiet. Clark remained upstairs for the most part. He didn't receive guests and barely acknowledged Lucy when she came to bring him food or a drink. Finally Ellie told him he was going to have to come downstairs and at least make his presence known. Too many friends were dropping in to pay their respects. Too many faces that Ellie didn't know or didn't remember. Besides, she had a nursery paint job to supervise.

A car coming down the highway turned left in front of Moss, right at the entrance to the park at the lake. His left leg was severed just above the knee. A massive cut had slashed away a large section of his forehead. Missy, not wearing a seat belt because it hurt her still tender bladder, went through the windshield and, according to the EMS personnel who had attended to her at the scene; was dead when they got there. They applied CPR from the lake all the way to Longview, but she never regained consciousness. Moss was attended to by a man who had witnessed the wreck. He had been driving his truck behind the car that had veered into Moss's path. He had placed his belt across the portion of Moss's left thigh that was still intact and used a tire tool to twist it into a tourniquet until the blood flow was all but stopped. He, too, had found Missy and knew that she was gone. An air ambulance transported the agent to a hospital in Tyler and after several surgeries he was moved to Longview to a critical care ward.

One afternoon almost two years later, as they passed in the hall, Ellie stopped him and said, "I'm going back to New York, Clark. Maybe it's time you should sell this house. Move somewhere where all the darkness and bad luck doesn't exist. Start over fresh somewhere. Some place that H.J. can be free from the shadows of everything that happened." He pondered that thought a long time. It was on his mind as he lay his head down on the pillow on the bed he and Missy had shared. He fell asleep with that notion going through his brain.

The suffering and the loss and the grief had returned to the mansion. They were certainly no strangers to the giant house that sat up on the hill with manicured lawns bordered by a long row of pine and oak trees running along its east side.

In all its grandeur, it looked like a sad house.

## A final thought:

The great East Texas oil field is playing out now. Most of the low hanging fruit, as they say, is gone. Sucked out of the ground and used up.

The ebb and flow of men and machines working the once mighty field, has slowed to a trickle. The majors are long gone. Their oil camps, full of small houses for workers, shuttered and sold off. The machine shops along with pump and tool suppliers closed or greatly reduced in both size and numbers. The trucking companies, once busy day and night delivering pipe, and mud and fresh bits to drilling sites, now drive roads in the Dakotas or Colorado or far, far West Texas in fields producing wealth at depths two and three times that of the great East Texas Woodbine pool.

To be sure, there is some shale drilling, keeping the field alive. Ironic as it may seem, directional drilling –

what they used to call 'slant-hole drilling' – seems to be the savior of the oil business. Drilling at a very acute angle into shale and locked away oil sands, to retrieve Earth's riches is now the name of the game. A process that long ago gave to so many so much and took away from others an equal measure is now looked upon as the norm.

Men like Rusk and Harvey and even scoundrels like Scroggins, all made themselves wealthy either drilling slant-holes or fighting those that did. And today those same men would have to stand back and watch as talented petroleum engineers, aided by 3-D computer models, run drill-strings almost horizontally into strata that reluctantly gives up its black, sticky treasures.

Irony of the field: things that were once wrong are now right. Things that were once impossible are now done daily. And the riches continue to flow, ever so slowly, from deep beneath us.

**About the Author**

John Crawley is a graduate of the University of Texas at Au
In addition to penning his numerous novels, he built a
thirty-year career in advertising, specializing in TV and
Radio and helped build dozens of national brands.
He has taught creative writing and advertising at
East Texas State University (now Texas A&M Commerce),
TCU, as well as guest lectured at North Texas University,
SMU and LaVerne University in California.
John is an award-winning photographer, an avid cook,
a devoted husband and a guitar and mandolin picker. He
occasionally finds time to fly fish and to ride his bikes.
John is married with three grown children. It is rumored
there is a cat about the place, too.

In recent publications, I have been including previews of future work, or short stories as gifts to my dedicated followers. To that end, I add to this book an essay entitled *The Cardboard Men.*

I originally penned a version of the story way back in 2012. I had been on a vacation to Madrid, Spain and while there ran across an old man, stooped over, carrying what appeared to be his life's possessions on his back in a cardboard box. I took a photograph of him and then thought nothing more about it.

Early the next year, Ted Karch and I were planning a project – a coffee table book of photography and poetry. The shot of the old man and his cardboard box popped up and we began to discuss it. What would we do with it? What would I say about it?

I thought about the shot for some time, then one day, I had the chance meeting with Oliver Gold. A real fellow who was really down on his luck. He had been fleeced in a bad divorce proceedings, lost his job and his home but not his will to go on. And go on he did. And it was from that brief meeting, and subsequent encounters with him, that I put together this essay.

I had planned to include it in my short story collection called Lincoln Texas, but for whatever reason, the editor and I decided to withhold it. Now it appears in this work, as a gift to you for spending time with my words and me.

Please, enjoy.

— John Crawley

# The Cardboard Man

He is the cardboard man.

He sits on a cardboard pallet and has a cardboard hut next to him where he lives, cold nights, hot nights, wet nights and dry nights. What he owns, he carries on his back in a cardboard box.

His feet are shod in cardboard. He has a pillow that is made out of rolled-up newspapers flush with yesterday's headlines and a striped blanket that looks as if it hasn't been washed in a hundred years.

He looks as if he hasn't been washed in a hundred years.

His name is Oliver Gold.

You probably don't know Oliver Gold.

I know I didn't.

Not until he asked me if I had some change. I looked into his tired, hungry eyes and said I did. I gave him a twenty. His eyes lit up and he actually smiled. He invited me to sit. To talk.

You fool…you say. He's just going to buy wine with it.

So? I say. You're probably having a cocktail as you read this. The only difference is that you are in your wood-paneled study, in a nice home in suburbia somewhere, the TV blaring in the background and you don't have to make a living on the street.

Oliver Gold might not either, except he lost his job, lost his family and then got taken for everything he owned by an unscrupulous lawyer representing his wife.

Sorry lawyers, but this guy was the worst example of what your profession can do. Oliver pleaded with the judge for some leeway, but the judge, who was up for re-election needed money and votes so, he sided with the attorney who promised to deliver votes and cash and Oliver was left out in the cold.

No home. No car. No money.

When I say no money, Oliver had nothing. He got a job for a while working in one of those big electronic warehouse stores, but when HR found out he was living out of cardboard boxes – they canned him. Undesirable.

There's no labor union representing Oliver Gold and the cardboard people. Hell, for that matter there's no government representing them either. Washington points to Austin and Austin points to Dallas and Dallas points to the cardboard people and says, "Keep moving. Don't stop here."

They are on the outside looking in.

Oliver Gold is the cardboard man. I sat next to him on the curb and talked with him for an hour. He didn't cry. He didn't try and hard sell me with a pity story; he just told it like it is.

Here's what I came away with. Oliver Gold is a good guy. We're going to try to get him in a halfway house and find him a job. But the real thing I learned is that judges should not be elected. There is too much graft in elections.

I'm starting to feel that way about Congress, too; but they don't seem to have as much control over the life of Oliver Gold and the other cardboard people, as do local judges and politicians, who want the men and women like Oliver Gold to just go away. Make the problem go away.

He's a cardboard man.

But he has a name. And that night, thanks to some very decent people who came to his aid, Oliver had a home.

It is not in the suburbs, because you wouldn't want him there. Too close to you and your family. Too close to your nest egg and your slice of the American dream. But at least it's not in a cardboard box. Not that night, anyway.

Now here is the scary thing. You and I could be a cardboard person just as easy as Oliver Gold. Think about that huge mortgage. That credit card debit. Think about how tenuous your job probably truly is. What if the downturn stays down for another two years? Can you hold out? What if that big client walks? Does your boss think enough of you to cut his bonus to keep you on?

Oliver Gold is not one of us. But we could all join him. Don't kid yourself.

It's that close. That close to being a cardboard person.

I saw Oliver not long ago. His step was brisk and his head was held high. He waved when he saw me.

"No cardboard," he said.

I nodded.

"I got a job. I deliver pizzas."

With a car?

"No." He laughed. "I can't afford a car. But I've got a bicycle. And I get by. Rain isn't the greatest. And the cold sucks. But I can get my delivers done fairly fast and the pay is decent enough."

Do they pay you a salary?

Sure. Not much. It's hourly. But he gets a lot of free pizza. The downside is the government gets its dirty hand in there for some. The salary not the pizza.

He grins. "But not the tips. Them tips is all mine." He pauses. "You was good to help me back then."

I wave him off. It was nothing.

"May have been nothing for you, but for me it was life changing. I'm back on my feet. I'll make it fo sure now . Fo sure. And if I don't, I got me a bunch of cardboard pizza boxes to build a new house."

He grinned. "What goes around comes around. You know?"

I did.

He is still, to me, the cardboard man. But he was at least happy about it. I just wish the government didn't have their hand stuck in his earnings. Of all of us, he can afford it the least. Why not raise the rates on the 1 per-centers and leave Oliver Gold alone?

There's an idea.

Leave the cardboard people alone.

I heard on the TV last night that the police raided a squatter's camp under a freeway in Dallas. Thirteen were arrested and two were injured when a fight broke out. Apparently the cops got rough with an old lady and two of the homeless men jumped to her rescue and they were beaten rather badly.

At the end of the article, which was praising the police for clearing the cardboard people out of the city center, was the name Oliver Gold. He had been one of the men beaten by the police.

I double-checked. Oliver Gold. It was him.

Defending a woman. A bit noble of a thing to do. And then to get your brains bashed out.

Oliver died. Little was made of it. Died in police custody. A brief ceremony at a pauper's grave and then covered with dirt.

The police were never brought to trial. It was never investigated. It was swept under the carpet, as they say. Forgotten and put away.

Just like Oliver's life. Swept up. Forgotten. And put away.

I wonder how long one of those cops would last as a cardboard person?

I got to meet the D.A. for Dallas County the other night. He is running for reelection. I asked him about the Oliver Gold investigation. He said he didn't know anything about it.

I told him the circumstances and he shrugged.

"The cardboard people are a true menace to our city. It is a problem we are going to have to clean up. If elected I will...blah...blah...blah..."

Oliver Gold is gone. He is no longer a part of the problem. He isn't a measure of the menace. He is simply dust now. Dust to dust. Oliver is resting.

I saw a man carrying his worldly possessions on his back the other day. Carrying it all in a cardboard box.

He sleeps in a cardboard box. He wears cardboard shoes and spends his days filling his cardboard box with things he might try and sell. Tonight, he'll lay his head down on rolled up newspapers with the headlines of the day. There's a story on the front page about clearing out the homeless. But there is nothing in the story about solving the problem of the cardboard people.

It is easier to keep them moving than it is to find a solution to why they exist in the first place.

Made in the USA
Coppell, TX
17 June 2024

33624451R00151